BOOK II OF THE PAIN SERIES

MICHAEL D'AMBROSIO

Queen of Pain: Book II of the Pain series
Copyright © 2024 by Michael D'Ambrosio

All rights reserved. No part of this publication may be reproduced, distributed, or transmitted in any form or by any means, including photocopying, recording, or other electronic or mechanical methods, without the prior written permission of the author, except in the case of brief quotations embodied in critical reviews and certain other non-commercial uses permitted by copyright law.

ISBN
978-1-959314-34-9 (Paperback)
978-1-959314-35-6 (eBook)
978-1-964982-20-5 (Hardcover)

TABLE OF CONTENTS

I.	A Gathering Storm	1
II.	The First Strike	26
III.	The Bitch is Back	50
IV.	About Lilith	81
V.	Complications	98
VI.	Failed Alliances	122
VII.	Orpheus - 2	146
VIII.	A Setup	173
IX.	The Trap Unfolds	201
X.	The Aftermath	228

1
A GATHERING STORM

Two months had elapsed since Marina liberated the people of Yord and was crowned queen. With help from militia Commander Britt Sykes, her close friend Rebecca, and Fleet Commander Sheena Brice, she gradually grew into her role as a leader of her people.

As the birth of Rebecca's baby drew near, Marina lost contact with her liaison and closest friend, forcing her to leave the palace on a regular basis to interact with her people. Still recovering from her addiction to the Stardust stimulant, she suffered from periodic spells of nausea and hallucinations. Determined as always, she refused help and took the consequences in stride.

Dressed in her usual leather pants and black bodice with no bra or T-shirt, and black boots, she wore her dark hair draped down on her shoulders. Over the leather attire was a regal red, velvet cape and a simple tiara with a small ruby embedded in it. Marina refused to wear anything more than that as a symbol of her royalty when she mingled with her people. She felt she was no better than any of them and chose to retain her old attire as proof.

Without Britt, who was away for a lengthy period of time, or Rebecca for guidance for friendly conversation, she was lonely. Strangers filled the palace, repairing and restoring its interior. The distraction of noise pressed her to leave the palace frequently for strolls into town for some semblance of solitude.

As Marina marched through the center of the Palace District, she observed the simple activities of the townspeople. Many business owners started the tedious process of cleaning and stocking the stores with some opening for the first time in a long while. Two cafes were adorned with banners promoting their return. Meanwhile, the streets were filled with many people; some shopping, some looking for work.

Marina's militia security urged her to take an escort but she always refused. She did, however, request that they maintain a presence in the major cities of Yord to keep order and ensure the reconstruction was carried out in an orderly fashion. She was well aware of the 'opportunists' that showed up at times like this, looking to take advantage of the less fortunate.

Several people greeted Marina as she made her way along the cobblestone streets. She listened to their comments and stories courteously. Once she learned to relax and enjoy their company, she became a favorite among the people. She entertained them with her own stories of her encounters with Victor and how she discovered the truth behind her missing parents. With each passing day that she spent among the people, she felt more like she belonged there.

A familiar voice called to her from the street, "Marina, look at you!"

Marina recognized Dix, her former handler, and responded giddily, "Well look what the cat dragged in."

Dix approached her with open arms and they hugged. He was a dark-skinned man in his fifties with a shaved head and a distinct gold tooth in front of his mouth, easily noticeable when he spoke.

"Have a hot job for me, Dix?" Marina kidded.

"Nope. I'm done with that business."

Marina was surprised by his response. "What happened?"

He grinned sheepishly and explained, "The whole courier experience was about preparing you for this. You weren't transporting contraband; you were helping the rebel movement."

Marina was stunned. "You mean all that secrecy was just to push me to take the throne?"

"Uh-huh," he answered slyly.

"Rebecca, Kat and Severin?"

"Uh-huh. Everything had a purpose that would lead to this."

Marina paced about with her hands on her hips in shock. She couldn't believe that anyone could con her like this. Dix backed away nervously and assured her that he would never have forced her to take the throne. It had to be her decision.

"What did the data chip have to do with all this?" she inquired curiously.

"That was real," Dix replied. "Your actions prevented a war and enabled us to break up a link between a mole in the Fleet and Balthus' smuggling operation. You took it much further than they expected though."

"Rock and Tulley were assholes," she retorted, thinking about her hostile encounter with the two agents.

"But those assholes have a lot of respect for you now. They'll make valuable allies in this new order."

"New order?" she questioned, baffled by the reference.

"There's rumor about a large corporate organization wanting to take over the galactic trade circuit. That's nothing new, though."

"So, what about Kat?" Marina asked, growing ever anxious for more details. "I think you owe me an explanation about your relationship with her."

"Ah, yes... Kat," he mused. "The plan wasn't for you to meet her; only to obtain the package."

"Oh, I met her up close and personal all right. More personal than I cared for."

"Let's go for a walk and we'll talk about her purpose."

"I figured her purpose out," Marina sniped. "And for my efforts, she has a marker on me already."

Dix paused with a concerned expression. "That's not good," he replied. "Care to explain?"

Marina glanced at Dix and wondered what bothered him so about her obligation to Kat. They continued to walk.

"Kat will use that marker and in a big way," he warned.

Marina chuckled at his concern. "I think Kat and I have an understanding," she said confidently.

"I certainly hope so," Dix replied, staring at her suspiciously.

Marina stepped in front of Dix and blocked his path. Looking into his eyes with a somber expression, she pressed for an explanation about his relationship to Kat.

Dix fumbled for words and told her it was complicated. He attempted to pass Marina but she blocked him again, determined to get an explanation from him.

"You're not leaving until you tell me. We had an agreement that, if I took the throne, you'd tell me what goes with the two of you."

Dix reluctantly revealed, "Kat is my niece. She, like you, also has the powers of a Seer."

Marina was stunned. "Then why did she ask me to destroy the crystal?"

"Because, like Victor tried, either of you could be held hostage for the use of its powers."

Marina grew more confused and asked, "How does that benefit her?"

Dix looked away shamefully and then reluctantly continued, "Kat turned to a powerful cult of witches to enhance her ability to channel the crystal's powers without the use of a crystal. Since you destroyed it, she believes she is the only one who can see the future."

Marina folded her arms and recalled her first meeting with Kat. She remembered her words, alluding to their intertwined fates. "Does Kat know I can see elements of the future without the crystal?"

"No," he responded uneasily, "but she'll want to make sure."

Marina pondered for a moment and then inquired, "What's her deal?"

"Our families were killed by Victor's men ten years ago. She wants revenge on everyone for what happened to them, including you."

"Me?" blurted Marina, failing to understand the connection to her.

"Yes, if you would have taken the throne back then, they would still be alive."

"That's bullshit!" she shouted angrily. "How could I have prevented that?"

Dix shook his head, indicating his reluctance to tell the story. She stared him down persistently, determined to know how she failed them. "Do you remember when you first met Rebecca?" Dix asked.

"Of course," she said, wondering what the relevance was.

"Do you remember the bookstore - the woman and the child?"

Marina thought hard and remembered that day. "Yeah, Victor's men burned it to the ground. The woman and child died in the fire, as I recall."

"That was my sister and nephew - Kat's mother and brother."

Marina was appalled and felt sorrow for Dix as she recalled that horrible night. It hurt her to think about the people who died holding out against Victor's forces until she emerged from obscurity to defeat him. It hurt even more, now that she knew she might have saved Dix's family members if she wasn't so damn stubborn. "So, Kat may well have a vendetta against me," she surmised aloud.

"Just watch your back, Marina," he warned. "That's all I'm saying."

Marina stared down at the ground with remorse in her eyes. Then she looked up and suggested, "Perhaps the three of us should have lunch and clear the air."

Dix sighed and replied sadly, "It would be nice if my niece and I could meet and get along for once. She's the only family I have left."

"I'll ask her the next time we meet," she mentioned. "I'm sure she'll pay me a visit soon enough."

"Only if she wants something from you," he said uneasily. "She never leaves her station."

They walked again past a number of shops. Dix was amazed at how the townspeople responded to her. "I see you've improved your people skills," he kidded.

"I'm still struggling with this, Dix," she confessed. "I'm used to being the unknown, unseen specter that creeps in and out of people's lives; not the center of everyone's attention."

"It'll take some time. The important thing now is to define your allies and enemies. Being the ruler will make you a target, more so than before."

"I'm not one to be intimidated. You, of all people, should know that," she reminded him.

As they continued walking, Dix mentioned, "You have become like a daughter to me. I don't want you to get hurt."

"What about my courier assignments?" she commented cynically.

"They weren't dangerous enough?"

As the two strolled around the perimeter of the palace, Dix continued, "Kat can be a formidable ally but she never does something for nothing. I did what I could to have your back, but sometimes you made that quite difficult with your aggressive tactics."

Marina hugged him, much to his surprise. "And you did well. I'm still here."

Dix returned her affection and then left. Marina wondered how he managed to run his operation for so many years in plain sight of Victor and the Fleet without being discovered. More so, she was amazed that she was so successful in his operation during that time. Until Victor set his sights on her, she was the elusive mystery woman with a violent reputation.

As Marina walked along one of the side streets, she developed a throbbing headache that forced her to sit for several moments on a wooden bench. She sweated profusely and trembled. Some of the townspeople gathered and inquired if she needed help, but she refused. Then the hallucinations began.

A vague image of a blonde woman in a Fleet uniform appeared. Six figures in blue Fleet uniforms appeared next. The image faded and another appeared. Marina fought the female officer. The image faded and she regained her composure. The vision made no sense to her as Commander Brice was the only Fleet officer she knew and Brice was a brunette. When the headache finally subsided, she disregarded the hallucinations as only that and resumed her walk.

An old, gray-haired friend Dora emerged from the crowd and greeted Marina with a hug. In her late sixties, she wore a long skirt and pullover sweater. She emphasized how proud she and her husband Clem were of Marina for defeating Victor and assuming her new role as queen. Marina could never thank them enough for risking their lives months earlier to save her when the mercenaries hunted her. She sensed that Dora was bothered by something and invited her inside the palace where they could talk in private.

The two sat in the large conference room with the doors closed. Dora took Marina's hand in hers and revealed, "I knew your grandmother many years ago. She was a great warrior, much like you. She trusted few people outside the circle of priestesses in the temple and I was one of them."

Marina grew anxious to hear more about her family history and was attentive. Dora continued, "Your grandmother foretold that new Seers would be revealed when the last priestess died."

"Why would she speak of that?" asked Marina, surprised by her remark. "Did she expect me to die young as well?"

Dora chuckled and placed her arm around Marina's shoulders. "Remember, Marina: you are different. You were not a priestess but, with the crystal, you were the very power they protected."

Marina was stunned at this news. "But I destroyed the crystal," she confessed. "What good would that do?"

"The power of the crystal is in you. By your very presence among new Seers, their skills will manifest themselves."

"Do you have any idea who these new Seers might be?" Marina asked eagerly.

Dora removed her arm from around Marina and nervously fidgeted. Marina noticed and urged her to relax and confide in her.

"I do not know for sure," Dora admitted. "I do have my suspicions, though."

"Why is this relevant to me?" Marina asked curiously.

"If these Seers fell under the influence of the wrong people, they could put you in danger."

"From whom would they fear?" Marina asked, surprised by Dora's revelation.

"There are many who would gain from controlling young Seers as well as yourself," Dora explained.

Marina stood and paced the room uneasily. Finally, she accepted the fact that she was involved, whether she liked it or not. "What can I do to help?" she asked.

Dora grew somber and instructed her, "When you find the new Seers, take them under your protection. Teach them how to use their skills for the good of their people."

Marina became concerned as she never anticipated a responsibility like this to be cast on her. She was far from the role model that the young girls would need to guide them. "I don't know if I can, Dora," she fretted. "I don't even know how to use my own skills."

Dora disregarded her apprehension and insisted, "Promise me you'll do your best to care for them. Kara may be of use in finding them and will need your protection as well."

Marina reluctantly agreed to seek them out with Kara's help. Dora stood and hugged her once more. "You are a great and wise ruler. I know your parents would be very proud of you."

Marina became teary-eyed at the thought of her parents watching her attempt to rule their kingdom. When Dora departed the room, Marina was more perplexed than ever. After finally bringing freedom to the people of Yord, was it possible that there was as much to fear now as there was under Victor's rule? She ascended the stairs and spent the afternoon in the meditation room, searching for answers to her new challenge.

★ ★ ★

Commander Sheena Brice marched down the corridor of Fleet headquarters in a neatly pressed, blue officer's uniform with her long, dark hair tied up in a bun. Her piercing brown eyes and tight body projected an intimidating appearance.

Sheena was never comfortable at headquarters and preferred the sanctity of her command ship, the *S.F. Argo*, away from catty politics. Her older sister, Severin, encouraged her to 'play the game' with the beaurocrats, but she never had the patience nor the tolerance for the pettiness that her sister did.

She grew teary-eyed as she recalled her sister's murder at the hands of mercenaries in an ambush on Orpheus-2. It haunted her that her sister didn't deserve to die like that, especially on her own space station.

At the end of the corridor on the third floor, two sentries were poised at the entrance to a high-security room, known as the Red Room. This room contained the most high-tech monitoring equipment in the galaxy and was designed with airtight security. Red Rooms were also used for high level briefings to ensure their secrecy.

The sentries blocked Sheena's entry to the Red Room while she positioned herself in front of the retinal scanner to gain access beyond the steel door. When the device acknowledged her identity and beeped, the sentries moved aside, allowing her access. The clicking sound from ten latches around the perimeter of the door meant she could enter. Nervously, she turned the handle and pushed open the steel door. Glancing back at the sentries, she gave them a sharp stare for not assisting a senior officer with the door. *Just another example of the lack of discipline that develops when an organization gets fat, dumb and happy*, she thought to herself.

Once inside, she immediately sensed the eyes of fifteen administrative officers on her. As they stood to acknowledge her, she announced, "Commander Sheena Brice of the *S.F. Argo*, reporting as ordered," and then saluted with her right fist over her heart.

The officers responded in kind and took their seats. At the head of the table sat General Duane Witty, a gritty-looking, older man in his fifties with beady eyes, like those of a snake. He wore a black, two-piece uniform with no identification; symbolic of his supreme leadership in the Fleet. Sheena had rarely spoken with him and when she did, it was only in passing.

Sheena took her seat and the meeting began. There was much discussion about a new weapons technology that would enhance all existing weaponry for the Fleet but was delayed due to contractual issues with the developer. Witty emphasized that the issues were being addressed appropriately and progress would continue shortly. Sheena wondered who had the knowledge and the facilities in the private sector as well as the financial backing for the research and development of something so advanced.

After another hour of mundane discussions about how the Fleet will increase the scope of its control and improve training among the ranks, Witty directed his attention to Sheena. "Commander Brice, I understand that you've had interaction with the Queen of Yord."

"Yes, sir," she answered, wondering why that was a concern.

"What do you think of her?" he inquired curiously and stood. He was an imposing figure, looking down at her with those eerie black eyes. Sheena was uncomfortable with the question and responded defensively, "It is not my position to judge, only to enforce the code of the Space Fleet."

The General was amused by her response and walked behind her. "And why is that?" he continued with arms folded. "You are a veteran officer with much experience."

Sheena quickly responded, "As an officer of the Fleet, I am trained to obtain facts and recognize threats to the Fleet."

"Do you see the queen as a threat to the Fleet?"

Sheena grew more concerned with his distinct interest in Marina. "Not at this time, sir," she answered casually.

"That's it?" he asked, somewhat surprised. "Not at this time?"

"Yes, sir."

"Does that mean that she will be a threat at some time in the future?" he continued.

"That remains to be seen," she answered uneasily. "I have not seen or heard anything to indicate she would be a detriment to the Fleet."

"And you would tell me if you learned of something, wouldn't you?"

Sheena stood and faced Witty. She did her best to remain respectful and follow protocol but she had to question his motive. "Sir, is there something that I need to be briefed on regarding the queen?" she countered. "I don't understand the line of questioning here."

"At ease, Commander," he ordered, smiling cunningly at her. "I just wanted your opinion on things."

"Sir, what things?" she pressed.

"It's nothing, Commander. Please take your seat."

Sheena sat down and wondered what transpired at headquarters that led to her unofficial inquiry about Marina's loyalty in front of other officers of equal or greater rank. Something was amiss and she was determined to find out what it was.

When the meeting ended, Witty requested that Sheena stay for a few moments. Once the room emptied, he informed her that soon she'd be patrolling the fifth sector for an extended period of time with two other vessels, the *S.F. Hydra* and the *S.F. Mantis*. Sheena thought that was strange, but said no more.

As she left the conference room, Colonel Sandra Lennox intercepted her in the corridor, standing in her path. Lennox, middle-aged and buxom with short blond hair, seemed determined to intimidate Sheena.

"Can I help you, Colonel?" Sheena asked uneasily.

"Just a warning, Commander Brice; I suggest you choose your friends carefully."

"I feel as though I'm missing something here, Colonel. Would you care to explain?"

The Colonel was fixated on her with an icy stare and then explained, "There are big things happening that will require all of us to make sacrifices. Make sure you're on the right team or else."

"Or else what?" she challenged Lennox.

Colonel Lennox ignored her and walked away, leaving Sheena more confused than ever. Something big was happening and, so far, nothing she heard made sense.

As she returned to the transportation bay, she recalled what information she knew about sector five. It was on the other side of former alliance members' territories and beyond that was unexplored territory. It made no sense why three Fleet warships would be positioned out there. More so, she wondered how the alien races in that region would perceive their presence at their backside.

When she reached the transportation bay, the militia commander Britt Sykes had just stepped off his transport. He immediately caught her attention in his black militia jacket over his tan shirt and tie with the insignias of his command. Sheena knew he was close to Marina and considered warning him.

"Good morning, Commander," he greeted her and saluted as he walked past.

Sheena saluted and then paused. "Excuse me, sir," she beckoned to him. "Can I have a minute of your time?"

Britt stopped and turned back, making eye contact with her. "Of course," he replied pleasantly. "What can I do for you?"

"Is the queen in any sort of danger?"

"None that I'm aware of," he answered, somewhat surprised. "Is something wrong?"

Sheena hesitated as she considered the risk she was taking in suggesting the Fleet had issue with Marina. Then she threw caution to the wind and mentioned, "The general has a particular interest in her loyalties to the Fleet."

Britt drew closer to her and, sensing her concern, spoke slightly louder than a whisper. "Do you sense a problem with that?"

"I'm not sure. He made several inquiries as to what I thought about the queen and if there was anything to indicate she was a threat to them."

Britt pondered her remarks and assured her, "I will pass that along to her. I'm sure it's nothing but I'll let her know just the same."

"Look, sir," Sheena continued with a concerned tone, "I've been assigned to a long-term patrol in the fifth sector with two other warships and I suspect it's somehow relevant to the queen. Trust me when I say that something isn't right here."

"I understand," he reiterated. "We'll look into it."

"Thank you, sir," she said, feeling confident that he understood the importance of her message. "Marina and I have become really good friends and I respect what she's been through for her people."

"Right now, that friendship means a lot to her," Britt replied. "She's having a tough time getting over her past demons."

"Well, thank you for your time, Commander Sykes," Sheena responded and continued toward her ship.

Britt watched her curiously as she left. He, too, wondered why the Fleet's leader would have such an interest in Marina. He glanced at his watch and continued to his meeting with the Industrial Development Committee and the Fleet leadership.

* * *

The crew of Sheena's warship, the *S.F. Argo*, greeted her with salutes and smiles when she boarded. Sheena immediately requested a meeting with her intelligence officer, Lieutenant Lars Kannel. The crew sensed her concern and the importance of their meeting. Glancing uneasily at each other, they watched the two officers intently.

The two left the bridge and entered her quarters: a long narrow cabin that housed her living accommodations as well as her work area. It consisted of three rooms: one for personal space; another for a private work area, fitted with secure communications equipment; and the general meeting area with a long, glass table where they now sat.

Kannel took a seat at the oblong table surrounded by ten chairs. Sheena sat across from him and folded her hands. He knew she was concerned about something and gave her his utmost attention.

"Lars, I need you to do me a very important favor," she requested. "Can you look into all the prisoners held captive here at headquarters recently?"

Kannel was surprised by her request. "Of course, ma'am. Am I looking for someone in particular?"

"Perhaps someone who reneged on a contract with the Fleet that has ties to Queen Marina," she explained, somewhat unsure of the answer herself. "It may have something to do with why we're being deployed to sector five with the *Hydra* and the *Mantis*."

"Yes, ma'am, I was just informed from our sister ships of the unusual mission. I did a search on sector five as soon as I heard and there is nothing of note that occurred there since the war ended."

"That's why I find it strange," she responded. "There was talk at the meeting that someone developed vital technology for the Fleet but may have reneged on the deal, resulting in a delay. It's a long shot but that person could be in their custody."

"There shouldn't be any prisoners at this time in headquarters," he informed her as he considered the possibility of an incarceration of a scientist or engineer. "Prisoners are usually transferred to the Kappa-Rigo prison facility once they're processed."

Sheena pondered his response and then instructed him, "See if anyone is in custody now or was recently held here for an extended period of time."

Kannel replied as he stood, "Yes, ma'am. I'll get on it right away."

"And please, not a word to anyone about this. I don't know what tree we're shaking and, more importantly, who's in it."

"I understand." They saluted each other and he left Sheena's quarters. Sheena was determined to find out what was going on before their deployment. If she disobeyed her orders to report to sector five, she contemplated how severe the consequences could be. She was also concerned by how the information she learned could relate to Marina as well.

Then she recalled her first encounter with Marina in the unexplored territories. Victor was defeated and Marina's alien cruiser ravaged the militia's pride ship, the *Scorpion*. Sheena's orders were to destroy any and all outlaw ships in the unknown territory. Perhaps, she considered, Marina wasn't supposed to survive her encounter with Victor and they were sent to unknowingly eradicate everyone who would know what happened to her. But why the Fleet would engage in something like this made no sense. She needed answers.

★ ★ ★

A shuttle with fancy emblems and logos painted on its hull docked inside the transportation bay of Fleet Headquarters. A large "K" for Kronos Enterprises with wings stood out between fire-breathing dragons and swirling ghosts overhead with expressions of fear on their faces.

Two Fleet soldiers escorted a bearded man in a suit, the vice-president of Kronos Enterprises Tripp Sexton, toward the shuttle. When the engines shut down, another bearded man also in a suit, Jack Klingman, stepped off with a brief case in his hand. Klingman was the president of Kronos Enterprises and was supported by very wealthy investors because of his profitable string of successes across the galaxy. The two men shook hands and walked away from the shuttle.

"Have you made the arrangements I requested?" asked Klingman.

"Of course," replied Sexton. "Everyone is on board with the schedule." Klingman patted him on the back.

"This was a long time coming and now… now we're on the verge of achieving our greatest success."

Sexton looked down at the ground as they walked, exhibiting doubt in his expression. Klingman noticed and inquired, "What's wrong, my friend?"

Sexton hesitated in front of the elevator. He gestured for the soldiers to leave them. The two men entered the elevator without their escorts.

"I don't understand why we're offering to share power with IDC and the Fleet. Do we really need them?"

"Look at the big picture, Tripp. We're using them to dismantle all the technical obstacles. The Fleet will handle the alien races and then we'll have them handle IDC. By then, they'll have very little to fight with. When all is done, we're the last men standing."

The elevator stopped on the third floor and the doors opened. The two men stepped out. "And you are confident that our support groups will come through?" inquired Sexton.

"Look, we're paying people a lot of money... a lot of money to make things happen. It's the kind of money that gets results."

"So, we're investors now, huh?" kidded Sexton.

"Only until the hostile takeover occurs. Then we're gods." The two men laughed.

"Do you foresee any problems?" asked Sexton.

"Only the damned chip," replied Klingman. "And that stupid bitch who reneged on our deal."

"Offer her more money," suggested Sexton.

"Already did. She won't budge," he answered disappointedly. "It's a moral issue with her."

"What can we do to change her mind?"

"Oh, I already have people working on it. Give it a little time and she'll come around - piece by piece."

The two men chuckled again. "I understand the chip was delivered to the station but disappeared a few months ago," Sexton mentioned.

"Yeah, a pair of Internal Security dicks claimed to have misplaced it," complained Klingman. "We're working that angle as well."

"I'll see what I can find out," Sexton volunteered. "If it's out there, I'll find it."

As they approached the conference room, Klingman remarked, "Everyone has a price and sometimes it isn't money. Sometimes it's a little deeper. Get my drift?"

The two men laughed sadistically. They paused before reaching the door to the Red Room. Klingman commented, "The universe is the limit for us and we're going to take all we can... once we get that chip or the bitch's cooperation to reproduce it."

"This weapon is really that powerful?" asked Sexton.

"And more," replied Klingman confidently. "It's the range of the targeting system that makes it exceptional."

They stopped at the door and performed their retinal scans. The scanner beeped and unlocked the door. The two sentries stepped aside and allowed them access. It was unusual for civilians to have access to the Red Room and for their identities to be in the computer system was a big deal.

★ ★ ★

Britt met with a panel of two Fleet officers, the two Kronos leaders, and three members from the Industrial Development Committee. One of the Fleet officers was Colonel Sandra Lennox. The other was Captain Devon Jeffries, the commander of Orpheus-2 and the replacement for Severin, Sheena's sister, after her death.

The three IDC representatives consisted of a young oriental man, Dr. Haney; and a middle-aged, dark-skinned couple, Drs. Marjorie Janus and Tyrus Ford. All were from affluent areas of the galaxy. Jeffries looked strangely familiar to Britt but he couldn't recall from where.

Britt was uneasy with administrative duties as this was much different than developing battle strategies, ordering subordinates into battle or fighting insurgents. He knew he had to tread carefully, being the babe in the woods among a pack of wolves. The Fleet and the militias always co-existed but never really cared for each other. He was unlikely to be treated with anything more than cursory respect.

When he studied the faces of the Kronos and IDC representatives, he recalled that civilians weren't permitted to have this level of access and found that odd. He was fortunate to be granted his access to this security level and only because of the militia's new affiliation with the Fleet after Marina's coronation.

After hearing their initial discussions about investing in big-ticket projects around the galaxy, Britt was amazed at the wealth that still existed for companies like Kronos, despite the squalor that befell the alliance worlds for so many years. He wondered where these people hid to maintain their status at the top of the food chain during the conflicts.

The meeting included a slide presentation about the value of metals, their availability throughout the galaxy and where the market was headed. Intergalactic development was nonexistent during the Great War with the Weevil and prices skyrocketed when resources became scarce.

Britt learned that, despite the high cost of materials, thirty satellites were staged on the unexplored outskirts of the galaxy for surveillance of other worlds to ensure safety and secrecy. He was aware of the expensive project but assumed it was a private sector venture group for the Fleet. Money buys a lot of contacts and loyalty in business.

Plans for rebuilding the central shipping hub called GSS, which belonged to an alien race called Galleans during better times, were discussed as well as who would control commerce throughout the galaxy from the hub.

Jeffries mentioned that tariffs would be required to support the Fleet's involvement over such great distances. This caught Britt's attention as they had no right to levy taxes without Marina's consent. He kept his silence for the time being and listened as other concerns were presented.

The issue of containment of certain alien races was raised by Dr. Haney. He fretted the possibility that these races might interfere with their projects by launching an assault on the defenseless GSS. Colonel Lennox assured him that it wouldn't be a problem under her command.

Sexton interceded and explained the advantages of a network that controlled communications and routing throughout the galaxy. They would not let that advantage slip away.

Britt had heard enough. "When did commerce and communication become a negotiable and taxable item without the queen's consent?" he questioned them sternly.

Sexton answered calmly, "Control of commerce in the sector is a very lucrative business."

Klingman added, "And there are other sectors just like it, waiting to be controlled as well. We will have the power to dominate everyone. Imagine, no more wars."

"With the new technology we're obtaining, we'll be rich beyond belief, once we begin operations," announced Sexton eagerly.

Dr. Haney stood and attempted to clarify their position to Britt. "IDC will control all commerce in the galaxy from GSS while Kronos manages commodities acquisitions and trades. The Fleet will maintain enforcement of our network and its needs."

"It's needs, huh?" remarked Britt snidely.

Jeffries reminded everyone that the Fleet would enforce the provisions of the plan to ensure all parties cooperated; however, there would be expenses for that protection.

Klingman grinned like a Cheshire cat as he pondered the anticipated successes and assured Britt that all would be well-compensated.

Britt stood and slammed the table with his fist. "You people have no right to take control of any territory you please, especially from other races! You have no right to levy any tax without the queen's consent! And you sure have no right to set up your own trade organization! You are out of line!"

The others were startled by his outburst. "Remember, you are only here as a courtesy, Commander," Colonel Lennox warned him. "I suggest you get on board or get out."

"Look, Commander," Klingman said calmly, "You play ball with us and you'll be a very rich man."

Britt recognized what was happening and wanted no part of it. "Who negotiated all this without the queen's permission?" he inquired sternly.

"Come now, Commander. You think we haven't followed the proper protocol?" countered Lennox.

"That's right! You have no legal authority to do this," he warned them.

"Ah, but we do," responded Klingman. "The Council already approved it."

Now Britt was irate. "There is no council! They were officially disbanded by the queen for abandoning their people during Victor's takeover."

Lennox countered, "There are three councilors, recently appointed, who are acting on behalf of the people of Yord. This is just a continuation of the government that existed prior to the war."

"It was decided that the queen doesn't have that authority since her position didn't exist before the war," added Sexton sarcastically. "This is a new alliance and, as a democracy, we've all agreed it would be better served with her as a figurehead only."

"And what does General Witty say about this?" Britt challenged angrily. Everyone laughed, making him angrier.

"General Witty doesn't believe in subjugating the Fleet to anyone, let alone a vagabond who declares herself queen," replied Colonel Lennox.

Britt leaned on the table again with piercing eyes and warned them, "Then you and General Witty will have to go through my militias and you'll be tried for treason when we take you into custody." He stormed out of the meeting and returned to his ship.

"We'll see who is tried for treason," quipped Klingman. "Lennox, give them a taste of what's to come. Deliver the package."

"I'd be happy to," she replied and left the room.

"Now, where does IDC stand in their progress?" inquired Sexton.

Dr. Haney replied, "We have completed the plans for the restoration of the galactic transport hub. The power dispersion modulator is nearly finished and we only require the program to operate the system."

Dr. Ford added, "The receivers have been installed and tested in all thirty satellites. Until the transmitter is operational in the GSS hub, there is nothing more I can do."

Dr. Janus spoke next and asked, "When can we expect receipt of the data chip?"

Sexton, now looking distracted by the question, rubbed his chin and replied, "We have two interrogation experts working with our engineer. I'm sure she'll have a change of heart about honoring the contract."

"And that means when?" Dr. Janus pressed for a definitive answer.

"Within the week, I assure you," promised Klingman.

"Meanwhile, Kronos is providing General Witty with a recommended plan of attack to disrupt the alien forces with his Fleet to prevent any resistance," added Sexton.

"Can we count on them to handle the situation?" asked Dr. Ford.

"Colonel Lennox is initiating the first phase now, regarding the queen," answered Jeffries. "The queen is the key to gaining the support of the militias."

"And the Fleet?"

"General Witty is already dispatching his forces as we speak, to handle the alien races."

"Then we can assume everything is on track," summed up Klingman. "I'm sure we can provide monetary incentive for anyone who gets in the way. If that doesn't work, then we'll just remove them altogether."

Sexton added, "We have a mercenary group that specializes in removing problems. Their leader is quite the aggressive female and her team has a very successful record. They'll handle the issue of the queen for us."

"This group also happens to be the new council that will overrule the queen on any matter," Klingman informed them. "Should be a smooth transition of power to our new council."

With that, the meeting came to a close and everyone departed.

★ ★ ★

An old, battle-worn cruiser arrived at the transportation center near the Palace District on the planet Yord. The hub, like most places on the planet, was bustling with activity as many of the city's former inhabitants returned to engage in restoring their facilities.

The hatch opened and Kat(arina), a tall, dark-skinned vixen of intimidating allure in her thirties, stepped off the ship. She breathed the air and savored its freshness. It had been many years since she left her safe haven on Magnus, where only recycled air was breathed.

Kat wore a regal robe with a tiara and sparkling eye shadow to compliment her platinum-colored hair. The dockworkers immediately stopped and gazed at her in adoration.

She fled Magnus, a small space station located halfway across the galaxy, after a hostile takeover by corporate mercenaries and sought to gain a foothold in the newly reborn alliance as Marina's ally and confidant. Accompanying her on the ship were six of her most trusted bodyguards who provided her security on her station.

Two of the bodyguards approached her and bowed respectfully. Kat acknowledged them and followed them away from the ship. The other four appeared at the hatch to her ship, wearing turbans. They stood guard with pulse rifles and swords.

The dockworkers noticed them and quickly left the area, fearing their intentions. They recognized Kat from the stories they heard over the years from crews that indulged in the contraband trade through Magnus. They also heard rumors that she was a witch with many powers.

"Should I acquire transportation for you, Kat?" Faust, her chief body guard, inquired.

"No, I think I'll walk," she replied, smiling. "It's a beautiful day."

Faust and another guard lagged behind, giving her space to shop and speak with several of the locals. Unlike the dockworkers, few of the locals knew of her and what she was.

The local townspeople shied away from her at the site of her bodyguards. Kat noticed and summoned them closer. "Obtain quarters for yourselves. We'll be here for a while."

"Are you sure?" questioned Faust uneasily. "There may be hidden perils here."

"I can count on the queen's protection," she replied assuredly.

"Let me know if you need anything," he requested humbly of her.

"Thank you, Faust," she responded. "I'm sure I'll be fine." The men left her and sought out lodging at a local pub.

Kat continued down the street and attempted to strike up conversation with many of the mothers and their daughters. Taking particular interest in the young girls, she initiated brief conversations with several. The mothers were quick to intercede and usher the girls away from her.

There were two young girls in particular that she took interest in: very perceptive, educated for their age and unintimidated by her presence. The girls, Kara and Ginna, were eager to have conversation with Kat, unaware that she was testing them for certain skills or powers. Kat's curiosity grew as she considered that they could be the new Seers. They talked at length about the girls' upbringing and their beliefs until Dora appeared and took the girls away from Kat.

★ ★ ★

Drizzle fell on the cobblestone streets of the Palace District as patches of fog enveloped the city. Cool air rolled off the mountains and created a chilling effect on the quiet city. Windows were no longer boarded up despite the disrepair of the local shops and second floor apartments.

As the shadows of evening stretched across the region, the streets emptied. Stores closed and only random candlelight in windows shone through the inky blackness.

Under cover of night, a dark-skinned man in his thirties, Franklin, and Willow, a tall, blond woman in her forties with a briefcase under her arm, stood outside the door of an abandoned apartment. Both were dressed in long coats with rain hats. Franklin rapped twice on the door. The two waited impatiently until the door squeaked and then opened slightly.

A bearded man in his early forties, Eddie, peered out at them. He promptly opened the door and allowed them passage. Once they entered, he peeked outside to ensure no one saw them and then closed the door. The lock rattled as he secured the door.

Eddie had a muscular build and was taller than both Willow and Franklin. Dressed casually, he held a glass of wine in one hand. The three of them ascended the creaky stairs and entered a dimly lit, two-room apartment.

A single candle on the table illuminated the small apartment unit. Bare cupboards and dusty counters presented the apartment with an eerie atmosphere. The windows were covered with cardboard and the few pieces of furniture, other than the table and chairs, were covered with sheets. At the center of the table was a half-empty bottle of cabernet wine and two empty glasses.

After removing their coats, the visitors sat at the dusty, wooden table. Willow set the briefcase on the floor and complained about the accommodations. Eddie folded his hands and ogled Willow for a moment. She wore a leather skirt and a white blouse.

"You can't afford a maid, Ed?" Willow complained, knowing she had his attention. "This place is a shit hole."

"I don't live here," he responded sarcastically. "It's abandoned, dumbass." Eddie rolled his eyes over her lame comment and poured the wine for his guests.

Franklin chuckled and joked, "Come on, Willow, you've been laid in dirtier places than this."

Willow responded irately, "I do have standards, you know." The two men were amused by her claim. She clenched her fists and bristled at them.

"Easy, Willow," cautioned Franklin. Willow pointed a finger at him, on the verge of an outburst but Eddie interrupted, "Alright, let's get down to business before Willow has an aneurism."

"Kiss my ass, you prick!" Willow shouted and shoved the table into his ribs. The glasses nearly toppled and Franklin grabbed the bottle before it could fall.

Eddie winced briefly and regained his composure. "Before we start, how about a toast to our futures ... our very rich futures?" he suggested.

"I'll drink to that," responded Franklin eagerly.

"Can't think of any better reason than that," Willow added and calmed down.

The three raised their glasses and tapped them in unison. Willow finished her glass and swapped it for the bottle on the table.

"Did you meet with your contacts?" Eddie asked Willow.

"Yes, I did. Kronos Enterprises was anxious to employ our services," she answered confidently and laid the briefcase on the table. "In fact, Colonel Lennox, a high-level Fleet officer, left us a 'starter kit' to celebrate our role with the team."

"And the Fleet is working with them on this... endeavor," Eddie remarked, searching for the right word. "Anyone else involved that we should know about?"

"IDC," answered Franklin.

"What the hell is IDC?" he asked, curious.

"The Intergalactic Development Committee." Eddie glanced suspiciously at him, wondering what IDC would have to offer in their deal.

Willow opened the briefcase and removed three smaller cases. Inside each case were four cylindrical glass ampules, each five inches long and an inch in diameter.

Eddie took one out and studied it. "What do we have here?" he inquired.

"It's a man-made virus capable of wiping out whole towns in only a few hours," Willow explained. "And our orders are to use them on the towns closest to the Palace District." She handed a list to each of them. "Take one case and do your thing. They expect to see results by noon tomorrow."

"This is really big!" exclaimed Eddie "Right up our alley!"

"I love this part of the job," Willow remarked and guzzled the contents of the wine bottle.

The two men watched with amused expressions. "You still swallow like a seasoned whore, Willow," Eddie teased. "How do you do it after all these years?"

"Same as you, asshole. Lots of practice," she replied cynically and wiped the wine from her lips.

"And one hell of a reputation," Eddie added giddily.

Willow licked her lips seductively and unbuttoned the top three buttons on her blouse. She smirked at him, drew a dagger from a sheath on her leg, and stuck it in the table between his fingers. Two small blotches of blood appeared on his fingers. "Try me," she dared him. "I haven't changed."

With an arrogant grin, Eddie held his hand up and stuck his tongue between the injured fingers, flicking it twice at Willow. She pulled the dagger from the table and pointed it at Eddie, nearly touching the tip of his nose.

Eddie stopped smiling and warily pushed the dagger away from his face. He knew Willow wouldn't hesitate to cut him if she was 'in the mood'. "Who do you know at Fleet?" he inquired, trying to maintain a focus on their objective.

"That's my business," she answered as she leaned back in the chair and smiled confidently. "We aren't the only ones who want to get rich, you know," she answered confidently. "I have my sources."

"I like it," remarked Franklin enthusiastically. "Reminds me of the job we did on Minos Major ten years ago."

"Save the stories for someone who cares," sniped Willow. "I don't get paid for stories. Only kills."

"Remember, Willow, we were making hits when you were scrubbing shit stains off the floors for the Council," chided Eddie.

"Screw you, jackass!"

"Look," interceded Franklin, "We're the first stage of the plan. We're here because Kronos knows we'll get the job done."

"What about the militia?" asked Eddie curiously.

"General Witty is handling them," replied Willow. "Once we deliver the goods, I'll get the queen in line and we'll be off to a rich new life."

"I'm concerned about the queen," Franklin commented. "She won't go quietly."

"She'll go down on me if I tell her to," snapped Willow. "I'm gonna own her before this is over."

Eddie countered, "Whoa, Willow! Not every woman is as easy as you. Queenie won't go down on your good looks alone."

Franklin chuckled at them. He enjoyed watching Eddie get under Willow's skin. He knew she always took a liking to Eddie, but he had no interest in her other than business and screwing.

Willow stood and slapped his face. "I'm never easy, Ed. You should know that by now."

Eddie stood and grabbed her by her arms. He kissed her passionately. Willow shoved him away angrily. "Marina will do whatever I tell her to do and I mean 'whatever'," she vowed, while staring him down.

"Ah, you want to make love to her, don't you?" taunted Eddie as he attempted to kiss her again.

"That bitch killed my sister," countered Willow. "I want revenge for what she did to her."

"And that's it?" he questioned, still not convinced of her intentions.

"Maybe I want her squeal like a pig," Willow joked and then resumed a long, wet kiss with Eddie. "You know I always get what I want," she added and massaged Eddie's crotch, panting gently as she grew more excited. Eddie winked at Franklin and caressed Willow's breasts through her blouse.

"You haven't changed, Willow," remarked Eddie playfully. "I like that."

"We can stop right now, if you like," she warned.

Franklin stood and chided, "What? And deny yourself a moment of wet pleasure?"

Willow grabbed each man's crotch tightly and warned, "I can find a place for these on my mantle ... with the others I've collected over the years."

"I'm cool," replied Franklin nervously.

"Don't damage the goods," griped Eddie. "I get it."

Willow released her grip on the men. She was used to having her way and enjoyed it. With the former council members dead, thanks to Victor, she now had the opportunity to take control of the kingdom that her predecessors let slip away.

Franklin and Eddie were always the muscle who covered her back in the past and allowed her to meddle in Council affairs until the palace fell into Victor's hands. She learned much during those times, including how to avoid the mistakes made by her peers.

"Why not just kill the bitch?" inquired Eddie.

"Kronos is concerned about her allies outside the sector," she grumbled.

"They don't want any surprises until after things are in place."

"What things?"

Willow and Eddie embraced each other and kissed again. Willow rubbed his crotch and replied, "Important things placed where they belong."

"I have an important thing to place…" he started but Willow placed a finger to his lips for silence.

Franklin walked over to the couch and sat comfortably, hoping to witness his partners in some act of debauchery. Eddie slid his hand under her skirt and nibbled on her neck affectionately. Willow sighed with pleasure, but then grabbed his wrist and yanked it away. He groaned and placed his hands on his hips in frustration. Over the years, Willow was notorious for getting him aroused and then ending their encounter just when it got interesting.

"Our plan is a go, I assume" Eddie concluded disappointedly as Willow pulled away from him. He sat on the couch next to Franklin with a glum expression.

"Yeah, it's a go," Willow answered arrogantly. She put her coat on and walked toward the door as if the two men weren't even there.

"You're not leaving already, are you?" inquired Franklin, also disappointed.

"I'd love to stay and watch you two do each other but I have to prepare for the queen's demise," she answered curtly.

"Kiss my ass, Willow!" hollered Franklin.

"That was your job last week," she shouted sarcastically and descended the stairs.

Once the door slammed shut, the two men laughed giddily. "You know, Eddie, she is such a bitch," remarked Franklin.

Eddie put his hands behind his head and smiled. "Yeah, but she's as good a lay today as she was twenty years ago."

"Amen, brother," added Franklin.

II
THE FIRST STRIKE

The afternoon air was warm and a strong breeze added to the comfort of her walk. As Marina eased through the throng of people, everyone acknowledged her with smiles or a wave of the hand, while some even greeted her with friendly words.

One woman pushed her way through the crowd into Marina's path and asked for a moment of her time. Marina assumed that it must be important for her to make such a bold effort and escorted her away from the crowd.

The woman introduced herself as Magdalena and that she was once a maid to Marina's parents. The two women sat on a concrete bench outside the transportation center and conversed. Marina enjoyed the opportunity to speak with friends from her parents' past and learn more about them.

"The turn of events with my parents changed everyone here," Marina commented. "I'm truly amazed at the dedication of all these people to help restore the Palace District as well as the other cities and towns."

"Your parents gave us hope," Magdalena said humbly. "We enjoyed living under their rule and seeing how everyone, both human and alien, could co-exist in friendship and peace."

"I really want to bring that back to Yord," Marina admitted with a determined look. She pondered for a moment, wondering how time could change one's life so quickly, but then turned her attention back to her visitor. "So, what can I do for you, Magdalena?"

Much like Dora earlier, she grew uneasy and hesitated. Marina placed her hand on the woman's shoulder and assured her, "I won't bite you. I'm learning to adjust to public life just as you're adjusting to having your freedom again."

Magdalena finally made her request. "Can you find a place for my daughter in the palace? I think she'll serve you as well as I served your parents."

Marina was pleased by the request and happy to honor it. "I'm sure I can accommodate her. What is your daughter's name?" asked Marina curiously.

"Ginna," Magdalena replied proudly. "She is young but she has many skills."

"Tell Ginna to come see me and I'll make sure she is taken care of."

Magdalena knelt before her and thanked her. Marina was touched by the woman's devotion. When they stood, Marina instinctively hugged her, something new to her behavior. Magdalena was stunned by the queen's affection toward a commoner.

"You are always welcome to see me at the palace. Perhaps we can talk further about the way things once were," suggested Marina. "I'd love to hear more about your memories of my parents."

"I would be honored, your Highness. Now I must return to work. I have wasted far too much of your time."

"It was a pleasure," insisted Marina.

"Thank you so much," Magdalena repeated and disappeared into a passing crowd.

Marina startled herself, realizing that she showed outward affection toward a stranger. A year earlier, she would never have considered it. Glancing back at the transportation center through an open bay door, she noticed an old cruiser docked at the end berth. She knew she had seen it someplace before. Then it struck her: it was Kat's vessel from Magnus. Marina smiled, knowing it was only a matter of time before Kat came to collect on her marker with her. She wasn't concerned as Kat saved both Britt's and her lives. She felt an obligation to repay that debt.

No sooner had Marina resumed her walk, an older gentleman approached her, dressed in a long robe, sandals, and a worn top hat with holes in the side. Marina's first impression was that he was a joker, looking to entertain her. When he spoke, she knew by his tone that his purpose was much more serious.

"Good afternoon, your Highness," he greeted her formally.

Marina returned the greeting and waited curiously for him to state his business.

"May I speak with you?" he requested. "It's quite urgent."

"Of course," answered Marina, as they walked through the crowd.

"I am Drago and I was your parents' personal engineer for things like the underground facility and mechanic for *The Reaper*."

Marina was impressed and remarked, "So you are the brains behind the labyrinth of surprises."

"You could say that," he replied humbly. "I am sorry for the fate of your parents. They were good people."

Marina appreciated his sympathy and asked, "What can I do for you, Drago?"

"I wish to discuss modifications inside the palace to ensure your continued safety, since many of the former devices and accesses have been compromised."

"And what would it take for you to indulge in this project?"

"Under your parents' rule, I resided on the palace premises and was fed regular meals. That was necessary to maintain secrecy and isolation from anyone who suspected my mission. However, I make no demands or requests of you."

"What about payment for services?" she asked, expecting the punch line to his visit. "Surely, your services are of value."

"No payment," he replied proudly. "It is my honor to serve your Highness as I did your parents."

Marina pondered his offer briefly and then responded, "I'd prefer to wait until the other work is completed and the palace is secure before addressing your proposal. That would ensure your continued secrecy."

Drago bowed to her and replied, "As you wish, your Highness."

Marina reconsidered and countered, "I do need some interior work done on my ship - something to complement the exterior, if you get my drift. Could you help me with that?"

"Yes, your Highness. Might I suggest you move the ship to the base beneath the palace sometime soon? Let everyone think that it's been returned to the Calamaari fleet or even scrapped... for your own safety."

"Should I be concerned about my safety, Drago?" Marina asked curiously.

"Human nature dictates that the events of the past often repeat themselves at some point. It is better to be prepared as one never knows what the future holds."

"Thank you, Drago, for sharing your wisdom with me. You are welcome in the palace and will have your previous accommodations as well."

"I am grateful, my Queen. I will not disappoint you."

"We will speak later about your modifications to the palace. I'll inform my procurement officer to provide you with whatever materials you need."

"Thank you for your kindness, your Highness. I will inspect the interior of your ship and begin at once."

"And thank you for your concerns."

Drago bowed and departed her presence. Marina was amazed at the concern for her safety by strangers and pondered if her parents experienced the same profound respect. She also considered that, perhaps, she was too trusting with the man and should be careful with him. Later, she would test his sincerity and ensure his loyalty.

It was difficult for her to put her past behind her and now she had one last item to put to rest. Drago was right that *The Reaper* should be stowed somewhere out of sight. Marina sensed she would need it again one day and what better place to hide it than the secret base beneath her own palace. *Perhaps, after the renovations to it,* she considered.

Continuing her march through the town, Marina's mind swirled with thoughts of rebuilding the kingdom and establishing ties with former alien allies.

A woman's shouts caught Marina's attention. She promptly pushed through the crowd to investigate. When she arrived at the source, a gnarly man in dress clothes held a woman's arm tightly behind her back.

"Just give me the names and I'll leave you alone," the man warned. He released her arm and pushed her backward.

"I don't have to tell you anything!" she cried. "Now, go away!"

As she turned to leave, the man grabbed her by the shoulder and pulled her back. "You're going to die anyway, so save yourself the pain and cooperate with us."

"Screw you!" shouted the woman.

The man raised his hand to slap her but Marina interceded and bent his arm painfully behind his back.

"What's the meaning of this?" she questioned him angrily.

The man was mortified when he realized it was Marina. "It's nothing, your Highness. I'm just trying to help these poor people by meeting with their civic leaders."

The woman introduced herself to Marina as the leader of the town's civic group. She eagerly revealed to Marina how the man wanted a list of all the civic leaders and their locations.

Marina's face turned red and she increased the pressure on the man's arm. She considered breaking it but refrained.

"You shouldn't have interfered," he uttered, nearly in tears. "You don't understand what's at stake here."

"Then tell me; why are you threatening my people?"

The man refused to answer. Marina grew impatient and lifted him by his arm onto the tips of his shoes as his shoulder nearly dislocated. "Don't make me ask again," she warned him.

"Alright!" he cried. "I'll tell you."

When Marina released her hold on him, he clutched at the arm gingerly.

"Start talking," she ordered.

The man looked about suspiciously and then spoke. "Kronos Enterprises wants to..." Suddenly, the man quivered and fell to his knees. He looked up at Marina pleadingly and then fell to the ground dead.

The people around them panicked and retreated from the area. Marina examined the man and found a small red welt on the side of his neck. When she looked more closely at the wound, she discovered a small needle protruding from a tiny hole in the middle of the welt.

"Damn it!" she shouted angrily.

"What happened to him?" asked the woman nervously.

"Poisoned dart," Marina responded angrily, as she scanned the area for any sign of a shooter.

Four militia soldiers approached the area, performing their routine patrol. Hearing the excitement, they hurried and reported to Marina. She ordered them to conduct a search for the killer. In addition, she instructed them to take the body to the palace for identification. The soldiers, concerned by the murder, promptly followed her orders.

"Thank you so much, your Highness," the woman said appreciatively.

Marina raised her hand for the attention of everyone around them. "If anyone else threatens you, I want to know immediately. This is your home and no one can threaten you here."

An elderly man stepped forward from the crowd and informed her that he was threatened if he didn't reveal the relatives of the civic leaders as well. Two more women also revealed that they had been questioned forcefully.

"I'll get to the bottom of this, I assure you," Marina promised and stormed off toward the palace. It roiled her that some corporation had the audacity to bully her people like this in plain sight of her palace. She was eager to speak with Britt about the incident and turn the matter over to his militia for resolution.

Willow peeked through the curtains from the hotel across the street, grinning deviously, as she watched Marina leave the area. "Next time, it'll be you and me, Marina," she whispered to herself as she dissembled her compact dart gun and tucked it inside her jeans.

Marina stormed through the crowd toward the palace, angry but aware of her perception to the others. Everyone was anxious to catch a glimpse of her and tended to impede her path more than anything.

When she reached the palace steps, she paused to regain her composure. She couldn't let her anger deter her judgment during her first real challenge. Her people looked to her for leadership and she needed to provide it.

Four men carried the corpse through a side entrance of the palace. One of the men stopped to speak with Marina. He informed her that it would be a few days before someone would arrive to identify the poison.

"I don't care about the poison," Marina replied tersely. "I want to know who he worked for and where he's from."

"I will coordinate with the militia immediately, your Highness," the man promised and hurried after his peers.

To the western (left) side of the palace grounds, her cruiser *The Reaper* was parked. It was the last remnant of her past lifestyle and one that she dreaded parting with the most. The ghostly painting on the hull cast a three-dimensional effect as if it were an apparition, reminding her of the ghosts of her past. Marina approached the ship and opened its hatch with a small transmitter on her wrist. The device was small and subtle, like a cheap trinket, used to operate the security feature for the hatch.

Once the hatch opened, she stepped inside and was distraught by the poor interior of the ship. The furniture was moldy and water-stained. The snow and ice from Ithaca rotted the craft's once beautiful interior.

Marina suddenly grew light-headed and was forced to sit down at the hatch. She feared it was another consequence of her withdrawal from the Stardust she once was addicted to. But then, a frightening illusion formed in her head. People in several towns were dying. They pleaded for her help but she could only look on in horror. The hallucination ended.

A young female voice from behind startled her. It was Kara, her twelve-year old friend. Marina was pleased to see her and greeted her with a hug.

"Are you okay?" asked Kara, looking worried. "You seemed frightened."

"I'm fine. Just a little dizzy spell," Marina lied, hoping to avoid discussing the recurring spells.

"You saw something, didn't you?" questioned Kara.

"Sometimes," Marina answered sheepishly. "It comes and goes." She realized that Kara knew more about her than she let on.

The two enjoyed their conversation until Kara mentioned something that startled Marina. "My mother told me before she died that, when you returned, you would train the new Seers to defend Yord."

Marina was baffled by the remark. She frantically searched for an appropriate response and countered with a question, "And you were concerned that I wouldn't be there for them?"

Kara placed her hand on Marina's arm affectionately. "I know a lot of things about you. You're a special person."

Marina's expression turned somber. "Did your mother know you were one of the new Seers?" she inquired, testing Kara.

"She wasn't sure but told me that I would know when the time came."

"And are you?" Marina challenged playfully.

"I don't believe I could ever be what you are," Kara replied cryptically.

"I'm a fighter, but not gifted as you are."

"I'm not gifted; just stubborn," Marina kidded.

"As am I."

Marina was surprised by her response. It was well-crafted and if she knew of her powers, she wasn't telling.

Kara recalled other stories her mother told her at bedtime when she was much younger. Marina then related some of her bedtime stories that she was surprised to remember, mentioning repeatedly how they were happier times back then.

"What made you so strong and cold-hearted?" Kara asked curiously. "You are filled with so much hatred."

Marina was stunned by her question. She was amazed that Kara could see that inside of her, recognizing her burden. Despite her new life as queen of her people, Marina did harbor hatred toward those who wronged her in the past. One thing she excelled at was holding a grudge. "I have many demons in my life. Every day I battle them."

"What do you think caused these demons to grow inside you?" Kara asked.

"When my parents disappeared, many friends turned to foe over greed and power," explained Marina bitterly. "No one cared about me or the alliance or anything else that my parents built. It was as if they never existed."

Kara became nervous, feeling Marina's rage grow as she spoke of it.

Marina continued, "One thing I will not be is soft. Many people suffered because of traitors and soft leaders. That won't happen again."

"How can you protect us? Grandmum says that there are many who would hurt us for personal gain and even kill us."

Marina pondered her question, realizing that Kara just admitted to her calling as a Seer. "Perhaps I can bring you to the palace and we can learn from each other. I'm new at this Seer business as much as you are."

Kara was excited by the idea of training with Marina. "That would be great!" she exclaimed.

"We'll talk more on this later," Marina assured her. "Us Seers have to stick together."

"I'd like that," replied Kara. She went to the hatch and glanced back at Marina with an innocent smile. "Thank you," she said and left the ship.

Marina peered out and was amused, watching Kara skip giddily down the street. Then she realized the responsibility she had taken on. She shuddered at the thought that there could be a next generation of Seers. It was supposed to be over when she destroyed the crystal. Now, it was starting all over and she was forced into the middle of it with someone she cared very much for. Sighing with disappointment, she sat on the moldy couch and fell fast asleep. The withdrawal symptoms often left her feeling exhausted.

As she slept, she dreamed that Kat came to Yord to take the girls from her. Marina stood at the transportation hub and waited to confront her outside her ship. When Kat appeared, she smiled at Marina and greeted her affectionately. Baffled by her friendly demeanor, Marina questioned her presence. Kat informed her that they must work together if they expect to survive. She swore her allegiance to Marina, if she would allow her to stay with her. Suspicious of her request, Marina reluctantly agreed.

When Marina awoke, she recalled everything about the dream as if it was real. *Was Kat really here?* she asked herself, unsure if the dream had any substance to it. She promptly ordered one of the sentries to check the transportation hub for Kat's ship and then dozed off again.

Drago entered through the open hatch with his tool box, and set to work gutting the interior of *The Reaper*. Marina had just awoken when he entered and was pleased to see him. They spoke at length, while he removed the water-stained panels from the hull.

Marina questioned him about his suspicions for her safety and was amazed at the knowledge he had about groups that thrived during the war. Drago proved to be much more than an engineer. *Perhaps*, she considered, *he could help solve the issue of the murder that arose recently in the city and who the murder victim worked for.*

"Drago, have you heard of Kronos Enterprises?" Marina asked nonchalantly.

Drago paused with a panel in his hands and responded uneasily, "Why do you ask, my Queen?"

"Just a name I heard crop up in town today," she lied. "I was curious what they're about."

Drago turned to her and replied in a somber tone, "Kronos is supposedly made up of the wealthiest and most powerful individuals from the galaxy. No one knows for sure who they are and, based on the fate of those who dared to pry, I don't think you want to know."

"I see," responded Marina curiously. She closed the hatch for privacy and related the story of the man who was killed earlier in front of her.

Drago set down his crowbar and rubbed his eyes as if pained. Marina placed her hands on his shoulders and assured him it was safe for him to speak his thoughts with her.

"You don't understand, your Highness. If Kronos is here, then we are already in danger. They are bad news."

"How is it they escaped detection all these years?" she countered.

Drago broke into a sweat and reluctantly explained, "They are about a technology for a long-range targeting system, mining valuable ores from planets and controlling all commerce in the galaxy."

"Why now?" inquired Marina curiously. "Why would they choose to start such projects now?"

Drago took a seat across from Marina. He debated revealing the truth about his knowledge of Kronos and finally relented. "There was a technology developed to heat and cool the atmospheres of planets to enhance weather for agriculture."

"That doesn't sound so bad," Marina commented, unsure of the problem.

Drago continued, "A private group wanted the technology to use as a weapon that could fire a powerful laser from any or all of thirty satellites strategically located along the perimeter of the galaxy and fitted with a special device to magnify the beam even more for precise targeting. The core weapon would have to be mounted at a central host station first to be operational."

"That could have long-reaching effects, particularly with our allies," Marina remarked with concern. "How effective is this technology?"

"The key to the accuracy of the targeting system is a software program that was developed specifically to direct this new type of laser beam to all thirty of the receivers on satellites where they could then be magnified and fired at targets in seconds. If used for war, it has the potential to destroy large targets like entire planets from a significant distance," explained Drago somberly. "The programming software was stored on a data chip that vanished. No one is sure what happened to it."

Marina considered the ramifications of Drago's words. "How far do you think Kronos would go to find it?" she asked.

"This weapon would eliminate the need for warfare," he answered. "Imagine taking out your enemies from your main base, no matter where they are. It would end warfare and subjugate races across the galaxy and control all commerce."

"Is that so bad?"

"It would also allow the owner to control everyone and everything, anywhere in the galaxy. You work for them or you die."

Marina was shocked by his information. "How do you know all this?"

Drago became teary-eyed and explained, "My wife, Lilith, developed that technology for peaceful purposes. One day, two men from Kronos came to our home and requested she give them access to her research facility." He paused to wipe tears from his eyes and then continued, "When she refused; they took her away. I never saw her again."

"I'm so sorry, Drago. When did this happen?"

"A year ago," he responded sadly and bowed his head.

"Did they get their hands on the software?" Marina asked curiously.

"No. I set off the self-destruct sequence in her lab and destroyed everything. All that remained was the data chip."

"Did the chip ever appear?" she pressed with her questioning.

"Rumor had it that the chip was on the black market and several groups bid for it six months ago."

Marina thought back to the data chip she surrendered to Severin. She wondered if was ever turned over to Fleet Security and if it could possibly be Lilith's. "What happened at the bidding?"

"The chip never appeared," he replied. "Many believe Victor had the other bidders killed off to obtain it. When someone who claimed to have the chip arranged for the transfer, several groups came to intercept it but it was never found. Some believe it was turned over to the Fleet but there is no record of it and no one can attest to seeing it."

"Thanks so much, Drago. I will look into this and see what I can find out about Lilith's status," she assured him. When she opened the hatch to leave, Drago gently grabbed her by the arm and pleaded, "Be careful, my Queen. These people are ruthless and dangerous."

Marina touched his arm compassionately and reminded him, "So am I. That's how I got this far."

She left the ship and entered the palace. It was late afternoon and the workers departed for the day, leaving the palace eerily quiet. Gazing out the second-floor window at the palace grounds, she was excited to see Drago return to her ship with more materials. His commitment, like that of many others she met, was inspiring.

As she sat alone on her balcony, two militia soldiers rushed into the room and informed her of mysterious outbreaks in several towns. Marina was mortified when they related the mounting number of deaths, already in the thousands. She feared that her premonitions were accurate and increasing in frequency.

Immediately she met with two officers and instructed them to inspect surveillance footage from the transportation hubs in each town. There had to be evidence of those responsible somewhere. Suddenly, she felt overwhelmed and grew nauseous. She sensed another premonition but was interrupted by one of the sentries. He informed her that Kat's ship was still docked at the transportation hub.

I knew she'd come to me, Marina thought to herself. Oddly, she welcomed the idea of meeting Kat again soon. With no one around, loneliness took its toll on her. Her days battling Victor with Britt and Rebecca by her side seemed like years ago instead of months. Life was much simpler than compared to her time as queen.

Within a week, Drago finished his work on *The Reaper*. Marina needed something to help her through this latest bout of detox and Britt was still a few days from returning. She had over five thousand deaths to explain and no answers. After careful consideration, she decided it was time to move her ship underground and revisit her past. Marina was anxious to explore the underground facility that existed under her palace and wanted an opportunity to revisit her youth.

When she boarded the ship, she was overcome with awe by the work Drago performed. The moth-eaten furniture was replaced with a Gothic-style couch and tables. A wine cabinet was installed on the left hull and stocked with red glass cups mounted on gold stems. The sound system was upgraded and the server was scanned and cleaned to free up large amounts of memory for updated programming.

An oak cabinet with glass doors was mounted on the forward wall next to the hatch. The background was red velvet with black trim. Eight new jewel-encrusted daggers were mounted around two leather, spiked gloves. There was also a black, conical helmet with eight cutouts around the perimeter for Marina's dreadlocks. A new wig with dreadlocks and her signature silver flash grenades was mounted on a hook inside the display. Marina pondered how Drago knew so much about her secret past and her attire. *Was my life as 'the courier' that well known?* she asked herself. More and more, she realized her prior life wasn't so secret. Only to her did it appear so. Under cover of night, Marina piloted her ship down the steep cliffs to the cave beneath the palace.

The facility was constructed inside the cliffs behind and well below the palace as a security measure. The only outside access was through the narrow cave used by Marina to dock her ship. Once inside the cave, the cruiser glided smoothly toward the underground base, using its advanced guidance system to maneuver through the darkness and past the rusted gates.

Marina found it strange that the gates were partially opened and was concerned that someone, most likely Victor, had gained access to the facility at one time. If so, then the base and temple were no longer the safe haven that protected her parents so many years ago.

There were twelve docks, capable of mooring from ten to twenty ships based on size. Empty boxes, broken crates and scattered papers littered the discolored steel surface. Rust-colored streaks revealed deterioration of the base walls as moisture seeped through several cracks in the stone walls.

Once the ship hovered alongside the first steel dock, electro-magnets energized automatically and secured the ship tightly to its moorings.

Marina stepped out with her pistol drawn, unsure of what to expect. She placed her hand on the 'close' pad on her ship and watched as the hatch closed.

There was one stairwell to access the palace from the base and another from the temple. The facility was only manned on a few occasions during the war and, even then, Marina's parents protected its secrecy from the outside world. It was powered by a fusion reactor with several automatic features for maintaining its operability without human interaction. Gradually, areas of the base illuminated and the ventilation system activated, replacing the stale air with a steady flow of fresh air from natural ducts in the cliffs.

Equipped with several shops designed for repairs to the ships, there was a variety of rigging devices and tool boxes at the entrances. A control center with high-tech equipment from that period was fortified with adequate food supplies to survive for months if needed.

Across the deck from her were sculptured cement stairs that led to the temple's entrance. She ascended the stairs and paused in front of a steel door. The silence was eerie as she felt chills run down her spine.

Placing her hand on a scanner next to the door, she waited patiently. The device beeped twice, recognizing her identity, and the door quietly slid open. She stepped through and glanced back to ensure the door closed securely and no one had followed.

Accessing a long corridor, memories of her childhood with the priestesses returned to her. She reluctantly entered the Temple of Icarus and reminded herself of her vow to never come back there again. But here she was. *How ironic*, she thought.

Once inside, she was surprised to see that the temple was still in excellent condition. In the center of the main chamber, a small fountain sprang to life and fed steaming hot water into a small pool. Marina recalled being bathed daily in the pool by the priestesses. *Perhaps they weren't so bad after all*, she kidded herself.

The temple's hidden passage to the wine cellar originated on one side of the altar, a marble structure of exquisite craftsmanship that the priestesses worshiped at. Above the altar was an image of two moons over the planet portrayed as large eyes in the sky looking down upon the people of Yord.

In front of the altar was a golden, high-back chair with red velvet cushions. Marina recalled that the head priestess sat in that chair when she addressed everyone after prayers each evening. After all these years, everything appeared the same. Curiosity got the better of her and she sat in the chair. Feeling a warm sensation over her body, she was startled by a woman's voice. "Marina, you must take back what is ours from those who will betray us."

Marina shuddered as she recognized her mother's voice. She tried to stand but couldn't. *Is this another premonition?* she wondered.

The voice continued, "You are surrounded by danger. There are many who seek to take control of your powers and your domain for personal gain."

"Mother!" Marina cried out.

"You have many battles ahead of you but, fear not, you will never be alone."

A vague image of her parents formed in front of her. She trembled at the sight of them. The image vanished and she was then able to stand.

"Mother! Father!" she called but there was no response.

Marina stood and approached the pool. Steam rose in the air from the bubbling waters. Tempted by memories of its soothing affect, she removed her cape and slowly undressed.

Without the bruises, daggers and the wig that were trademarks of her prior life-style, Marina was an image of beauty.

Knowing that her parents had not abandoned her and that she avenged them when she reaped her revenge on Victor, she changed her outlook on life and brought closure to their deaths. Since she took up residence on Yord, she ate regularly and worked out privately, maintaining her fighting skills. Her body was one to die for and she was proud of it. After all the years of physical punishment, now she was finally rewarded for her efforts. Despite her cold-heartedness, she was learning to show affection in her own way toward others.

The one thing she craved was her time with Britt. Their duties put a premium on their time together and frustrated Marina to no end. As she slid into the pool, she was overwhelmed by a series of visions that left her unsteady and light-headed. Faces of people she knew as a child filled her thoughts. The chamber grew foggy and a chilly breeze swept across Marina's face. She felt helpless with no weapons to protect her and lay naked in the pool.

"Relax, Marina. You're safe down here," a woman's voice startled her.

The fog cleared and Charisse, the priestess from her childhood, stood before her.

"Charisse, I thought you were dead!" blurted Marina.

"Only that part of my journey has ended. We have many important things to accomplish."

"We?" replied Marina, confused by the reference.

"Yes. Your journey only started when you took the throne. There is much to develop, including the freedom of your people and your parents' empire... your empire."

Marina was stunned by her words to her, 'your empire.' "What else could I possibly be cursed with?" she complained. "I never wanted this life."

"But it's your destiny, as are the events that will soon unfold before you."

"What are these events?" questioned Marina uneasily.

"In time," answered Charisse calmly. "Remember the lessons I taught you as a child and you will succeed."

"Tell me more!" demanded Marina.

The chamber was clouded by the mysterious fog again and Charisse vanished. Charisse's fading voice warned her, "Many will turn against you. Be wary of your allies."

Marina became alert and peered nervously around the chamber. Anger took over as she realized she would have more assholes to deal with in her life. "It just doesn't get easier," she grumbled. Just when she started to accept a serene life without violence, new enemies arose to stir her rage.

After what seemed an eternity in the steaming pool, she found her resolve to take on whatever cruel tricks life had in store for her. "Perhaps the old Marina isn't gone; she's just taking a break," she told herself. Feeling invigorated after the bath, she wondered if the waters held magical powers of strength for her.

When she strolled back to the altar, she remembered the secret passage to the temple. Only once had she ever seen it. The night that mercenaries raided the palace, Charisse carried her into a hidden stairwell that led down to the temple from the second-floor hallway.

Marina noticed a small bench next to the altar and instinctively raised the seat on it. There was nothing beneath it but then the wall creaked. It slowly rotated and opened, revealing a dark passageway.

"Ah, there it is," she said to herself, pleased that she found it.

Charisse's voice whispered from the darkness, "Have faith, child. I am with you." Then a small light formed in front of her. The light grew until she could see a stairwell just ahead.

Marina reached for the ball of light and held it in her hand. She was amazed that she could control the light. As she stepped onto the stairs beyond the rotating wall, it closed quickly.

Excitedly, she ascended the rickety, old stairs, wary of rotten or broken wooden steps. There were cement platforms every hundred steps where the stairwell changed direction. Her curiosity grew when she reached the second-floor hall but the stairs continued. This was new to her as she never saw the end of the stairwell. Her curiosity drove her to go forward. When she finally reached the top, she counted about four hundred steps. "Now that's a friggin' workout," she complained to herself.

The silence was interrupted by voices. The ball of light extinguished in her hand and tiny rays shone through holes in the wall from the other side. She peered through and saw three strangers in her parents' third-floor den. Eddie, Franklin and Willow sat pompously in chairs with their feet on the desk, puffing on cigars. Marina immediately grew nauseous from the smell. *Arrogant assholes*, she thought to herself.

Marina stepped across the platform toward another section of the wall and located the entrance to the corridor. She pressed the latch on the side of the panel, releasing the spring assembly, and the door swung open. Stepping through the passageway, she entered the corridor and stood outside the den. The secret door closed quietly behind her.

Marina's blood boiled as she felt violated by these people. She heard one of the men, Eddie, question his peers about an attempt for a conference with the alien leaders of her parents' former alliance. There was great concern that she would unite them and create a problem for Kronos.

Eddie remarked giddily, "I expect ol' Marina will have a hard time explaining the deaths of all those people."

"Wait until she finds out we were behind it," said Franklin, chuckling as well.

"Now that she knows what we're capable of, I think she'll be more than accommodating," replied Willow stoically. She didn't share the same satisfaction as her partners and only sought revenge against Marina for her sister Fiona's death.

"How do you know the queen will cooperate?" Franklin asked. "Kronos won't be happy if we turn this into a revolution. They want things taken care of quietly."

Willow reminded them, "The queen will do whatever we tell her to do. I'll see that."

"We're counting on you, Willow," added Eddie as he blew rings of smoke in the air for entertainment.

"And when we do break the news to her that she answers to us, she'll be surprised to find that she has no one to support her," Willow added confidently.

Marina couldn't contain her anger any more. She barged into the room and challenged them, "How about we resolve this right now?"

Willow was pleased to see Marina and taunted her, "You're just in time for your attitude adjustment."

"And I have an adjustment for you assholes!" she threatened. "You're trespassing in my palace and you'll answer for that."

Franklin approached her and poked a finger in her chest. "We run this kingdom, not you," he announced defiantly. "You're just a figure head for the people."

"Guards!" shouted Marina confidently.

"Guess what, Marina? No one's coming," taunted Eddie. "We took care of that already."

"Looks like you'll have to deal with us yourself," Franklin remarked confidently.

Marina tossed her cape on the desk and felt the adrenalin rush she always got when faced with confrontation. "Oh, believe me, you'll wish you had the guards to deal with instead of me." She stepped between them and assumed a defensive posture. "This is my kingdom and you don't belong here," she warned them.

Willow chastised her, "While you were out roaming the universe, I was the ruling authority over this kingdom."

"And look what you did with it," Marina chided. "It went to hell."

Marina grabbed Franklin's arm and twisted it behind his back. He yelped in pain. "Don't ever point that finger at me again or you'll lose it," she warned sternly.

"Let's get the formalities out of the way," announced Willow, unconcerned with Franklin's painful position. "Kronos wants you alive, very much against my wishes, but we have orders to bring you back with us."

"Kronos can kiss my ass," Marina shouted and yanked harder on Franklin's arm until he yelped.

"Come on, Frankie, suck it up," taunted Eddie.

"As such, I suggest you come peacefully or we will have to rearrange that little figure of yours into something much less palatable."

Marina fumed and yanked once more on Franklin's arm until he screamed. She released her hold and drove her elbow into the back of his head. Franklin staggered forward and fell to his knees, dazed from the blow.

Eddie and Willow charged at her. Marina instinctively kicked Eddie in the jaw and floored him. Willow threw a punch at her face but Marina blocked it and chopped her in the throat. Franklin staggered to his feet and struck Marina in the back of the head with a lamp. Marina fell to the floor, stunned by the blow.

Before she could move, the three were on her with daggers at her throat. "I don't have to bring all of you to Kronos," Willow taunted. "How about I start cutting off pieces until we come to an agreement?"

"Go ahead, if you think you have the balls," Marina replied weakly.

"You are nothing, Marina," declared Willow. "From this day on, you'll answer to me and do whatever I tell you. Got that, *bitch*?" Willow then planted a big kiss on Marina's mouth.

Marina smirked and mocked her, "A little mouth wash for that dog breath wouldn't hurt."

They were perturbed by Marina's arrogance, even when she was disadvantaged. Eddie stood and unbuckled his pants. "We're gonna have some fun with you, girl!"

While lying on her back, Marina head-butted Franklin and knocked him off of her. With her free hand, she grabbed Willow's wrist and turned the dagger away from her face and directed it toward Willow's cheek. Before Eddie could react, she kicked him in the groin. Eddie gasped and fell to his knees. She struggled to her feet, still wrestling with Willow over the dagger.

With three knee kicks to Willow's side, she gained the advantage and pressed the knife against her cheek until a line of blood appeared. Then Willow surprised her by dropping to the floor and head-butting Marina in the stomach. Instinctively, Marina grabbed Willow's head and rammed her knee into her forehead. Willow fell backward onto the floor, weakened from the blow.

Eddie got to his feet and charged at Marina. She quickly took up a defensive position and delivered three chops to Eddie's throat, followed by a big kick to his groin again. Eddie fell to the floor, gasping for air, while coiling up in a fetal position.

Willow stood up awkwardly but hesitated to attack out of concern for Eddie. Marina took advantage of her hesitation and threw three punches at her jaw, staggering her. Willow winced from the pain but instinctively kicked Marina in the jaw, flooring her. Willow then lunged on top of Marina. Each woman held the other in a choke hold and, despite turning blue from asphyxiation, neither would yield.

Franklin crawled to his knees alongside them and punched Marina in the side of the head in desperation, leaving her dazed. He cried out in pain as he broke his hand. Marina's grip on Willow loosened from the impact. As she lay stunned, Willow retrieved her dagger and stood over Marina. "You're gonna beg for mercy before I'm finished with you."

Marina wanted to reply but couldn't. She tried to regain her senses and stand, but still reeled.

"I hope you like what we did to your loyal followers, Marina. How many are dead - nine... ten thousand?" Willow taunted.

Marina hadn't realized the number of casualties was so high. She felt hopeless and death didn't seem so bad right now. Ten thousand people died on her watch and she'd have to live with that or take it to the grave with her.

Kara and Ginna, both twelve-year old girls, peered in from the hall and were horrified by Marina's predicament. They both cried out to Marina.

Willow grew irritated by the site of them. They didn't need witnesses to spread stories of their transgressions toward Marina among the townspeople yet.

The girls closed their eyes and raised their hands upward. Eddie and Franklin saw images of spiders crawling all over their bodies. They frantically dropped their daggers and shook as if possessed to remove the imaginary arachnids. Willow imagined her abdomen split open and her intestines seep from within. She dropped her dagger and clutched at her stomach to hold them in.

Marina took advantage of the illusions and shoved Willow aside. She threw several punches at Willow's face, leaving her barely conscious. Then, as if possessed by a mad demon, she turned on Eddie and Franklin with a series of kicks to the head, followed by chops to the throat and knees to the midsection. All three of her assailants lay disabled on the floor with spasms from the pain.

Turning to her new Seers, Marina beamed with pride as she realized she found her Seers or rather they found her. Even better, they already knew how to use some of their powers.

Willow struggled to her feet and surprised Marina from behind. "Stay away or I'll kill her," she warned the girls and pressed her dagger against Marina's neck. Marina was undaunted and instinctively grabbed Willow's wrist, twisting until the dagger dropped to the floor. Willow howled in pain as Marina delivered an elbow to her jaw and floored her.

The girls again raised their hands upward. Willow imagined black worms crawling over her body and forcing themselves into her mouth.

She gagged and coughed uncontrollably, shuddering until she was nearly unconscious. When the girls lowered their hands, Willow sobbed, while reeling from her spasms.

Marina stood and nodded in approval to the girls. She requested they leave and say nothing of the attack. With Willow helpless on her knees, Marina gripped her throat with one hand, pulled her to her feet, and punched her repeatedly with the other. After a number of blows to her face, Willow gasped and was nearly unconscious once more.

"You tell your friends at Kronos that I'm coming for them - every one of them. Got that, *bitch?*" Marina shouted, her blood boiling with rage.

Willow forced a smile and replied arrogantly, "I will have you before you know it. I eat bitches like you for breakfast."

"Then it's time to go on a diet," Marina mocked and slammed her head against the wall. Willow fell to the floor and was out cold. Marina was pleased by the sight of blood streaming from several cuts on Willow's forehead above her eye and her cheek. *Perhaps the violence is more of an addiction than the Stardust*, Marina considered.

Four militia soldiers rushed through the door, led by a young Lieutenant Marcus, while three others apprehended the men in the hall. "Are you alright, your Highness?" Marcus asked nervously.

"Of course," Marina replied. "I want these three imprisoned. If they resist, kill them."

The soldiers were surprised by her fierceness. Unaware of the young girls' role, they assumed Marina manhandled her assailants alone. They jerked Eddie to his feet. He was barely coherent as he glared at Marina.

Marcus, young and dark-skinned, threw Eddie down and stood over him with his foot on his chest. "Don't ever screw with our queen again or I'll kill you myself."

Eddie sneered at him but said nothing as Marcus backed away.

"You can't do this to us," Franklin uttered. "We have protection."

"I'm your Queen," Marina announced defiantly as she stepped into the hall. "There is no protection that will save you from my wrath, asshole."

She gripped Franklin by the neck and punched him in the gut. As he doubled over, she kneed him in the nose and broke it. He fell to the ground, clutching at his disfigured nose with blood streaming over his hands.

The soldiers were amused by Franklin's misfortune. He struggled to his feet, blood streaming down his chin now and onto his shirt. "This isn't over, I promise you," he groaned.

Marina smiled and delivered a kick to the side of his face. He dropped to the ground, grasping frantically at his dislocated jaw.

"It is now," she remarked defiantly. "I'll speak to Kronos myself while you three are rotting in a nice cell." Franklin moaned in pain and stayed down.

"Well done, my Queen," Marcus commented proudly. "I will see to it that security is tightened around the palace and I will personally monitor everyone who is permitted entry. Please forgive our failure to protect you. It won't happen again."

"No worries," she remarked. "I needed a little workout."

"I will have the medics tend to your wounds," he assured her.

Marina wasn't used to that kind of treatment. She chuckled and replied, "What wounds? I'm fine."

Willow came to and snarled at her, "You cocky-ass bitch!"

Marina pulled Willow to her feet by her hair. She warned her, "If I ever see or hear you again, you'll be in shackles and serve every citizen and soldier of Yord for the rest of your life, *peasant*!" She shoved Willow to the ground and stared her down.

The soldiers pulled Willow to her feet again and pushed the three of them toward the door. Marina stopped Marcus and inquired, "What is your name?"

"Marcus, your Highness."

"Well, Marcus, I like your attitude. Thanks for your help."

"My pleasure, your Highness." Marcus bowed and pursued his men with the prisoners.

When the room was empty, Marina fell down and lay on her back, staring at the ceiling. Her head still spun and she felt nauseous. *No sense complaining,* she thought to herself. *You've been through worse.* After an hour alone on the floor, she summoned enough strength to stand and then left the den.

Marina stopped at regular intervals because of her injuries and took a while to make it to the palace entrance. Now, she had to hide her pain and look strong before exiting the palace. After a deep breath, she opened the door and stepped out, pretending all was well.

Outside the palace, a man with a cane waited to see her. When she reached the bottom of the steps, she took notice of him. He looked so familiar but his face was scarred and he walked with a terrible limp.

"Do I know you?" Marina asked.

"You did once. I was a different person before the Fleet did this to me."

"And you are?"

"Tulley. Remember the data chip?"

Marina was stunned. Tulley looked as if he aged a hundred years. "Where is Rock?" she asked.

"He is still imprisoned at Fleet headquarters along with someone else who is very valuable to you."

"Why do you come to me?"

"You are the only one who can stop what's happening."

"What's this about, Tulley?"

"The data chip and Kronos Enterprises," he uttered and continued after a brief pause. "When we found out that they were involved, we hid the chip for everyone's sake."

"And who is this person of value?" Marina asked curiously.

"She owns the information on that chip. They torture her every day in hopes of gaining access to the chip or the information on it. She can help you stop Kronos, but you need to act soon before she breaks." Tulley turned and limped away.

Marina called to him, "Is this woman named Lilith?"

Tulley looked back and smiled with broken teeth. "You're smart," he replied. "Perhaps not smart enough, though. Watch your back."

"How did you manage to escape?" she inquired. "I assume you were a prisoner as well."

Tulley glanced back once more and replied with a sordid grin, "The same way as you on Orpheus-2. The chip is there." He turned the corner and disappeared from her sight.

Marina wanted to ask more but thought better of it. The image of Tulley's emaciated frame haunted her. He and Rock were two tough sons of bitches. She then recalled on Orpheus-2 that she and Rebecca escaped from Victor through the HVAC ducts, which took them down to the transport bay.

Still stunned by the night's events, she spent the evening in the safe confines of her ship in the underground base.

The appearance of Kara and Ginna at the palace gave her some relief as she now knew the identity of two new Seers. In the morning, she would have to figure out what to do with them. Panic set in as she wondered how many more Seers were out there. This was a responsibility that she really didn't want.

III
THE BITCH IS BACK

The beautiful flowers and shrubs that once adorned the garden were overgrown with weeds and unsightly bushes. Two men tilled the ground at the back of the garden, while others repaired the damaged wall surrounding the palace.

Marina walked across the palace courtyard and sat on a cement bench. She hoped for guidance for the young Seers from the spirit of Charisse or maybe even the ghosts of her parents, but there was no one to help her.

Dix arrived at the palace in search of Marina and was escorted into the garden. Looking concerned, he sat next to her and inquired, "Are you alright?"

"Of course," she lied. "I had to squash a few insects last night but it's handled."

"You'd best be careful with those 'insects'. I understand they are part of a powerful group and should be feared."

"Well, I've already started weeding them out. I think they know not to underestimate me."

Dix was greatly concerned now. "What happened?" he asked uneasily.

"A few thugs claimed to be councilors. They were under the misconception that they run Yord and that I'd take orders from them. When I clarified their misunderstanding, they required a lesson from the old Marina."

Dix looked horrified. "You didn't kill them, did you?"

"No, but I think they know who's in charge around here. I did have some well-timed help to handle them."

"And they were?" he pressed.

"It's not important right now," Marina lied to protect the girls' identities.

Dix placed his hands on Marina's arms and warned, "You're messing with dangerous people, who have connections in powerful places."

Marina folded her arms and glared. "They weren't so dangerous when Victor turned on them," she replied cynically. "If he handled them, so can I. Besides, what makes them think they can rule anything here?"

"Just be careful, Marina. Don't underestimate them either."

Tired of the topic, she sighed and replied, "I've imprisoned them and plan on keeping them there for a long time."

"Don't underestimate them," he repeated.

"I won't. Thanks for your concern."

"What's happening with the outbreaks?" he inquired. "People are scared and fleeing the neighboring towns."

"I don't know that I'd call them outbreaks. They were planned."

"You think this is a message to you?" he questioned.

"Oh, I'm sure it is. My visitors told me so in no uncertain terms."

"Watch yourself, Marina," he warned. "Let me know if I can do anything to help." Dix stood and left her, glancing back with concern as he exited the gates.

Marina hated that those around her were frightened. While she appreciated their concern, she needed her courage. These warnings from Kronos and company only undermined that. She knew Kronos was bigger than Victor ever hoped to be and she could expect worse from them.

In the past, her Stardust addiction provided her the courage she needed to overcome her obstacles. Now that she was clean, she had to face this head on. She hoped that her parents or Charisse would show her guidance through her dreams and premonitions, but she also knew that she had to make her own decisions.

Later that afternoon, Marina stood at the bottom of the concrete steps in front of the palace and scanned the palace grounds. She watched as a group of men tied thick ropes to one of the palace gates and hoisted it upright. They maneuvered it against the wall, where the damaged hinges could be cut out with a welding torch and replaced. She stared at the ground and feared her loneliness. This wasn't how things were supposed to be.

Britt arrived and ogled Marina from across the courtyard. He wore his dark uniform with the stars of militia commander on his shoulders. Having just returned from Fleet headquarters, he was anxious to speak with her. He noticed her depressed expression and knew that look all too well. Something was wrong.

When he approached her, he was stunned at the bruises on her face. "What the hell happened to you?" he asked frantically. "I told Marcus to watch your back!"

Marina rushed to him and embraced him. They kissed passionately and then Britt pushed her away, waiting for an explanation.

"Marcus did fine," she said, smiling for the first time in a while. "I just needed a little workout to shake the rust off." She stared at him hungrily, hoping for some sign of affection.

"What else is wrong?" he inquired anxiously, knowing full well where Marina would go with the question. She missed him and, no doubt, wanted some private time with him.

"Apparently Kronos is concerned about me," she mentioned to his surprise. "They want me stopped."

"How do you know?"

"Long story," she remarked disinterestedly as she placed her arms around him and kissed him."

"Anything else wrong?" he asked suspiciously.

"This is what's wrong," she replied and kissed him again. "Not enough of it."

Britt looked around nervously to see who watched. Marina frowned and folded her arms disappointedly. "I thought we were past this?" she complained.

"I'm still getting used to it," he confessed. "Besides, I have a reputation to keep up."

"I'll fix that reputation. On your knees, boy!"

Britt laughed at her and countered, "How about I put you over my knee?"

"I might like it," she joked and kissed him once more. They held hands and entered the palace.

"I heard you had a problem last night," he mentioned uneasily. "Did I hear right that you were attacked?"

"Just a few thugs. Nothing I couldn't handle, though," she replied confidently. "Marcus took them away."

"I'll have them executed immediately."

"No, I want them tried for treason and then punished. I need my people to know I stand for them."

"Well, at least you didn't kill them," he joked.

"I sure wanted to. I think your young officer Marcus did too."

Britt grinned and revealed, "Marcus is my most trusted officer. I have big plans for him."

Marina was pleased with his choice and considered she might have plans for Marcus as well. She appreciated his outspoken loyalty to her and knew she could count on him. The two held hands and entered the palace.

"We need to talk about some things that occurred at Fleet Headquarters," Britt informed her.

"How about over dinner?" she suggested. "I have some things to discuss with you as well."

"It's a date," Britt replied. "I have a meeting first and then I'll come by for you."

Two very old men waited outside the conference room on the first floor. Britt nodded to them and they acknowledged him. "Duty calls," he replied disappointedly. Britt kissed Marina and they parted ways.

Marina inspected the first-floor repairs before going upstairs. A dozen women scrubbed the walls and floors, oblivious to her presence. She noticed that Marcus' guards kept a watchful eye on everyone and that Marcus frequently passed through the palace to ensure security was tight.

Despite their vigilante watch, Marina ascended the stairs, wary of anything suspicious. Even with Marcus' assurance, she studied each face as she passed, remembering who had access to her palace.

As she walked along the second-floor hall, she was pleased to see that the lighting was operable and the walls had been painted. The ceramic tile floor still required work but she was happy with the overall progress.

At the end of the hall was Charisse's meditation room. Marina entered and sat next to the stone table. The image of Charisse's brutal death at Fiona's hands still burned in her brain. As if on cue, an apparition of Charisse appeared. She gazed adoringly at Marina from behind.

As Marina pondered the past, Charisse's voice startled her. "Fear not, my child for I will always watch over you," she said compassionately.

"Why are you here, Charisse?" Marina inquired curiously.

"You are surrounded by enemies," she warned. "Trust no one."

Marina grew uneasy with the repeated warnings. "Who are these enemies? Can you tell me?"

Charisse glided closer to her and placed her hand on Marina's cheek. Marina felt a chill where the hand touched her. "You will be forced leave this land and fight a war greater than your parents."

"Against whom?" Marina asked uneasily.

"There are few who can be trusted," Charisse replied cryptically. "You'll know who they are when the time comes."

Marina stood and questioned her. "How will I know who will fight for me?"

"When the time comes, all who are true will stand with you," Charisse revealed as her apparition faded.

"Wait!" pleaded Marina. "Don't leave." She fretted as the apparition vanished. Marina paced the floor and considered the warnings.

Kara and Ginna stood in the doorway and startled Marina. "Come in, girls," she invited them anxiously. "I was just thinking about the two of you."

"Would you like some company, your Highness?" Kara asked. "You were talking to yourself."

Marina chuckled and knelt down next to the girls. "First of all," she explained, "call me Marina when we're in private. You are my children now."

The girls were pleased by her reference to them. Ginna inquired, "Why are people trying to hurt you, Marina? You are here to help us."

Marina sighed and placed her arms around the girls' waists. "The universe is full of bad people. They will do anything for money and power."

"Is power a bad thing?"

"It is if the person uses it to hurt good people," Marina explained.

"Who were the people who attacked you?" Kara asked again.

"They work for some very bad people who want to destroy our kingdom."

"Can you stop them?" asked Ginna uneasily.

"I think so. I need a really good plan, though, because they are a very big enemy."

"We can help," Kara offered eagerly.

"You already did," Marina replied, while stroking the girls' hair affectionately. "I wasn't prepared for them and you saved me. I'll make sure that doesn't happen again."

"What can we do to help?" asked Ginna.

Marina pondered for a moment as she considered how to keep them safe. "I would like you to stay with me so I can protect you."

"Will we live with you?" asked Kara anxiously.

"Yes, but not here. I have someplace else in mind. Get your things and bring them here."

The girls eagerly left the room. Marina was concerned for their safety just by her association with them. She knew she just escalated the fight with Kronos by humiliating Willow and her thugs. No doubt, they would retaliate more seriously with their next move and now the girls were in play as well.

Marina wondered how the girls knew where to find her and how they knew she was in need of companionship. Perhaps that was their role as Seers to know when to appear. She sat for an hour and pondered what the future held for her. Finally, she grew frustrated and accepted the fact that she'd have to face her enemies head on and alone. She left the palace and sat on the front steps.

When Britt joined Marina on the palace steps, she leaped into his arms like a little girl. They kissed and hugged several times before Britt set her down. "How was your meeting?" Marina inquired.

Britt handed her a disk and explained, "This is a gift from the historians. It details all of your parents' allies as well as how they handled their enemies. Basically, it's the blueprint to their alliance."

Marina eyed the disk excitedly. "Britt, this is wonderful!" she blurted. "Thank you so much." She kissed him passionately.

Britt grew somber and suggested, "Why don't we get something to eat? We really need to discuss some issues."

Marina grew agitated, wondering what else could go wrong. She also resented the fact that her man returned home and is occupied with issues other than her.

They sat in a small café not far from the palace, sipping wine while dining on steak and fresh vegetables. Britt revealed that Marina's assailants were taken away from the palace prison by Fleet personnel on orders from

General Witty. They also confiscated the corpse of a man who died in town recently.

"Damn it!" shouted Marina. "How could you let them do that?"

"I had to," he replied apologetically. "They've invoked the rules of jurisdiction established by your parents and we're not ready to handle them in a confrontation yet. I've recalled several of my ships to help out, though it will take several days for their arrival." He then explained in detail what was discussed at the meeting and how they informed him that he was only there as a courtesy.

Marina related her experience with the troublesome man in town earlier and how he was assassinated. She also mentioned that she wanted the corpse identified and who he worked for. Despite the setback, they decided to upgrade the security and increase the militia presence around the Palace District.

Britt informed her that his medical officer determined that the outbreak in several towns was from a man-made virus and the towns were deliberately targeted.

Not surprised, Marina warned him that she would not hesitate to return to her old ways, if necessary, to protect her people. Britt tried to dissuade her from that idea and assured her that he would handle things. He recommended that she meet with the IDC and Kronos Enterprises with backup to make them aware that they are violating her sovereignty.

Marina expressed concern for her people and her desire to protect them. Britt informed her that his men monitored all the transportation hubs on the planet and were verifying identities of everyone passing through, both recently and presently. "If we're lucky, they'll find a link to the assassins," he said confidently.

"Don't waste your time," replied Marina. "I know who they are."

Britt waited anxiously for her to reveal their identities, but Marina liked having his undivided attention. She paused long enough for him to press her for a reply.

"The three false councilors were behind it. Willow was kind enough to inform me that she was responsible for nearly ten thousand deaths."

"Then we need to get her back here!" exclaimed Britt. "She has to be tried and executed."

"Good luck with that," chided Marina. "If Witty got her out of here, you know he won't send her back."

"We'll see about that," he responded angrily.

Frustrated with the news, Marina changed the topic and spoke about how they could spend some time together on a short trip to Andros-5 where her father often hid from his enemies during the Great War. Britt agreed to her offer but, to her disappointment, at a later date.

When they returned to the palace, Marina eagerly led him up the stairs to her bedroom. They embraced and kissed hungrily for several minutes. This time, Marina would hold him hostage until they made love.

Later that evening, they lay in bed together, both spent. Marina wondered if her parents had this much difficulty spending quality time together and then recalled how they were always forced to leave her at the worst moments. Sometimes she missed the days of being a loner with obligations to no one. Other times, she wanted to belong to someone, particularly Britt. She glanced over at him but he was fast asleep. She lay awake and wondered what their future held.

The next morning, Britt left the palace early to handle business with the militia captains. Marina awoke with a fresh attitude and renewed stamina. After a hot shower and breakfast, she left the palace for her daily stroll through the town. There was much to consider after the previous day's events and now she knew the identities of her new Seers.

After Kara and Ginna's performance to rescue her, she had decisions to make. Most importantly, she needed to ensure the girls' safety, especially since Willow was now aware of their powers? But then, she fretted retribution from Kronos itself.

Who should I fear most? she questioned herself. In the past, she always knew her enemies before encountering them. Here, she still wasn't even sure who the real enemy was.

Marina searched through the crowd, unsure what or who she expected to see. Two of Britt's soldiers rushed toward her urgently.

"Your Highness!" called the lead soldier. "Come quickly!"

Marina feared what could have happened now and hurried after the two men. She followed them into an alley lined with dumpsters. Several other soldiers stood in front of two dumpsters where a pair of legs could be seen protruding from between them.

"Who is it?" Marina asked uneasily as she approached.

"I believe it's a friend of yours," answered one soldier. "That's why we summoned you."

Marina peered between the dumpsters and recognized Dix's body. His throat was slashed from ear to ear. The letter 'K' was carved in his forehead.

Marina was enraged that Kronos would dare send her a message like this. She ordered the soldiers to take Dix's body back to the palace and arrange a decent burial. Her concern for friends and allies alike grew and she was determined to make her new enemy pay.

Two of the townspeople arrived with a gurney and picked up the corpse. They were escorted by the soldiers back to the palace. Marina followed them and stormed up the steps to the entrance. There was no hiding her emotions now. The bitch was back.

Marina sent two soldiers to locate Kat and request her presence at the palace immediately. She entered the conference room on the first floor and sat at the table. Tapping her fingers, she contemplated where to begin her response against Kronos and the councilors.

Drago appeared at the door and asked for a brief moment with her. Marina gestured with her hand for him to enter. He sat down across from her and hesitated, aware that something significant was on her mind. Marina looked up at him with a fierce look that startled him.

"I'm sorry, your Highness. Is this a bad time?"

Marina leaned back in her chair, looking tired, but still smiled at him.

"I always have time for you, Drago," she assured him, despite her anger. "What can I do for you?"

Drago discussed the existing passages in the palace and recommended some changes to maintain security of the base below. Marina listened patiently and then changed the topic, catching him off guard. "Can you design body armament?" she inquired.

Drago was baffled by her request and asked, "What kind of armament are you looking for?"

She pondered briefly and then replied, "I'd like something that I can use on my arms and legs in hand-to-hand combat."

"You don't like the items I stocked on your ship?" he asked nervously.

"Oh, I love them. Don't get me wrong about that. I want something dirty; something that reeks with death. Something that's... well, me."

Drago fretted at first but then became amused by her request. He was apprehensive about the task but agreed he could handle it. Marina then emphasized that she needed it soon, due to changing circumstances. "You'll have whatever materials you need," she assured him.

"Yes, my Queen," he replied anxiously and left the room.

Marina considered what exactly Dix's killers wanted from her. She wasn't going to cooperate with them so a stronger response was likely to be taken against her. There were too many variables to narrow down the potential threats for retaliation against her and her people. Frustrated, she stared at the disk Britt gave her in hope of an answer and pined over her dilemma.

Kat entered the palace and met with two of the soldiers. One of them ordered her to wait while the other summoned Marina. She was patient as the remaining soldier stood uneasily next to her. Kat, sensing his unease, placed her hand on his shoulder. "Relax, good sir. I mean you no harm."

"I'm sorry, ma'am," the soldier replied politely. "I can't help but feel your presence."

Kat placed her hands affectionately on his cheeks and replied in a soothing tone, "So long as you remain true to your queen, you have nothing to fear from me." The soldier breathed a sigh of relief and assured her that he would.

Marina and the second soldier appeared at the conference room entrance. Kat smiled, anxiously awaiting Marina's approach. "I wondered when you would summon me," Kat remarked. "It's been a long time since we've been together."

"Yes, and I know you well enough to know that you don't do something for nothing. I am in your debt and you are here to collect."

Kat's eyes widened with surprise, followed by a look of disappointment. "Marina, how could you think that of me?" she replied hurtfully.

Marina gestured for her to enter the conference room. "I saw your ship at the transportation hub," Marina commented, not revealing that it was through the premonition. "I was quite surprised you came here." She approached the window and stared out at the garden of weeds and newly turned dirt.

"It's good to see you again," Kat mentioned coyly, eager for some sign of affection.

Marina stood motionless at the window and announced somberly. "Kat, I have some bad news." Kat backed away and waited for her to explain.

Marina turned to her and placed a hand on her shoulder. "Dix was murdered today in town."

"What?" Kat exclaimed, stunned by Marina's words. "By whom?"

"His throat was slit and the letter 'K' was carved in his forehead," Marina informed her. "Use your imagination about who was behind it."

"Then it has started," she replied sadly. "Where is his body?"

"Downstairs, next to the wine cellar," she replied sadly. "I've arranged for a decent burial for him." She embraced Kat and revealed that he was like family to her.

Kat wanted to believe Marina, if even for compassion, but Marina appeared lost in other thoughts. "I appreciate that," replied Kat, unsure where their relationship was going. "You have become like family to me as well."

"I'm glad to hear that," Marina replied.

Kat hugged her and promised, "I will use no magic or hallucinations against you. Things are different now and so are we."

"I'm well aware of that," Marina responded, tears streaming down her cheeks. "I could really use your support, Kat."

"And you shall have it. We do have important business to discuss, however," Kat mentioned. She eyed Marina with a seductive smile and added, "I missed you, for what it's worth."

"Come upstairs so we can talk in private," Marina requested and led her up the stairs to her den. She went to the window and peered out at the city. Kat approached her, strutting like a fox to her prey and placed her hands on Marina's shoulders. When Kat hugged her from behind, Marina savored her touch. As much as Kat intimidated her, she knew how to make Marina relax. Kat slid around and stood in front of her, still with her arms draped around her shoulders. "You're looking well, my Queen."

Marina was still uncomfortable being addressed that way. She suspected that Kat's visit included a request for a favor and pondered the possibilities. Not one to shy away from trouble, she placed her arms around Kat's waist affectionately and pushed her toward the wall. Kat relished Marina's forcefulness as Marina pressed herself against Kat. Their lips were just a breath apart. Marina recalled her confusion about whether she enjoyed Kat's liberties on her or her repulsion to being violated.

"What brings you to my humble palace?" Marina inquired suspiciously.

"Some things have transpired on Magnus... terrible things," Kat explained dejectedly. "You are the only person I trust during these trying times."

"I knew we'd meet again, just not so soon," Marina remarked and gazed into Kat's eyes seductively. "We are two of a kind."

Kat felt her will melt in Marina's arms and she breathed deeply, awaiting the feel of their lips together, tongues entwined in a romantic interlude. She leaned closer to Marina, dying to taste her once more. Marina touched her cheek delicately but then backed away. Kat was crushed by the abrupt, unsatisfying end to their encounter. "That was rude," she complained.

Marina faced Kat and responded, "I have some difficult problems right now and so do you. I need answers quickly."

Kat stepped toward her smoothly as if she glided on air. She placed her hands on Marina's hips and leaned toward her until, again, their lips nearly touched. "We had something good once, Marina. We can help each other through these dark days."

"And what of your problems?" countered Marina. "I suspect they outweigh mine."

Kat attempted to kiss Marina once more, but she again rebuffed her. "You are still all business, I see," Kat remarked disappointedly. "I really hoped we were beyond that."

"Maybe later," she replied coldly. "Explain your visit, Kat."

Kat attempted to coax Marina onto the couch next to her but Marina stood her ground. Frustrated, Kat's hands dropped to her lap. "I'm here as your ally," she admitted. "There is a storm brewing of immense proportions. You and I, my dear, are standing right in front of it."

"What do you know and how?" Marina questioned her.

Kat patted the cushion next to her, gesturing for Marina to sit. Marina folded her arms and grew impatient. "Answers first, then maybe we'll play."

Kat became more frustrated and explained, "An evil empire is on the rise. You and your people are in grave trouble."

"Does this empire happen to be Kronos Enterprises?"

Kat was impressed by Marina's awareness of Kronos. "Very much so," she answered. "We are about to embark on a long and difficult road. There will be many casualties before this is over."

"We?"

"Yes, Marina. Our fates are intertwined, regardless of how we feel about it."

"There is no ill will here, Kat. I just prefer to know the rules of the game before I play."

"As I told you already; I'm your ally. We need each other to survive." Marina peered out the window to the palace grounds. Kat stood and followed her. With arms around each other's waists, they were silent for several moments. Then Marina spoke. "Why did you come here, Kat? You never give anything away, especially information, for free."

Kat stroked Marina's hair and admired her beauty. Marina waited patiently for a response.

"Kronos sent a team of highly trained mercenaries and imprisoned everyone on Magnus. Then they destroyed my station. I have no home."

Marina was stunned by the news. "How did you escape?"

Kat revealed that she saw Kronos' team coming in a premonition and fled with her closest body guards.

Marina felt the anger return that she thought was gone forever. After the sacrifices that were made by friends to help her vanquish Victor and Fiona, now this new enemy reared its head. Perhaps Rebecca was wrong about becoming a gentle, caring ruler. She recalled her old motto as a courier: Get soft, get dead.

"You have strong emotions. Share them with me," Kat requested.

Marina paced the room, becoming agitated as she spoke. She revealed what Dix had told her about Kat; then the incident in town with the dead man. Finally, she informed Kat about how their relationship was going to be: friends, not lovers.

Kat was disappointed, but knew that fate would have its final say on whom and what they were. Reluctantly, she requested, "Can I count on you for protection and asylum?"

Marina countered, "Can I count on your loyalty?"

Kat placed her hands on Marina's arms delicately and replied, "I only ask one thing from you: my family could have been saved if you had been decisive that horrible day. While I have put that behind me, I only ask that you don't fail me in that respect again when critical times come, and they will come."

Marina was surprised by Kat's candor and replied, "So you have no vendetta against me?"

"At first I did but I realized that both our survivals are dependent on our actions together."

Marina willingly accepted her terms. Kat then swore her loyalty to Marina regardless of her demands.

"There is one other thing I need to know?" Marina added. "What information do you have about a new group of Seers?"

Kat beamed as this was a topic she so wanted to discuss, but feared arousing Marina's suspicions.

"If you must know," Kat replied, "I believe the new Seers will be the key to defeating Kronos. I don't know how or when but we will need them."

"Do you know who they are?" asked Marina, testing Kat's knowledge.

"No, I do not," answered Kat. "It is imperative that we find them, though, and prepare them for what is coming. They need to be trained and cultured in their skills. If not, then none of us will survive."

"Thank you for your honesty." Marina showed her appreciation with an affectionate hug. "We'll speak more on this later. I do have some pressing issues to deal with."

"I look forward to it," Kat replied and left the room.

Marina stared out the window, considering whether or not she could trust Kat with the new Seers. She knew Kat's powers were more developed than hers but Kat did have the dark element of witchcraft in her.

★ ★ ★

Later in the evening, Kara returned with her grandparents, followed by Ginna and her mother, Magdalena. Marina briefed the adults on the events that took place and why she feared for their safety

Kara's grandfather, Clem, reported that the people were becoming restless and feared for their lives after the deaths in the neighboring towns. He also mentioned that some disgruntled residents demanded action by Marina to protect them. Those were gathered at the palace gates.

Marina took the girls to the temple where they were safe. She discussed a training regimen for the girls that featured mind control exercises, emotional control, and an education/history on the planet since her parents' rule began. She wanted the girls to understand what Yord once was and how she aspired to return to those days.

Dora and Magdalena were more than happy to work with the girls. Clem preferred to return to town and keep an ear on the local population for any information pertinent to Marina. Marina was pleased with the arrangement but wondered why the women were secretive of their knowledge of the girls' powers from her.

She left the palace and went into town to seek out Kat for her advice. Kat was usually easy to find, with her entourage of body guards at a local pub. As she walked past the transport hub, she noticed one of the Fleet's vessels docked at the far end. The vessel bore the insignia of a Fleet flagship and immediately caught Marina's attention. As she studied the huge ship, two men came from behind and discretely placed their pulse pistols against her side.

"Walk to the ship or we'll execute the wench," ordered the bearded man, as he pointed to Kat's unconscious body at the ship's hatch.

Marina was furious but managed to keep her cool. She turned toward them, unintimidated, and looked them over. The men were middle-aged and dressed in suits. One of them, Jacob, was bald with a mustache while the other, Henley, had a short beard.

"When you speak to me, you will address me as 'your Highness'," she instructed them defiantly.

"I'll call you 'bitch' if I damn well please and you'll like it," he boasted. Henley laughed as he enjoyed his partner's brazenness.

Marina noticed that some of the townspeople gathered nearby, suspecting there would be trouble. She faced the crowd and announced, "It's okay, everyone. These men are just ..." she paused and elbowed Henley in the throat. He fell to the ground, gasping for air.

Immediately, she kicked Jacob in the back of the knee with a leg sweep and punched him in the bridge of the nose as he tilted sideways, off balanced. She wrestled his pistol away from him as he fell to the ground. Henley aimed his pistol at Marina but she kicked it away and stomped on his jaw several times. She held on tightly to Jacob's arm and used him for leverage to deliver a karate kick to the side of Henley's jaw. He fell to the ground in agony as he clutched at his jaw. Marina then reached her free arm around Jacob's neck and bulldogged him face first to the ground.

Jacob staggered to his feet, eyes bulging with hate. The crowd was amused by Marina's dominance over the men. Some even cheered.

Marina tossed Jacob's pistol away and taunted both men. She held her bare hands out and challenged them. Henley slowly got to his feet, bristling with rage. Jacob nodded to him and then rushed at her. Marina repeated her earlier tactics but swapped targets. She spun and delivered a karate kick to the side of Jacob's jaw while she wrapped an arm around Henley's neck and bulldogged him face first to the ground. Both men stayed down on the ground, dazed and badly injured from their wounds.

Bowing to the crowd, Marina picked up the pistols and stowed them out of sight under her cape. The crowd suddenly grew quiet and retreated.

Marina knew that someone of significance approached her from behind. When she turned around, Colonel Lennox stood a short distance away from her in uniform with six of her subordinate officers.

Marina recalled her earlier premonition where a blond woman and six accomplices threatened her. She also remembered that in a second premonition, she fought someone like Colonel Lennox. It boosted her confidence knowing these premonitions were reliable.

"How nice of you to come visit me, Colonel," Marina replied cynically.

Colonel Lennox disregarded Marina's quip and walked toward her with an air of arrogance about her. "You assaulted two businessmen under my protection," she accused Marina. "As such, you're under arrest for assault and battery."

Marina felt her blood boil by the colonel's arrogance. Again, she maintained her composure and asked innocently, "What men, Colonel?"

When Lennox pointed to Henley and Jacob, Marina drew a pistol and fired one shot into each injured man's head. "I didn't assault them, Colonel; I killed them."

The townspeople cheered for her. Marina bowed to them and continued to chastise the officer. "Let me be clear, Colonel, if they assaulted me on your orders, then you are the one who is under arrest and will be imprisoned for quite a long time, assuming I let you live. After all, treason is punishable by death."

Lennox pointed her finger into Marina's face and warned her. "You have no...," but Marina grabbed her finger and broke it, cutting Lennox's threat short with a brief yelp in pain. The officers each drew their pistols and targeted Marina. She promptly twisted the colonel's arm behind her back and forced her to her knees, holding the barrel of one of her pistols against her head.

"Drop your weapons and leave now," Marina ordered them, "or I put a hole in her thick skull."

"Shoot her!" shouted the colonel as she groaned in pain. No one ever mocked her like that before and she wasn't going to take it from Marina now.

Britt and a dozen militia soldiers emerged from the crowd with their pistols aimed at the officers. "I don't think that's a good idea, Colonel," he announced and approached her. Lennox' officers put down their weapons and stepped back.

"You'll all pay for this," Lennox warned. "The Fleet doesn't take orders from anyone!"

Britt announced a series of charges against Lennox and her men for their aggressions against Marina. The crowd cheered as the militia surrounded and handcuffed the officers and Lennox.

"You see, Colonel, we could have discussed this like human beings but unfortunately, you chose the wrong means of communication," explained Marina. "I don't respond well to threats and I do love to indulge in hand-to-hand combat."

Lennox threatened to bring the Fleet down on Yord and destroy it. Britt informed her that she would now be imprisoned and tried for treason for her statement.

Marina interceded and ordered that the officers be returned to their ship and Lennox released. Britt was miffed by her orders but complied.

Lennox sneered at her and said confidently, "I knew you'd see it my way."

"No," replied Marina. "I just thought I'd give you a chance to show your men how tough you think you are."

Marina dropped her cape and handed her weapons to Britt, but still wore the belts around her thighs with the daggers. Britt rolled his eyes, dreading what was to come.

"You stupid bitch," Lennox uttered and drew her pistol, thinking that she now had a distinct advantage.

Marina laughed as she dropped to one knee. Instinctively, she drew two daggers and fired them at Lennox. One embedded in her thigh ; the other in her abdomen. She kicked the pistol from Lennox' hand and karate chopped her in the throat. Lennox writhed in agony on her back.

"A bitch, maybe," Marina quipped, "but stupid, that would be you, you little prig." Lennox wailed and floundered like a spoiled child in a tantrum as she clutched at her damaged leg and abdomen.

Marina leaned over and offered a hand to help her up. "On occasion, I can show some compassion to my vanquished enemies." When she took Lennox's hand, she snapped it, leaving it hanging limply from her wrist. Lennox again wailed in pain. "Unfortunately for you," Marina remarked, "this is not one of those occasions."

"This isn't over," Lennox cried as she clutched at her broken wrist and held it close to her body.

"If we ever cross paths again, Colonel, it'll be the last breath you take. Understand?" Marina warned and retrieved the daggers from her body. She was pleased, knowing that she humiliated her, a permanent reminder to Lennox not to underestimate her in the future.

Marina turned to Lennox' men and warned, "If you dare stand against your queen, you will suffer a worse fate, I assure you."

Lennox could only cry and plead for someone to help her. Her officers were permitted to usher her back to the ship. Britt's men took Kat from the officers' custody and carried her back to the palace.

The crowd cheered for Marina as she donned her cape and stowed her knives. Britt placed his arm around her waist and kissed her cheek. He was proud of her, despite his misgivings about her return to a violent nature.

The Flagship departed from the hub and darted into the late afternoon sky. Marina knew that she just lit the fuse that would start a full-scale war as the Fleet would retaliate and soon. She marched back toward the palace alongside Britt, with his soldiers following from a distance.

"Do you think it's a coincidence that the Fleet appeared so soon after my visit from Willow and her cohorts?" she asked Britt.

"It's possible. There are a lot of people involved in this: the Fleet, Kronos, and IDC. Maybe others we don't know of yet."

Marina suggested to him that it was time to meet the IDC leaders and then visit Fleet headquarters with General Witty in an attempt to learn who the players are in this plot. He urged her to delay such a move until they better ascertained the situation, but Marina had her own idea about handling them.

★ ★ ★

The next day, Marina entered the guest bedroom on the third floor of the palace. Kat slept soundly under silk covers. She studied Kat and wondered how much their fate was really entwined and how much she could trust her. Even more so, she knew it would be impossible to hide anything from Kat, even for a short time. Kat's telepathic abilities were extraordinary along with her magic skills.

Faust sat nearby, looking dejectedly over her. He took it personal that she was apprehended and beaten when he was responsible for her protection. Marina pitied him. His loyalty was unshakable and his intelligence led her to believe that he was more important than a body guard.

Marina sat on the edge of the bed and laid her hand on top of Kat's. She wanted so badly to believe in her but her trust issues stemmed more from herself than from Kat. As she thought back to their previous encounters, she recalled that Kat did save both her life and Britt's. She likely wanted a marker for her services and Marina was concerned about what that marker could be.

Suddenly, Kat's eyes opened and she squeezed Marina's hands affectionately. "You came to my rescue, my sister," she said appreciatively.

Marina frowned at her and replied, "I honestly didn't know they took you. It was coincidence that I went to the transportation hub."

"I saw it in a premonition," Kat revealed. "You proved that you will do what it takes without delay."

"And that means what?" Marina asked, unsure of what Kat was leading up to.

"It means that you are all in and I can count on you."

Marina felt embarrassed for withholding information from Kat. "There are some things we need to talk about, Kat."

"Such as..."

"I do have information on the new Seers."

Kat's eyes widened with joy. "Please, tell me!"

"Come on, Kat. You already know what I know."

Kat giggled at Marina and teased, "You are so naive."

Marina was baffled as she wondered if perhaps Kat didn't have the ability to read her thoughts.

Kat explained, "Our thoughts are like highways. Some intersect. Some don't." Marina was at a loss of words to reply. She felt ashamed for doubting her. "I could intrude on your thoughts," continued Kat, "but I won't. If I am to gain your trust, I need to prove that to you."

"I appreciate that but right now I have serious matters to deal with. I need to punish those responsible for the many deaths of my people."

Kat sat up attentively and suggested, "I can be of help, if you only ask."

Marina considered her offer and then informed her, "I have to go to the International Development Committee and meet with their leaders."

Kat grew concerned and warned, "Not alone!"

"It's better that way," she replied determinedly.

Kat placed her hands on Marina's shoulders and reminded her, "They will imprison you or worse, kill you. They are part of this whole plan to do whatever evil they aspire for."

"Then I'll go as someone else," Marina declared confidently.

"Faust and I can go with you and the three of us will pose as Marina's ambassadors," Kat suggested. "Marina officially will not be there."

"Now that I can do," Marina agreed. "When can you travel?"

"I'm ready when you are," replied Kat. "They bruised my pride more than anything."

"For what it's worth, I'm glad to see you're okay," she said cheerfully and then left the room.

Faust shook his head in disbelief. Kat stared at him, uncertain of his rationale, until he explained, "The queen doesn't mind putting herself in danger. I have never met anyone like that before."

Kat placed her hand on Faust's shoulder and informed him, "Ah, Faust, you have to understand. That is the secret to her success. Unfortunately, it is up to us to make sure she survives to achieve her goals."

Faust pondered Kat's words and asked, "What goals might they be?"

Kat enlightened him that Marina was destined to be the central figure in their future. She admitted to him that, despite her own powers, fate would have Marina as their leader.

"Does Marina know this?" he asked curiously.

"Not quite. She doesn't realize what the universe is capable of and how it is her responsibility to maintain balance. My purpose is to help her achieve that in any way possible."

Faust affirmed his loyalty to both women and assured Kat that he would not allow her to be in danger again. Wherever she went, either he or his men would accompany her.

* * *

At noon, Kat returned to the conference room with Faust to meet with Marina. They found her staring out the window from her seat at the table with a grim expression. Kat approached and placed her hand on Marina's arm, gazing at her with a soothing stare. "You are troubled, my dear."

"I'm afraid so, Kat. I believe it's time to go to war with these assholes and I need a plan."

"I'm glad to see you are decisive in the matter," replied Kat, looking pleased.

"We're leaving immediately for the IDC as we discussed earlier - as Marina's ambassadors."

Kat was surprised by the urgency and requested, "Would you share what you know of the Seers with me, Marina? It could have significant consequences for us."

"We'll speak later on the ship. I prefer to keep this quiet."

Kat understood and departed to assemble her things for the trip. Marina went down to the underground base and boarded *The Reaper*. She felt the return of the rush that once overcame her when she courted danger. Eagerly, she piloted the ship from the base up to the palace courtyard, landing in front of the palace for all to see. This was her statement to all: The bitch was back and on the prowl for her enemies.

After opening the hatch, she suddenly grew light-headed and sensed another premonition coming. This time she tried to embrace it. Sitting back on the couch, she closed her eyes and let the images come to her. A cloud formed in front of her and she felt herself glide to another location. The cloud cleared and she appeared in a large laboratory equipped with industrial equipment. Computerized stations were connected to the equipment and the monitors displayed bar graphs of power ascension levels.

Marina scanned the lab and noticed a dark-skinned couple in lab coats, Drs. Ford and Janus, arguing in front of a gigantic machine that resembled a futuristic telescope. She thought that was strange and approached the couple to question them. Then she felt herself slipping away from the facility. The cloud appeared and she again felt herself glide through space. When she opened her eyes, Kat was next to her and Faust just closed the hatch for their departure.

"Are you okay?" asked Kat nervously.

"Yeah," she answered in an uncertain tone. "I just had the strangest experience."

"Tell me about it," urged Kat.

"I found myself at the GSS hub and saw two of the IDC technicians. It was so freaking weird," Marina uttered, somewhat embarrassed, and went to the bridge.

Kat glanced at Faust uneasily and followed her. Faust took a seat at a small table in the rear of the craft. It worried him that Marina had mysterious qualities about her much like Kat. Neither woman made sense to him in his attempts to protect and serve them. In the back of his mind, he feared what a conflict would lead to between them, each with her own unique abilities.

Marina piloted the ship from the palace. Now she was anxious to find out the truth about the premonitions. She understood that they could be a valuable weapon for her if they were, in fact, real. Kat sat next to her, anxious to know more about them.

"Tell me what you saw," Kat pleaded anxiously, wanting to know how advanced Marina's powers had become.

"It doesn't matter," replied Marina. "We have a job to do."

"But what do you mean 'you were there'?"

Marina hesitated as she sought words to explain what happened to her. Then she replied, "It's complicated. I don't know how, but I was there."

Kat tried to fathom how she could do such a thing. It was certainly not in her powers, or so she thought. Then she considered that Marina could have other powers that she hadn't detected.

Marina contacted Britt and informed him that they were in route to IDC and he should keep his forces on alert. She feared that the Fleet or Kronos' assassins would attempt another attack on her people while she was away.

Britt assured her that everything was under control and he'd wait anxiously for her return. He wasn't pleased that she left without discussing her intentions with him and feared she was returning to her old, reckless self.

When Marina revealed the premonitions to Britt, he rebuffed them as coincidences and lingering effects of her drug addiction. She was frustrated with his stubbornness and more concerned that something dreadful would happen to her kingdom during her absence if he didn't heed her warnings. She reluctantly ended the transmission with him.

Marina stood and ordered Kat to stay put until she returned. Kat pressed her to talk to her about her thoughts and plans but Marina instructed her to be patient and remain there.

At the rear of the cabin, Marina sat next to Faust and studied him. Faust appeared to be napping but quickly opened his eyes and stared back. "Is there something I can do for you, your Highness?" he asked curiously.

"I believe you would give your life for me," she remarked.

"Of course, I would, your Highness," he replied humbly.

"Call me Marina," she requested cheerfully.

"Thank you, your... I mean Marina."

"Kat trusts you more than anything. I believe I can, too."

"I owe Kat my life and, thanks to your parents, we aren't slaves to the Weevil."

Marina looked down at the floor and frowned. "I fear my battle with Kronos may be as difficult as my parents' battles," she confessed.

Faust touched her hand and said confidently, "I have faith in you my Queen and I will be there for you, if required."

"Thank you, Faust." Marina returned to the flight deck, feeling that Faust's loyalty gave her a sense of family with him. He was becoming like a brother to her.

Kat eyed her suspiciously as she wondered what Marina was up to. If she probed Marina's thoughts, she'd know and that would damage any trust they built so far. She grew frustrated with Marina's procrastination to discuss the Seers and the premonitions with her. She folded her arms, while staring deliberately at Marina.

Marina operated the communication equipment and attempted to contact IDC. After several tries, she received a response from one of their operators. She informed them that she needed to speak with Dr. Janus. After another delay, Dr. Haney responded.

"What can I do for you?" he replied pleasantly.

"If Dr. Janus isn't available, I'd like to speak with the Gallean curator of the station. There are some technical issues that I have questions about."

Haney hesitated and then replied, "The Galleans have departed and no longer control the station."

"Why is that, Dr. Haney?" she questioned accusingly. "They fought a war to get back what belonged to them."

"I'm sorry, but we now control the station. Is there something I can help you with?"

"As a matter of fact, there is. What is your role, I mean IDC's role, at the station?"

"I'm afraid I can't answer that," he replied. "It's classified."

Marina's ire began to build. "That station belongs to the alliance and I have the right to know whatever goes on there."

"I'm afraid you don't have that authority," he replied arrogantly. "You see, we only answer to Kronos Enterprises, not you."

"Then you and the queen will be having a face-to-face discussion on this matter very soon," she responded angrily. "And, I promise, you won't like it."

"I look forward to it," he replied and ended the transmission.

Marina screamed and shouted, "That miserable little prick!"

"Easy, Marina," cautioned Kat.

"I'm gonna tear him apart!" she yelled until her voice crackled.

Kat resumed the transmission. "Attention, sir, we formally request permission to land on GSS for a brief discussion of its current status," she explained in a sultry voice. "Our visit will be unobtrusive and cursory. We mean you no inconvenience."

"Stand by," the dispatcher replied.

"Thank you," replied Kat politely. "We appreciate your assistance." Marina glared at her, while Kat returned a sly smile.

The GSS facility was a space station built by the Gallean race as a means of organizing all shipping in the old empire. It was very advanced, compared to other space stations and satellites. For the time they operated it, trade was prosperous in the empire. Then, Kronos agents took the Galleans prisoner and executed them. The representatives from IDC were then assigned control of the station by Kronos.

On board GSS, Dr. Haney entered and shouted at Drs. Janus and Ford for bickering. Dr. Janus approached him and complained that the equipment couldn't handle the high temperatures at the source. Dr. Ford added that, without the program, they can only amplify the power to about fifty percent.

"Fifty percent is not adequate for the system to operate as a weapon," Dr. Janus complained. "What's the delay in getting the program?"

"We have to assume the program is gone," he said disappointedly.

"Then what about the designer of the program?" questioned Dr. Ford.

Haney rubbed his chin and answered, "The Fleet's working on it."

"They've been working on it for quite a while and we have nothing to show for it," grumbled Dr. Ford.

"Someone out there knows what happened to that chip!" she exclaimed angrily. "This is bullshit!"

"Ah, perhaps we can find out," replied Dr. Haney confidently. "Let's turn up the heat on Yord and see what happens. Rumor has it that the queen once delivered the chip to a source that lost it to the Fleet. She likely knows the whereabouts of the missing chip."

"Allow me to make the call," volunteered Dr. Janus. "I look forward to speaking with that dumb-ass Witty."

Dr. Janus left them and went into her office at the far end of the lab. She entered several codes into a device and sat in front of a large monitor. The sound of soft music filled the room as she waited patiently. The music stopped and General Witty's face appeared on the screen. "What do you want, Marjorie? I'm a busy man."

Dr. Janus unbuttoned her blouse and displayed her breasts under a black lace bra. She slid two of her fingers under the bra and massaged her right nipple in a circular motion. "Come, now, Duane. You always had time for me before."

"That was different," he replied coldly. "This is business."

Dr. Janus unhooked the front clasp on her bra and let it drop. She massaged her breasts with both hands and gazed at him with hungry eyes. "I miss you, Duane," she crooned. "You make me so... so hot."

"Damn it, Marjorie! What do you want?"

"I need a favor from you," she answered seductively.

Witty sighed and inquired, "What kind of favor?"

"I need you to launch a small assault on Yord for me." She stood and dropped her pants to the floor.

Witty's interest piqued as she stood in front of the screen wearing only her lab coat and panties. He became cooperative and responded, "What kind of assault?"

Dr. Janus sat down and placed one leg up on the table. She took her time responding and pleasured herself. Witty became uneasy as he watched anxiously. Finally, she responded, "I want you to generate casualties around the palace; lots of them."

Witty became excited as he watched her. His hand moved beneath his desk. He asked, "What for?"

"That bitch did a number on one of your senior officers. The plan was for her to be a non-issue at this stage. Perhaps a little friction at home will convince her to relinquish her power. She may even know a little something about that chip we've been anxiously waiting for as well."

"That won't be easy without Kronos' okay," he complained disappointedly, his voice quivering. "I'll see what I can do?"

Now that she had his support, she thanked him and promptly ended the transmission. Witty leaned back in his chair and groaned, "Damn, that bitch is hot."

After dressing, Dr. Janus returned to the lab and informed the others of her success with Witty. A male voice blared from the loudspeaker, requesting Dr. Haney contact the control center. He was informed of Kat's request.

Dr. Haney rushed to the control room, joined by Drs. Janus and Ford. When they arrived, Dr. Haney took over the transmission and inquired what purpose Kat had for coming.

"I represent Marina, the Queen of Yord and the new alliance," Kat informed them.

"And why does the queen have an interest in what goes on here at GSS?" Haney asked.

"We can discuss that when we meet," replied Kat tactfully. "I am her ambassador and would appreciate the courtesy of a face to face with the IDC senior leadership."

"Very well," relented Haney. "You have permission to dock."

On board *The Reaper*, Marina was impressed with Kat's handling of the situation. "Not bad," she remarked. "I think you make a great ambassador with words like that."

"The question," Kat countered, "is how long you can behave like an ambassador's aid and not beat anyone up?"

Marina quipped, "As long as they don't piss me off."

The ship glided inside the designated bay and secured to the dock. Once the outer doors closed and oxygen filled the bay, five armed mercenaries entered and approached *The Reaper*.

Kat stepped out, adorned in a loose, red robe with gold trim and a tiara. Faust escorted her, wearing his turban and a scimitar at his left side, his pulse pistol on his right.

Marina followed behind them, wearing a black hooded cloak, draped over her head to hide her face. Beneath it, she wore a gray, satin tunic with black, leather pants and stylish, black boots.

One of the mercenaries, a tall bearded man named Chilton, gestured for them to stop. "Identify yourselves," he ordered and held up a transponder.

"I am Katarina Tosci," answered Kat proudly. "This is Faust, my body guard and the woman behind me is...," she pondered briefly as she thought. "This is Shanna, my personal assistant."

Marina kept her eyes on the floor, stunned by Kat's choice of names for her. Shanna was her mother's name and she was rattled that Kat knew that.

Chilton seemed to care little about Faust and Marina. The transponder beeped after each name and he stepped back. "You may enter," he announced and led them down a series of corridors. After ascending two flights of stairs, they entered the control room for the station.

Drs. Ford and Janus entered from another door and approached them. Marina glanced up briefly and immediately noticed that they were exactly as she saw them in her premonition.

"What can we do for you, Ambassador Tosci?" inquired Dr. Janus.

Kat extended her hand in friendship to Dr. Janus and answered, "We have several concerns, based on rumors, regarding the GSS and IDC. The queen felt it would be appropriate to discuss these rumors and perhaps put them to rest."

Dr. Ford stepped in and chided them, "There is nothing here that concerns the queen. You can tell her to mind her business."

Dr. Janus glared at him until he backed off. "Please excuse my associate. He's been under a lot of stress lately."

Marina remained calm and kept her head down, while Faust stared down Dr. Ford. He had little patience for those who failed to show respect to Kat or Marina.

Dr. Janus pointed to a table with several chairs. "Please, have a seat," she invited them. Kat, Faust and Marina took seats on one side while Dr. Janus sat across from them. Dr. Ford left the room, looking disturbed by their presence.

"What are you working on here at GSS?" inquired Kat.

Dr. Janus countered, "What have you heard?"

"Something about controlling the weather on planets around the galaxy," she replied tactfully.

"There is some truth to that, although we haven't had much success."

"We've also heard something about a corporation called Kronos taking over with the intent of controlling all commerce in the galaxy," explained Kat. "What can you tell me about that?"

Dr. Janus became unnerved by Kat's question and hesitated. Before she could answer, Dr. Ford returned with Dr. Haney. Haney immediately demanded to know what they were doing there.

"Relax, gentlemen," urged Dr. Janus. "There's nothing to be concerned about."

Haney barked, "I'll be the judge of that!"

Ford remained in the background, smugly with his arms folded.

Kat stood and inquired arrogantly, "Who might this... person be?"

"This is Dr. Haney," replied Janus. "He is in charge of our project."

"And it is time for you to leave," he ordered.

"Do you have something to hide?" countered Kat. "You seem awfully defensive."

"If you don't leave now, I'll have my men throw you out!"

"Dr. Haney!" Janus chastised him. "These are guests."

"I don't care. Get them out of here."

"Very well," replied Kat. "The queen hoped that we could reach an amicable agreement, especially about a particular chip, but I see that won't happen."

Dr. Janus' eyes lit up with excitement. "A chip?" she echoed anxiously.

Kat led Faust and Marina to the door and looked back. "I believe I did. Thank you for your hospitality, Dr. Janus." Kat, Faust and Marina left the room and returned to the ship.

Janus angrily shoved Haney against the wall. "What the hell was that all about?" she shouted at him. "She knows something about the chip!"

"How was I to know?"

"You fool! We may have lost our opportunity thanks to your stupidity."

"Like hell!" he exclaimed and barged out of the room.

As the hatch opened on *The Reaper*, Dr. Haney stormed toward Kat. He reached for her with both hands and hollered, 'What do you know about the chip?"

Faust intercepted him and grabbed his arms. Haney promptly used a judo move to slam Faust on his back.

"That's uncalled for!" cried Kat as she knelt by Faust to assist him.

"And you," he threatened and grabbed her by the back of her neck. "You tell that queen of yours to..."

"Now, Marina had enough of his arrogance. She tossed the cloak aside and ordered him to release her. Haney immediately recognized her and replied, "So, Marina, we finally meet." He threw Kat to the ground and focused on her.

Marina stalked him and taunted, "I see Kronos took control of your toys here."

Haney seemed to delight in the challenge by Marina and took a defensive position. "I'm just borrowing their resources for now," he responded confidently. "They'll have nothing when this is over."

"A little boy playing adult games, I see," Marina jeered. She jabbed twice and jammed his nose. Haney winced in pain, but then responded with a karate kick to Marina's head and then a leg sweep that floored her. She was stunned by the speed of his counterattack. He chuckled at her and gestured for her to stand. Marina got up slowly, hurting from the impact, and prepared to fight again.

"Get on the ship, Marina!" shouted Faust. He struggled to get to his feet and drew his pistol.

"Save it for another day," Kat warned.

Marina charged at Haney and leaped at him. She wrapped her arm around his neck and attempted to pull him to the ground. Haney knelt down as he caught her and threw her over his head. Marina slammed against the wall and fell to the ground in agonizing pain.

Faust crept up on Haney and announced, "That's enough. We're leaving now."

Haney turned and chopped Faust in the throat. His eyes bulged briefly and he gasped for air. Marina panicked as she realized he was in desperate need of help.

Once more, Marina leaped at Haney. He rammed his fist toward her but she latched onto it and pulled him to the ground. Now that she finally had an advantage, she wrapped one arm around his neck from behind and shoved her thumb and forefinger into his eye. Haney screamed and lunged toward the wall. Marina's head slammed against the wall and she lay dazed. Haney raised his fist to pummel her, smirking as he relished his moment of victory.

Kat took the scimitar from Faust's hip and was about to decapitate Haney from behind when Janus and Ford barged into the bay. With pistols aimed at Kat, they warned her to stand down. Janus ordered Haney to back away from Marina as well.

"Get your people and leave now," ordered Dr. Janus.

Kat helped Marina to her feet and they dragged Faust on board. As soon as the hatch closed, Kat piloted the ship away from GSS. Marina tended to Faust. Aching from her injuries, she was sickened. Never in her life was she ever overmatched like that and it devastated her to think that she grew weak since her days as a courier.

When *The Reaper* was clear of the station, Kat switched to auto-pilot and checked on Marina and Faust. She was concerned by the extent of their injuries.

Marina lay motionless next to Faust, both exhausted and resting. Faust still labored to breath and gasped from time to time. Kat knelt between them and became teary-eyed when Faust opened his eyes.

"I have failed you and Marina, Kat," he uttered sadly, still wheezing. "I should have killed him immediately."

"No, you didn't. We handled the situation badly, not you." She turned her attention to Marina and lifted her into a sitting position. She nestled her head against her bosom and wept.

Marina awoke and looked up sadly at Kat. She said somberly, "I owe him my life."

"And I owe you mine," Kat responded. "We were lucky to escape."

Marina rolled over onto her knees and struggled to stand. "The next time I meet Hanley, he's a dead man," she vowed. "I'm going to…"

"Stop it!" shouted Kat. "Stop it already. You almost died. Isn't that enough?"

Marina grew agitated by Kat's words. "What am I supposed to do? He was going to kill you!"

"You were overmatched. We both knew it and yet you persisted."

"You were the one who wanted this," responded Marina angrily. "You wanted me to act when needed and not delay."

"Don't turn my words against me," Kat countered irately. "You know what I meant." She stood and paced the cabin, frustrated by the turn of events.

Marina was annoyed with her pettiness. "Look, we knew this was risky," she reminded her. "So, what are we gonna do about it?"

"I don't know," Kat replied despondently and returned to the flight deck.

Marina hugged Faust and whispered words of thanks into his ear. She stayed to comfort him until his breathing stabilized. He squeezed her hand and swore he'd avenge her.

IV
ABOUT LILITH

Sheena Brice sat at the desk in her office and studied charts of the fifth sector. She was baffled by the Fleet's decision to send three warships to an area of no significance. Further complicating her thoughts was the fact that no one cared about sector five. *It's as if they want me out of the way,* she thought to herself. *But why the other ships, too?* Then she recalled her discussion with General Witty and his concern over Marina's loyalty to the Fleet.

Lt. Kannel knocked and entered. "Good morning, Commander," he announced pleasantly.

"Come in, Lieutenant," Sheena replied and pointed to a seat at the conference table.

"I found out something very interesting about your request."

Sheena leaned forward with folded hands and listened intently. Lt. Kannel leaned toward her, concerned that someone might hear them, and whispered, "There are two prisoners that have been held there for over six months with no charges filed. They are listed as persons of interest but nothing more."

Lt. Kannel reached inside his uniform shirt and removed his comp/comm which is a computer-communication device. After pressing several keys, he displayed a picture of Drago's wife Lilith. The text beneath her picture described her as a scientist with many accomplishments in various science fields.

"I asked a friend in security about her," he continued. "He said she had a contract with the Fleet to provide the software for her project that the Fleet believes is owed to them and now she refuses to turn it over."

"What do they do with her all this time?" asked Sheena curiously.

Lt. Kannel replied, "They torture her every day with the standard tricks and still she refuses to turn over the technology, despite their tactics."

Sheena grew concerned as she recalled the mystery of the data chip and what her sister told her of it before her death. "We have to get her out of there somehow," she said frantically. "This technology must be very dangerous for her to resist their torturous methods thus far."

"They plan on butchering her to extract the information as soon as two 'qualified' individuals arrive from Kronos Headquarters," Kannel added.

Sheena tapped the table nervously and then asked, "What of the other prisoner?"

Kannel pressed several keys and a man's picture appeared. "His name is Rock Grant, a former Internal Affairs guy."

Sheena knew the name and recalled that two men worked with her sister Severin in the recovery of the missing data chip from Marina. "How long has he been incarcerated?" she asked curiously.

"Since shortly after your sister's death," he replied. "Quite ironic, if you ask me."

"And Kronos is sending their butchers to extract information from her. This smells real bad."

"Something else," he added. "Colonel Lennox is in surgery."

Sheena's eyes widened with surprise. "Why?"

"It seems she had an encounter with Marina and lost."

"What happened to her?" she responded, stunned by the revelation.

"A leg, an abdominal and… a hand injury," he announced sheepishly.

"Marina did that?"

"Sure did," he remarked. "And I'd say there is going to be retaliation against her in the worst way."

"We need to get the two prisoners before the butchers arrive and we have to warn Marina that she's in danger," Sheena contemplated aloud.

"How do we know who we can trust in the Fleet?" Kannel inquired.

"We don't and we can't do anything to arouse their suspicions either." Kannel waited for further instructions as Sheena considered the limited options they had. Finally, she directed him to delay their departure for twenty-four hours for security upgrades of the computer system. Kannel knew he could change the due dates in the computer system for the upgrades because of the length of their upcoming departure to make the request valid.

Later that evening, Sheena met with her officers and announced that Lt. Kannel was in charge until she returned. After a solemn goodbye, Sheena left the ship. Lt. Kannel sensed that Sheena was in danger but he was obligated to follow orders.

★ ★ ★

Sheena entered Fleet headquarters and proceeded to the elevator. The night shift desk clerk paid her no attention and focused his attention on a stack of files. Once inside the elevator, she selected level 'C'. The control panel prompted her to insert her ID badge for access to the restricted level. She inserted the badge and the elevator descended to level 'C'.

When Sheena stepped off the elevator, an elderly officer stood at the desk and glared at her. "This is a restricted area. You need to leave now."

Sheena calmly approached the officer and explained, "I do have unrestricted access or I wouldn't have gotten this far. Don't you think?"

The officer sat down, while eying her suspiciously. Sheena peered down the hall at both barred and solid doors on either side. She reluctantly requested the officer's help to find Lilith's cell.

"Can you tell me anything about the two prisoners in long-term confinement?" she inquired innocently.

"Why would you ask that?" he countered.

"I'm investigating a potential terrorist threat and I need to determine what risk level to assign headquarters."

"You think someone would try and break them out?" he asked, suddenly interested in her explanation.

"More likely, a retaliatory attack," she responded. "Obviously, I don't spend much time here at Headquarters but I was assigned to evaluate the value of the prisoners that are here."

The officer revealed the identities of Lilith and Rock. He mentioned that Lilith had information vital to the Fleet's defenses and she refused to divulge it.

"So, what happens to her?" Sheena inquired.

"They torture her every day, three times daily but she never talks. It won't be for much longer though. Experts have arrived to extract the information from her."

"Are they with her now?"

"For about three hours now," he replied.

"And the man?"

"He knows the whereabouts of a data chip with her program on it and refuses to reveal its location. They starve him and beat him daily but he never talks either. It can't be that hard to make them talk, if you ask me."

Sheena considered releasing the prisoners and taking them away but she'd never escape. Now that she knew who the prisoners were, she'd have to find a way to save them from the butchers.

"Thank you for your help," Sheena said and returned to the elevator. Unsure of her next move, she returned to her ship.

★ ★ ★

The members of the Fleet, the Industrial Development Committee and Kronos Enterprises met in an emergency meeting. Klingman sat back in his plush chair, content to let his second in command run the meeting.

Sexton walked around the table with a taut look upon his face. The other members sensed that something was wrong and wore concerned expressions. He paused by the window and stared out as if preoccupied with faraway thoughts. Finally, he spoke. "We've spent many years planning for this day and now it has come."

One of the IDC representatives, Dr. Haney, interrupted and inquired, "Has something occurred to endanger our plans?"

Sexton faced the man, quite irate over his interruption. "As a matter of fact, a few things have happened and I'm really pissed off about it."

"If it's about the queen, I don't think she'll be a problem anymore," explained Haney.

"And why is that?"

"She's licking her wounds right now."

Drs. Janus and Ford flinched as they knew what was coming. Dr. Janus interjected, "I advised Dr. Haney to restrain himself. There was no reason to assault the queen and her associates. She would have left peacefully with no knowledge of our goal."

"In fact," added Dr. Ford, "she wanted to make a deal for the chip she claimed to have."

"And what did you find out about the chip?" Sexton inquired.

"Dr. Haney's aggressive actions prevented any further negotiation."

Sexton walked calmly behind Haney and punched him in the back of the head. Before Haney could respond, Sexton rammed his head into the table several times and shouted at him, "You...stupid...shit! Do you realize what you started?" He released his hold on Haney and walked to the front of the room.

Haney looked up groggily as blood streamed down his nose from his forehead. "She's lucky to be alive," he mumbled.

"Do you know what a wounded animal does when it's trapped, you jackass?" Sexton yelled angrily. "It goes on the offensive. Marina has quite a history of destruction when on the offensive."

Haney wiped the blood from his face with his sleeve. "I'll go after her and finish her off," he assured them.

Sexton returned to Haney's side and grabbed him by the chin. "If you jeopardize my plans, I will take you apart, piece by piece. Do you understand?"

"Yes, sir," he replied humbly.

Captain Jeffries entered, accompanied by Willow, Franklin and Eddie. "Pardon the intrusion, sir," Jeffries interrupted, "but I believe you wanted to see these three."

"And here is another of my problems," Sexton remarked and smiled fiendishly as he approached Willow. "You assured me that you and your accomplices could handle the queen," he chided. "It seems that you've created quite a stir and put the militia on alert for any future acts of aggression."

"Sir, we had a little bit of a problem," replied Willow, "There were these two girls..."

Before she could finish, Sexton took out a small pistol and fired a red laser beam into Eddie's head. Eddie slumped to the ground with a blank expression and a small hole in his forehead.

"You were saying," Sexton said, amused by the shocked expression on Willow's face.

"There were two young girls that..." Again Sexton raised his pistol and fired another beam into Franklin's head. Franklin staggered backward and collapsed, with a hole in his forehead as well.

Willow became visibly upset and pleaded for an opportunity to get revenge on Marina. Sexton placed his pistol against her forehead and unbuttoned her blouse halfway down. The others in the room were amused at the humiliation he instilled on Willow.

"You have beautiful breasts, Willow. I'd hate to waste them because of a hole in your head," he warned. "But then, it might be more fun taking liberties with your corpse."

Willow struggled to contain her rage, but knew she had no recourse. Sexton glanced at the others and burst into laughter. Then, his expression turned serious. He rammed the butt of his pistol into Willow's face and knocked her senseless. She lay on the ground dazed with blood spewing from her broken nose.

Sexton pressed the intercom and called for security. Two Fleet soldiers immediately entered the room. "Lock her up in sector Charlie," he ordered.

The soldiers grabbed Willow by her arms and dragged her from the room. The other members applauded.

Sexton stood over Haney and suggested, "You should get your shit together and fast. I wanted a peaceful resolution to the queen's influence, not a war."

"Yes, sir," Haney muttered.

Sexton pressed his thumbs into Haney's eyes until he screamed for mercy. "Do you really understand?"

"Yes, I do!" cried Haney.

Dr. Ford glanced at Dr. Janus. Both grinned with satisfaction.

Sexton leaned on the table and glared at everyone. "Problem number three: Lennox decided to take matters into her own hands and, because of her disobedience, she is not nearly the person she used to be. Again, using violence against the queen has always proved unsuccessful. I pay you people a lot of money to be smart."

Klingman stood and informed them, "Lennox' ego nearly got her killed. It remains to be seen if she and General Witty are still of value to us. Perhaps the militia would be willing to work for us for the same generous fee."

"We will not tolerate any more failures," Sexton warned them. "This plan has already taken too long to implement and there is too much riding on it. Now, are there anymore issues that I need to know about?"

Captain Jeffries raised his hand half-heartedly until Sexton nodded for him to speak. "The Colonel received successful surgery to repair her injuries and I assure you; she is quite capable of resuming her duties. As for General Witty, he is currently rendering the alien races helpless."

"And why should we believe that?" questioned Sexton.

"General Witty will report to you directly upon his return," Jeffries replied. "In fact, I already know he's inflicted heavy casualties on several of the alien races already." He then went to the door and opened it. Standing in uniform was Colonel Lennox with gloved hands.

Lennox entered and stood before them. "As of this moment, we are at war with the kingdom of Yord. I don't tolerate failure and I don't expect you to either," she announced arrogantly. "I paid a price for underestimating my enemy, but now that vagabond who calls herself a queen will feel my wrath! I will exact payment from Yord for its resistance."

"But Colonel, how can we believe that after what the queen did to you?" Sexton taunted. "That must have been humiliating."

Lennox grabbed him by the shirt and warned, "Do you really want to find out?" She released her hold on Sexton and walked toward the door. "Don't ever doubt my resolve," she threatened the group.

Sexton shouted angrily, "This one woman has managed to humiliate three assassins, a doctor with martial arts skills, and a combat qualified colonel. That doesn't sound like the situation is being handled, now does it?"

Klingman advised her, "Stick to the plan, Colonel. We don't need heroics. We need results."

"You'll get results alright," she replied snidely.

Sexton aimed his pistol at Lennox and ordered her to stop. Lennox paused and turned. Before Sexton could fire his weapon, Lennox fired a laser beam at his knee from a pencil-like device. He screamed and fell to the floor.

Klingman rushed at Lennox from behind and held his pistol to the back of her head. Lennox immediately turned, and with a sadistic grin, pointed the device at his head.

"Stop it!" screamed Sexton as he used the table to support himself. "We need to work together, you fools!"

Klingman smiled and pushed Lennox's hand away from his head, while lowering his pistol. Lennox cautiously backed away and lowered her hand. Finally, calm was restored. Klingman instructed Lennox to refrain from any retaliation against Marina and her forces unless it's part of the plan."

Lennox grunted at him and left the room. Sexton dropped to the floor in agony, clutching at a deep hole in his knee. Blood seeped from the wound, trickling over his fingers.

Captain Jeffries announced proudly, "As you can see, the colonel is quite capable of handling herself. Any questions or concerns?" he asked arrogantly.

The room was silent. Jeffries approached the door and paused. "Don't ever underestimate the Fleet," he warned them. "We don't take kindly to traitors." He smiled mockingly and left the room.

Klingman announced, "The meeting is adjourned. We'll be in touch."

The IDC representatives hurried out of the room, followed by the Fleet officers. Klingman helped Sexton to a chair and called for medical assistance.

"The Fleet is gonna be a problem," Sexton grumbled as he clutched at his injured knee.

"I'll handle the Fleet," replied Klingman confidently.

★ ★ ★

Sheena stood on the bridge of her ship and considered how to rescue the prisoners. Lt. Kannel arrived on the bridge and informed her that the updates to their systems would only delay their departure by a day. He also mentioned that Fleet was not happy about it.

"We have to move fast," she remarked uneasily.

"And do what?" Lt. Kannel inquired.

"Request extra rations from the depot for our mission. Have them position the crates outside the cargo hatch for early loading in the morning."

"Why?" asked Lt. Kannel.

"I want you to place an empty crate out there as well. Mark it for 'frozen goods' but make sure it's empty and the side panel unsecured."

Kannel paced nervously and fretted over what his commander had in mind. "How do you expect to get away with this?"

Sheena replied, "When the cargo is loaded, close the hatch and leave."

"And you'll be...?"

Sheena stared at him uneasily and replied, "Hopefully in that crate."

"And if not?"

Sheena placed her hand firmly on Kannel's shoulder and said, "Leave immediately. If not, the entire crew is in danger." She turned and walked to the hatch.

Lt. Kannel gazed sadly at her as he knew she was risking her life. "Is the queen worth your life?"

Sheena paused without turning back. "Is your freedom worth fighting for?" she countered. "Trust me on this."

She left the bridge and retired to her quarters. Lt. Kannel, feeling quite concerned for her safety, made the arrangements for extra provisions to be staged for early loading prior to departure. He personally made sure an empty crate was marked appropriately and ready to place on the dock when the supplies arrived in the morning.

★ ★ ★

After dinner, Sheena entered Fleet headquarters and proceeded to the elevator. Once inside, she selected level 'C'. The control panel prompted her to insert her ID badge for access to the restricted level as before.

A different elderly officer stood at his desk and informed her, "Interrogation is in progress. You need to leave now."

Sheena calmly approached the officer and replied, "I need to meet the interrogators regarding another matter. It could jeopardize Fleet security."

The officer pointed down the hall, while staring her down. "If I get into trouble for this, I'm telling them that you pulled rank on me," he warned.

Sheena heard a woman scream and realized she would need to act fast. "I have permission to access the area," she replied and proceeded down the hall.

A woman's fragile groan made her shiver as she feared what methods of torture were used on her. When she reached the first door, she peered through the small window to the cell inside.

An elderly couple stood in front of a decrepit woman with no hair, handcuffed to a chair. The elderly woman, Firth, held a drill to the prisoner's head and drilled another of many small holes into her skull. The woman wailed and pleaded for someone to help her.

The elderly man, Grissom, held a grinder to two of her fingers and shredded them. Spatters of blood and bone sprayed the walls. "Anything you want to tell us now, Lilith?" he asked coldly.

The prisoner, Lilith, could only sob as the drill caused her to spasm each time it penetrated her skull.

Someone called to Sheena from the opposite door and startled her. She immediately recognized the emaciated, scabbed face of Rock, Tully's old partner, who hid the mysterious data chip. Sheena was appalled at Rock's physical condition. His shirtless body was covered with charred scabs and scars from brands. "Help me, please," he begged.

Sheen placed her finger to her lips for silence. She used her pistol to destroy the hand scanner for the lock. The cell door immediately slid open and Rock staggered forth.

"Wait here," Sheena ordered. "I have to help the woman."

Rock nodded and waited in the doorway. Sheena knew she was in too far now and had to finish. She opened the door to Lilith's cell and ordered the elderly couple to stand back.

"What are you doing, you fool?" shouted Firth. "We're so close to extracting the information from her."

"Extract this," Sheena said defiantly and fired a shot into the woman's kneecap. Grissom was horrified as he watched Firth fall to the floor in agony.

"I'm calling General Witty right now!" he exclaimed and reached into his pocket for his communicator.

As he raised it to his mouth, Sheena fired a shot at his hand. The communicator exploded into tiny pieces of molten metal. Grissom screamed and clutched at his burnt hand. "I promise you, you'll pay for this," he threatened with bulging eyes.

Sheena stepped toward him and belted him in the face with the butt of her pistol. Grissom staggered against the wall and fell to the ground. He stared down at several broken teeth and pooling blood on the floor.

"Don't touch him again," warned Firth through tears.

Sheena delivered a powerful kick to Grissom's forehead and knocked him unconscious. "You mean like that?" she chided Firth.

Firth struggled to her feet with the drill in hand. As she charged, Sheena leaped aside and kicked her injured knee. Firth dropped face first to the ground in agony and the drill slid across the floor.

Sheena quickly used her pistol and shot the handcuffs off of Lilith's wrists. "I'm here to rescue you," she instructed her. "I need you to keep quiet." Lilith nodded that she understood and stifled her sobs.

Rock peered in and saw his opportunity for revenge. He hobbled inside the cell and picked up the drill. Sheena was tempted to stop him but thought better of it.

He looked at her with a sadistic smile. "Get her out of here. I'm going to finish this."

"Come with us," Sheena urged.

"I'll catch up. Now get going."

Sheena understood that he wanted to die, exacting his revenge. She took Lilith from the cell and closed the door behind her.

Rock promptly dropped on top of Firth and drilled into her brain with the drill, while taunting her. Her screams brought chills to Sheena as she wondered if she did the right thing.

Grissom regained consciousness and pleaded for him to stop. "I'll be right with you, Mr. Butcher," he assured Grissom. Grissom sobbed and watched helplessly while Rock tortured his partner to death.

Sheena moved Lilith down the hall, leaving a trail of blood. Another voice called out to her. "Please don't leave me here."

Sheena set Lilith down and peered down at the last cell, which was barred. Willow waved frantically to her. Sheena looked back at the guard. Despite the muffled screams from Firth and now Grissom, the guard by the elevator paid no attention to them and perused a pile of papers.

Sheena freed Willow and questioned her about her imprisonment. Willow lied that she was recently arrested for what she knew about the Fleet's plans to conquer the sector on orders from Kronos. Sheena believed her story and opted to use her help.

Willow was bruised and beaten when she was placed in the cell but she wasn't tortured like the others. She helped Sheena move Lilith to the elevator with little difficulty.

The elderly officer stood up and shouted, "What's going on? I told you I'd turn you in if there was trouble!"

Sheena pointed down the hall and instructed him to apprehend the escaped prisoner. The officer was suspicious that Willow and Lilith were out of their cells and with Sheena, no less. He reached for his pistol.

"Fine," grumbled Sheena, realizing he wasn't buying her story. "Here's what's going on." She raised her pistol and fired two pulses into the officer's chest, killing him instantly.

"I hope you know what you're doing," snapped Willow. "You just killed a Fleet Officer."

"Let me worry about that," replied Sheena. She opened the door to a custodial closet and pulled the cart out. The trashcan on the front and the buckets on the side were empty. Mops and brooms stood upright in front of the handle.

"Lift her into the can," instructed Sheena. Willow obediently lifted the frail woman and set her inside the can. Sheena took a janitor's jumpsuit from the closet and tossed it to Willow. "Put this on fast."

Willow, sensing that this improved her chances of escape, eagerly complied. Sheena laid plastic bags over the top of the can and directed Willow to push the cart into the elevator. Once inside, Sheena revealed their escape plan.

In the early morning hours, there was no sign of anyone as they approached the dock. Sheena saw the crates and quickly searched for the one marked 'frozen goods'.

"Where is everyone?" Sheena asked Willow.

"Witty took his forces to attack the alien races that he believed were a threat to their plans."

"We have to stop them!" exclaimed Sheena. "That's an act of war!"

"Get us out of here first and then we'll worry about that," chided Willow, fearing what would happen to her if they were caught.

Sheena frantically searched the crates for the empty one. Captain Jeffries approached and watched her curiously. Sensing his presence, Sheena engaged him in conversation. Jeffries inquired as to what she was doing.

"I'm looking for a particular crate of wine cases," she lied.

Willow heard them and pushed the custodial cart toward the ship. Checking each rear panel of the crates, she discovered the empty one with the markings. Urgently, she opened the lower panel on the side of it and slid Lilith inside. As she hid the cart away from the crate, twelve Fleet security troops arrived and handcuffed Sheena. Once she returned to the crate, she quickly slid inside and pulled the panel shut.

"How could you do this, Jeffries? After all the time you spent with my sister, have you no sense of loyalty?"

Jeffries laughed at her. "Of course not," he replied giddily. "I knew she would be killed in that ambush. In fact, I set it up."

Sheena became enraged and struggled to get free. "I'll get you for this, Jeffries! I swear!"

"No you won't. I have a nice cell for you and two attendants who will make your body tingle in ways you never imagined."

Another security officer arrived and whispered in his ear, telling him of the fate of Grissom and Firth. Jeffries bit his lip in an effort to hide his anger. "Get her out of here now. Take her back to 'C' level."

Four security personnel escorted Sheena away. Jeffries glanced around the dock and instructed the remaining troops to watch for anyone trying to stow away on the *Argo*. The men spread out and waited.

The security detail took Sheena down to 'C' level to the cell next to Rock's. She was handcuffed to the wall and left alone. Tears filled her eyes as she fretted what would happen to her. Surely Witty would try her for treason.

Jeffries entered the cell with a smug look about him. "I am so going to enjoy this," he taunted and punched her in the gut. Sheena gasped and heaved.

"Where are the prisoners, Brice?" he demanded.

Sheena summoned her strength and stood proudly. "Their location is need-to-know only and you don't need to know," she answered arrogantly.

Jeffries paced back and forth in front of her, trying to control his temper. Her bold stare got the better of him and he punched her in the mouth.

Sheena's lip split open and blood streamed onto her uniform, staining it. Still, she managed to maintain her composure and stared him down.

"Where are the prisoners, Brice? I won't ask you again," he warned.

"And I told you, you don't need to know. You aren't as important as you think you are," she mocked him. "In fact, you're just a little rodent and nobody likes rodents."

Jeffries lost it. He grabbed her by the throat and shook her violently. When he hesitated, she spat a mouthful of blood on him. Again, he choked her until she turned blue in the face.

Rock crept out of his unlocked cell and peeked in at Jeffries. He still held the bloody drill in his hand that he used to kill Firth and Grissom.

As Sheena nearly lost consciousness, Rock slammed Jeffries in the head with the drill. Jeffries fell to the floor in tears, grasping at the side of his head.

Rock rolled him on his back and knelt against his chest. With a coldhearted and evil grin, he shoved the drill into Jeffries eye. Jeffries' screams filled the corridor. Rock then pushed the drill through Jeffries' other eye until it penetrated well into his skull. Jeffries sobbed uncontrollably.

Rock stood over him, feeling somewhat vindicated, and then drove the drill into Jeffries' groin, destroying his manhood. Rock gazed at him proudly and taunted, "How does it feel to be *my bitch*?" He hacked up a wad of phlegm and spat on Jeffries.

Jeffries' cries diminished to child-like whimpers. He was barely alive with severe head trauma and brain damage.

Rock tossed the drill aside and used Jeffries' key to unlock Sheena's cuffs. She dropped to the floor, still struggling to breathe. Once her breathing was stable, Rock helped her to her feet and escorted her down the hall to the elevator.

"Thank you so much," whispered Sheena appreciatively.

"Don't mention it," replied Rock. "At least now I have a reason to live."

"Why is that?" she asked weakly.

"By freeing you, I certainly pissed off Witty and that robo-bitch Lennox."

Sheena forced a smile, not realizing why he referred to Lennox as robo-bitch. They rode the elevator to the main floor with renewed enthusiasm.

Rock asked, "Do you have a plan to get us out of here?"

Sheena frowned and explained how her ship would have departed if she wasn't there on time. Rock shrugged his shoulders and replied, "It was still worthwhile to take out some of those scumbags. I didn't expect to make it this far anyway."

The elevator doors slid open and General Witty stood waiting with four of his sentries. "Well, Commander Brice, I hope you have a good explanation for this," he remarked sarcastically.

Sheena tried to think quickly and responded, "I did until that traitor Jeffries interfered."

"Then we'll go to my office and discuss it. Why is he here?"

Sheena glanced at Rock and then explained, "He's a very important part of my plan."

Witty stared at her, disbelieving, and gestured with a wave of his hand for them to follow him. The sentries stayed close to Sheena and Rock as a precaution.

"I'm not buying your story for one second, Brice. However, if your idea has merit, I'll give it consideration. Until I'm ready to discuss it with you, you and your accomplice will remain in my custody."

Sheena glanced at Rock. Both knew that their only hope was to sell her idea to him. "Can we talk about this, Sir?" she requested.

"Negative," replied Witty in a gruff voice. "I'll tell you when I'm ready to talk."

He pointed to the sentries and then at Sheena and Rock. The sentries escorted them away to a standard holding cell.

★ ★ ★

After an hour, the crate became stuffy and Willow grew nauseated by the smell from Lilith's unconscious body. She was tempted to kill her but then the odor would worsen.

The sound of a forklift's engine gave her hope. Soon the crate was lifted and set on board the *Argo*. Shortly after, the cargo bay hatch closed and the ship departed for its mission to the fifth sector.

Lt. Kannel immediately led a team down to the cargo bay and opened the crate. He was horrified to see that Sheena wasn't there. Willow explained everything that happened, hoping to buy their trust.

Lt. Kannel's medical people took Lilith for treatment and placed Willow in minimal security until her identity could be proven. He shuddered as he realized he was leaving without his commanding officer. Fearing his own capture and punishment, he refrained from his temptation to contact the dispatcher for information on Sheena's status.

Lt. Kannel went to Sheena's quarters and used her secure line to contact the militia on Yord and inform them of the Fleet's assault on former allies. When the crew raised questions about Sheena's disappearance, Kannel urged them to follow the orders she gave them earlier. Despite their concern for her, they obeyed.

Several hours after their departure, one of the crew approached Kannel and informed him of a missing shuttle.

"How the hell did that happen?" Kannel shouted at him. The officer had no idea and stood ready for discipline. Kannel immediately suspected Willow and sent a team to search for her. A security officer arrived with video footage that showed Willow boarding the shuttle and departing the ship.

"Find out where that shuttle is headed," ordered Lt. Kannel. He paced the bridge uneasily, still concerned about Sheena's well-being. His first charge as commander and he already lost a prisoner and a shuttle, which only made things worse.

Sheena sat across from Rock on a cot. He leaned forward in a steel chair with his hands folded, looking down dejectedly.

"I think we can convince Witty to trust us," Sheena whispered. "I have an idea."

Rock slowly raised his head and waited for an explanation. Sheena stood and paced the cell, while sorting her thoughts. She looked like hell with her uniform blood-stained and her hair disheveled. Her neck began to show signs of bruising from Jeffries' choke hold.

Rock took notice of the confidence in her demeanor as she began to articulate zealously with her hands. "If we can negotiate with Marina to help recover the chip, perhaps Witty will work with us."

Rock shook his head negatively at her. "And why would he do that?" he countered. "Besides, even if we had the chip, I sure as hell wouldn't give it to him."

Sheena knelt in front of him and continued, "We have to get out of here, right?"

"Yeah," replied Rock unhappily, "but we're not traitors."

"We're not going to be. If we can get back to my ship, then we can make efforts to recover the data chip. Once we have it, then Lilith can change the programming to sabotage it. It will be useless."

Rock still looked unconvinced. "There's an awful lot of 'ifs' to your idea, Commander."

"Let's start with phase one - getting the hell out of here."

"And you're assuming we know where the chip is hidden," he replied cynically.

"You do know, don't you?" she asked eagerly.

"I might. Then again, I might not."

"Damn it, Rock!" she shouted. "Work with me, will you?"

"Alright," he muttered. "Let's assume that I know where the damned chip is. Get us out of here first and then we'll discuss where it might be."

"That's fair," replied Sheena. "Just follow my lead when the time comes."

V
COMPLICATIONS

Kat eyed Marina conspicuously as she piloted the ship back to Yord. Marina noticed and remarked cynically, "Spit it out already. What's on your mind?"

"I was going to ask you the same thing," responded Kat. "Especially in regards to the Seers."

Marina frowned and explained, "I'm concerned that we'll have differences of opinion over the Seers and I want to make sure we're on the same page since this is new to both of us."

Kat placed her hand on Marina's thigh affectionately and responded, "There are many things I've seen and known. No matter what I want, the future is about you, not me."

"Can you translate that into something I understand?" Marina requested.

Kat carefully chose her words and explained, "I've seen enough to know that you are central to our group. You are our leader. I didn't choose it; fate did."

"I really didn't want that," Marina replied sadly. Kat didn't respond but waited for her to continue. "There are two Seers that I know of, each about twelve years old."

Kat's eyes widened with excitement. "So, you know who they are?"

"I do," replied Marina sheepishly. "I will need your help to train them or whatever else we're supposed to do with them."

"Of course," replied Kat enthusiastically.

"And I don't want them to know some of the things you consort with like black magic, black arts and anything... well, you know what I mean."

Kat breathed a sigh of relief and asked, "Is that what's been bugging you?"

"What do you think?"

"I promise - no black magic."

Marina smiled and placed her hand on top of Kat's. "Thank you, Kat. I really do want to trust you."

"And I believe I already trust you, my sister," she replied proudly.

Marina felt some emotion stir in her when Kat called her 'sister'. She had no family and Kat was quickly becoming exactly that - her sister.

★ ★ ★

Britt stood on the bridge of the *Monolith*. An alarm sounded and stirred the crew into action. As they hustled into position at their designated stations, one of the men announced, "Sir, two Fleet ships approaching at slow speed."

The captain, Joel Kemp, pointed to the comm/nav panel and picked up a microphone. The operator quickly raised the ships on their channel and pointed to the captain.

"This is Captain Kemp of the *Monolith*. Please identify your ships and your purpose."

A male voice replied over the speaker, "We've come to meet with the militia leaders at the palace."

"Your identity please," requested the captain.

"Standby, Captain Kemp."

Kemp glanced at Britt and remarked, "That's unusual."

Suddenly the ship rocked violently as it was pounded with cannon fire from the Fleet ships.

Britt rushed to the transmitter and changed channels. He shouted frantically, "This is your commander! All ships return fire on the Fleet vessels! The *Monolith* is under attack."

Five militia cruisers rushed to their defense. The ships exchanged cannon fire with the *Monolith* taking heavier damage.

An explosion rocked the bridge and sent sparks flying. Britt and Captain Kemp were thrown to the ground. Fire broke out from the power supply panels at one end of the bridge. Another blast brought an I-beam and several pieces of metal and ductwork down on the men.

The Fleet vessels then trained their fire on the Palace District. Buildings exploded as the residents raced toward the forest for shelter. The militia ships arrived and pelted the two Fleet vessels until they crashed onto the palace grounds in smoldering wrecks.

The *Monolith* was forced to land nearby with smoke rising from several ruptured sections of hull. Help arrived quickly from the other ships as the men attempted to rescue their friends.

On the bridge, both Britt and Kemp were unconscious and badly injured. Others cried out in pain as panels lay on top of them, some burning.

The front and side of the palace collapsed under the wreckage of one of the Fleet vessels, crumpled against the building. Inside the palace, Marcus crawled to his knees in the main lobby. He was horrified by the debris in front of him. He staggered out the front of the palace and climbed over the tail section of the burning ships.

The *Monolith* was a smoldering wreck a short distance away from him. He rushed to the ship in search of Britt. When he arrived, Britt was carried off on a stretcher by medical personnel and appeared unresponsive.

Marcus became frantic. "How could this happen?" he shouted. Then he saw Captain Kemp, also unresponsive, on a stretcher.

Marcus knew he had to step up and take charge. He boarded one of the battleships and requested all commanders to assemble for an emergency meeting.

As the commanders entered, a message came through from Lt. Kannel, warning of the Fleet's actions against the alien races and a possible assault on Yord. He was baffled by the late warning and disregarded it.

"They want a war, they got one," shouted one commander angrily.

As soon as the captains assembled, Marcus updated them on Marina's mission to the IDC and the recent attacks on the townspeople. They assembled all information on the location of Fleet ships in the sector and began with the development of a defensive strategy.

Marcus watched as the captains laid out a plan to defend the planet and surrounding stations from additional attacks. When they finished, Marcus interceded, "This is wrong. Look at the Fleet's numbers! They've taken heavy casualties on their forces already from the alien races."

"But they still outnumber us," replied one of the captains.

"I'll bet many of those ships are incapable of combat right now."

"Why did the Fleet vessel contact us with a warning about the assault on the alien races?" asked one captain.

"Perhaps not everyone is buying into this war," replied Marcus. "I believe Marina still has some allies out there."

"So, you think we should go on the offensive, Marcus?" asked another.

"Not yet. We need to consult with the queen and also assess what damage the Fleet ships have sustained. In the meantime, prepare for a major offensive. Let's give them something to think about."

The captains agreed with Marcus' plan and attempted to contact Lt. Kannel for more information on the Fleet vessels and their formations. Marcus then instructed the men to assist in search and rescue operations in the area.

One of the captains, an older man named Titus, approached Marcus alone. "You do realize you are just a lieutenant, Marcus."

"Yes, sir. I don't mean to overstep my bounds."

"You are doing well, but you will need someone of rank for support. Britt is a close friend of mine and he spoke highly of you."

"Thank you, sir."

"So long as you keep your instructions as suggestions and not orders, the others will work with you. Try to keep peace with them."

"Yes, sir," replied Marcus nervously, realizing he took charge of the militia captains in a crisis situation.

Captain Titus patted him on the back and offered assistance if he needed it. The two shook hands and Titus left him.

★ ★ ★

After what seemed like hours of silence between them, Kat pressed Marina again for information on the new Seers. Marina placed the ship on auto-pilot and turned to her.

Kat leaned back in her seat and became impatient. "Well, Marina, I'm still waiting," she remarked, growing annoyed with the delay.

Marina was about to speak but then her eyes turned white with no pupils. Kat panicked and feared she was having a seizure. She took Marina's hand and held it. Suddenly, she could see what Marina saw in her mind.

Marina imagined herself gliding through space until she saw the wreckage of many vessels belonging to the Fleet, alien forces and the militia. The carnage was devastating. Then she glided through space again to the Galactic Shipping Services transportation hub. Her body drifted through the outer shell to an empty corridor. She and Kat then glided down the corridor, wearing cloaks made of expensive material to an elevator. Someone called out her name from behind and she turned.

Dr. Haney appeared and hurled a dagger at her. This time, she was ready for him. Marina dodged the dagger and charged at Haney. He surprised her with a serious of martial arts moves and left her reeling on the floor. Just as he appeared to have her beaten, the image blurred and then she found herself alone in the GSS station. Screams filled the corridors and she rushed to see what happened. When she turned the corner, she discovered nearly fifty Galleans being slaughtered by Fleet soldiers and their corpses tossed into an incinerator.

People in lab coats entered the room and met with General Witty. "The station is secure, Dr. Haney," announced Witty. "Now build that device," he instructed him and walked away.

Marina shuddered and awoke. Kat lay back against the chair, gasping for air. The two stared at each other in disbelief.

"You were there with me!" exclaimed Marina.

"We saw what was," Kat replied sullenly. "There will be a price to pay."

Marina weighed the consequences carefully and then responded, "You and I have a destiny with Haney. He must die."

"If required to fulfill our destinies, we will kill him."

"I don't want to hear this 'if required' bullshit. He will die!"

Kat placed her hand on Marina's arm and reminded her, "We cannot change what must be."

"We can and we will," replied Marina determinedly. "I'm calling the shots, so screw fate and destiny and anything else that stands in my way!"

An incoming signal interrupted their conversation. Marina responded and spoke with Marcus. When he revealed the details of the attack on Yord and Britt's condition, the women were appalled. Marina ordered Marcus to make arrangements for a response but take no action yet. He promised an update on their situation and Britt's health as soon as he knew more and then ended the transmission.

Marina burst into tears. "I hate this life!" she shouted and buried her head in her hands. Kat stood and hugged Marina, encouraging her that Britt would pull through. Marina stormed off the flight deck.

When the ship approached Yord, Marina left her cabin and returned to the flight deck. She took her seat next to Kat with a determined expression on her face.

"Are you alright?" Kat asked uneasily.

"I am," she answered with a stone-faced expression. "When we land, I need to meet with Marcus."

"I sense a lot of anger in you, Marina. You can't let your emotions take control of you."

"My emotions have nothing to do with this. Revenge does."

Kat grew fearful of Marina's intentions but said no more.

The auto-lander pinged, indicating that they were locked into the tracking beam for the transportation hub. Faust entered the flight deck and sensed the tension between the women immediately.

"When we land, I need to know everything we have on those assholes: who they are and what they're capable of," she announced adamantly.

Faust suggested, "Perhaps we can learn more from your parents' former allies. They may have first-hand information."

Marina agreed with him and left the flight deck for her cabin with tears streaming down her cheeks. She couldn't let the others see her in such an emotional state.

After landing, Marina stepped off her ship and was appalled at the damage to the Palace District. The transportation hub was badly damaged as was much of the town. Many of the local people tended to the injured, sobbing from their misfortune and loss of life.

As Marina marched past them, several shouted obscenities at her for allowing the Fleet to attack them. She fought back her urge to reply and continued past them, thinking only of Britt.

As she approached the damaged palace, Marcus intercepted her. "Your Highness, Britt is on board the *Wasp*," he informed her. "I can take you there if you like."

"Is he going to make it?" she asked dejectedly.

"We don't know. The doctors are with him now, but he is unresponsive. His vitals are weak but steady."

"Then we'll tend to the more pressing issues. I'll see him later."

"What can I do to help?" he asked. "I want revenge on those bastards as much as you do and I'll do whatever it takes."

"How good a fighter are you?" she inquired curiously.

"I was number one in my class in all categories. I competed in the galactic tournaments and placed every time."

"Why did you not win?"

"My opponents were significantly bigger - Attradeans, I believe they were called."

"And?" she pressed, still wanting to know why he didn't win.

"I chose the wrong fighting class for the competition. Many of my moves were ineffective because of their size and strength."

"So, if you fought them today, would you win?"

"I certainly would," he responded confidently. "I let my emotions control my choices. Now, I know to outsmart my enemies first, and then conquer them."

Marina pondered his response and then changed topics, surprising him. "Is the wine cellar intact?" she asked.

"I believe it is. My men are clearing the wreckage around it as we speak."

"That won't be necessary. We're not rebuilding the palace. Have them go into town and help the people."

Marcus was baffled by her choice. Then, she instructed him to meet her in an hour at the wine cellar and departed. He climbed through the rubble to relay the new instructions to his men.

★ ★ ★

After surveying the damage to the area, Marina spoke with Drago briefly and followed him to the wine cellar. She watched eagerly as he unlatched a different wine cabinet than she expected and rotated it, revealing a new escape route.

"It's a shame the rest of the palace is in ruin," remarked Drago."

"I'm not concerned with the palace. We have more important things to deal with."

Soon Marcus arrived, followed by Kat and Faust. Marina led them through the open cabinet and onto a concrete landing. Once inside, the cabinet returned to its natural position and soft lights illuminated the stairs. They descended several flights of the stairs, periodically reaching a landing and then changing course.

At the bottom of the stairs was a locked steel door with a hand scanner. Drago placed his hand on it and pressed four keys. He stepped back and instructed Marina to place her hand on the scanner. Drago entered a code and the door opened. "After you, your Highness."

They entered the underground base through a conference room at the end of the massive dock. Marcus and Kat were silent as they followed.

"You've done well, Drago," Marina complimented him.

"Might I ask, if it's not too personal, your Highness, what your intentions are? Perhaps I can be of assistance."

"My people were burdened with heavy casualties. I can't do this alone so I have to rebuild my parents' alliance if I expect to stop this."

"And you have plan?" he inquired.

"Not yet," she replied disappointedly.

"I would think that Kronos will send a hit team for you next. The Fleet just lost two valuable ships to get to you and failed."

"I'm sure they will, too."

"My Queen, I will do whatever it takes to keep you safe. All you need to do is ask of me and I will obey."

Marina was overwhelmed by his commitment to her. "I will reward you for your dedication, Drago. It is much appreciated."

"That isn't necessary, your Highness. I am happy to be your trusted servant."

Marina offered him a permanent position on her staff for his dedication and promised to do what she could to reunite him with Lilith.

After passing eight docks and several repair shops, they accessed the command center for the underground base and took seats at a long table in the center of the room. There were monitors, computers, communications equipment and satellite control devices that had been in sleep mode for years. Their presence in the room brought the equipment back to life like ghosts from the past.

During the boot-up, Marina and Drago discussed potential threat areas outside the palace that provided ideal locations for snipers to target her.

Marcus informed Marina, "I received a coded message from a Fleet officer, Lt. Kannel, of the *S.F. Argo*. Witty's forces have also attacked a number of alien races."

Marina was stunned by his revelation. "Can we defend ourselves if they try again?"

"I believe so, but that's not all," Marcus mentioned nervously. "Lt. Kannel also informed me that Commander Brice is in custody at Fleet Headquarters, compliments of some traitor named Jeffries. She's been imprisoned."

"That's insane!" blurted Marina.

"He also mentioned that he has Lilith on board if that means anything to you. She's in bad shape and his medical team is tending to her."

Drago's eyes widened with excitement. "That's my wife!" he exclaimed.

"I need to know that he can protect Lilith from Kronos," Marina informed them. "She's the key to their whole operation?"

"And you're sure of this?" inquired Kat.

Marina explained how she learned about Lilith, the chip, Rock and Tully and that Kronos can destroy everyone with Lilith's technology.

In response, Marcus suggested they keep their communications to a minimum until they validated the information.

Marina was concerned that Sheena risked her life to free Lilith and now was a prisoner and likely branded a traitor. Suddenly, she recalled the name 'Jeffries'. She turned to Kat and asked, "Do you know who Jeffries is?"

Baffled by her request, Kat replied, "Not a clue."

"Severin's nephew on Orpheus-2," she finished her own question.

"Then why's he at Fleet Headquarters?"

Marina ignored her, occupied in a fit of anger now. She punched the wall and exclaimed, "That piece of shit played all of us, including Victor! I knew he couldn't be trusted."

Kat placed her arm around Marina's shoulders and attempted to calm her. "Let's take this one step at a time. We need a plan."

Marcus then revealed to them that the shuttle from the *S.F. Argo* was discovered in the mountains with no one on board.

"That's odd," she interceded. "Why would it be here?"

"There was a message scrawled on the wall, your Highness. It was addressed to you."

Marina and Kat glanced at each other and waited anxiously to hear more. Marcus continued uneasily, "Willow says your time is nearly up. She is coming for you."

"Things have taken a significant turn with all the aggression focused on me and my kingdom," Marina stated angrily. "It's time to play by my rules. For the record: the bitch is back."

Marcus urged her to let the militia handle it, but she had something else in mind. Marina stood and paced about the room, considering how to play both defense and offense against Kronos.

"Take me to Britt," Marina requested of Marcus. "Kat, you remain here. See what you can do with this equipment. Maybe it'll be helpful."

Marina and Marcus left the command center and took the stairs back to the wine cellar. As they climbed through the rubble and approached the *Wasp*, Marcus requested that Marina allow him to hunt down those responsible for the attack. Marina assured him that he'd have the opportunity to join her in taking down all those responsible.

At the open hatch, three militia soldiers stood guard. They moved to attention when Marina and Marcus approached and then stepped aside to allow them passage.

Marina was impressed with the bridge and the high-tech equipment the militia had on board their ships. She always envisioned them as pirates or rogues with primitive, outdated ships.

The officers on the bridge stood at attention and saluted her. Marina and Marcus returned their salute, the common fist over the heart, symbolizing loyalty. They exited through a hatch at the rear and descended stairs to a long corridor. At the end of the corridor was the infirmary.

They paused at the entrance and Marina steeled herself for what she was going to see. Marcus glanced at her before opening the hatch. She nodded that she was ready.

When they entered, Marina was appalled to see over twenty gurneys with militia officers and soldiers, badly injured in the attack, receiving medical care from the doctors.

One doctor recognized them and promptly came over. "Commander Sykes is at the end," he pointed to the right and continued, "but not responsive yet." He led them past the injured until they came to Britt's gurney. "I'm very sorry, your Highness," he said compassionately.

Marina broke down in tears when she saw him. A bandage covered a wound on his left cheek; his arm was in a sling and his knee was heavily bandaged. "What's the prognosis, Doctor?" Marina asked as she regained her composure.

The doctor hesitated as he studied Britt and then replied, "I just don't know. He has a severe concussion from a blow to the head. What concerns me is that something struck him in the chest and may have caused internal damage."

Marina reached out and touched Britt's hand. Marcus stepped around the other side of the gurney and did the same.

"We're still running tests and gathering results, your Highness," continued the doctor. "I assure you, we'll do everything we can."

"I know you will," she replied somberly.

Marina whispered to Britt, "They'll pay for this and when it's over, we're leaving all this behind." Again, she sobbed as he was unresponsive.

Marcus put his arm around Marina's shoulders for comfort. She turned to him and declared angrily, "It's time for revenge."

Marcus nodded in agreement and led her back to the bridge.

Several of the captains assembled on the bridge, waiting anxiously for orders from Marina. She and Marcus entered through the hatch and approached them.

Marina informed them, "I need you to protect the planet right now. This is where it all begins - our home."

One of the captains asked, "Shouldn't we retaliate, my Queen?"

"Not yet." She went on to explain the complications of the situation due to Kronos, the IDC and their involvement with the Fleet. Then she revealed that she would attempt to reassemble the alliance by recruiting their allies once more.

The same captain inquired skeptically, "But aren't they in shambles as well after the Fleet attacks?"

Marina stood in front of the man, somewhat annoyed with his negativity. "The Fleet incurred damage from those attacks as well. Do you know how much damage?"

"No, your Highness," he replied sheepishly.

"Then why would we blindly go after them without knowing what we're up against."

"I understand now, my Queen. Is there an attack planned for the future?"

Marina patted the man's shoulder and smiled. "We all want revenge for what happened. I promise you; we'll get that revenge."

The men were relieved to know that they would get retribution for their peers.

Marina then announced, "Marcus will be my liaison with you. He will relay my orders and requests. Please give him your utmost cooperation."

The men assured her they would. They saluted her as she left the bridge.

"Meet me on *The Reaper* tomorrow at sunrise," she instructed Marcus. "We're going to visit some old friends across the galaxy."

"Yes, your Highness," Marcus replied. He saluted her and left.

★ ★ ★

On *The Reaper*, Marina poured a glass of wine, while admiring Drago's handiwork on her ship. As if on cue, Drago entered and bowed to Marina. "I'm glad to see you are safe, my Queen."

"Yes, but many are not," she replied sadly. "A glass of wine for you?" she offered.

"No, thank you."

"What can I do for you?" she inquired.

"Have you heard anything more on Lilith?" Drago asked humbly.

"No, but I will soon," she assured him. "I need to make contact with the vessel that's caring for her."

"I can't believe they rescued her. I do feel as though I should be by her side," he said respectfully.

"And you will be soon. Right now, you're assisting me in bringing her assailants down in your own ways."

"Speaking of which, I understand you are leaving tomorrow," he commented eagerly.

"I am," responded Marina curiously. "Why are you concerned?"

"I have some gifts for you that I'm sure you will be most pleased with. Please do not leave without seeing me."

Marina's eyes lit up with joy as she considered what gadgets Drago might have created for her. "Can you come before sunrise tomorrow?"

Drago responded anxiously, "I look forward to it."

"As do I," she said giddily.

Drago bowed and left the ship. Marina finished her glass of wine and considered her parents' success in forming an alliance. She wondered how they managed to convince the alien races to join them and what she could do to repeat their success. Then her thoughts turned to Britt.

She felt herself slide into a fog and then sensed his presence. When she emerged from the fog, Britt sat in front of her in the palace garden. By the expression on his face, he was bothered by something. Marina paused behind him and rubbed his shoulders. She nibbled at his ear and kissed his cheek.

Britt reached around her waist and eased her in front of him. "Don't go down this road of violence again, Sweetie," he pleaded. "We'll work this out."

"Not now," she replied sternly. "You have something more important to tend to."

Marina sat on his lap and affectionately pressed her nose against his. Britt couldn't resist her big, brown eyes and kissed her hungrily. "This isn't the time, Marina," he blurted and tried to pull away.

"Then let's make time," she suggested anxiously.

Britt was reluctant to do anything without knowing Marina's plans for Kronos. Finally, she grew flustered by his resistance and sat down next to him. She was about to plead her case when the room grew cloudy. She felt him slip away from her and then she felt herself whisk through darkness.

Kara and Ginna entered the ship with their guardians, Dora and Magdalena. They were alarmed to see Marina in a trance, sweating profusely, and oblivious to them. Kara kneeled in front of her and gently touched her cheek. "Marina, it's Kara. Are you alright?"

Marina felt off-balance as she was falling through space. Suddenly, she gasped and became alert. "Ah, yeah, Kara. I'm fine," she responded with a glazed look in her eyes.

Dora soaked a rag and then dabbed it across Marina's forehead. Kara and Ginna each held her hands. Magdalena filled one of the wine glasses with water and offered it to Marina. She eagerly gulped it down and regained her composure. They spoke briefly about Marina's plans for the girls and what was expected of Dora and Magdalena.

Marcus entered the ship and informed Marina of the condition of the Fleet forces in the sector. She was pleased with the amount of damage incurred by the Fleet vessels and considered what advantages she now had at her disposal. Then she realized this was the time to trap Willow. The likelihood of an additional attack by the Fleet was minimal.

"Marcus, I want you to remove all palace security from the area," she instructed. "Without the Fleet to deter me from my priorities, I have one problem to take care of right now."

Marcus was baffled by her request and asked, "Why would we do that, my Queen? You'd be helpless."

"Exactly," she replied with a smile. "Whoever is coming for me, and it's likely to be Willow, will have a small team. They want this done quickly, I'm sure."

"Why do you say that?" he asked, trying to understand the method to her madness.

Marina looked at him disappointedly and countered, "Why else would Colonel Lennox make a personal appearance here on Yord to deal with me? I'm a thorn in their side."

Marcus had no answer. He excelled at military tactics but Marina was known for her psychological strategies as well as her battle tactics from her days as a courier.

Marina continued, "She's Witty's right hand in Fleet matters so we must have put a snag in their plans." Marina then informed him that, once the hit team was inside the palace grounds, she would handle them. Marcus' forces would ensure that none of them left alive.

Marcus reluctantly agreed to support her decision. He had his own idea how to protect her but Marina already selected Faust to stay with her.

"I understand your thinking, my Queen," replied Marcus uneasily. "But I don't want anything to happen to you."

"Why?" she teased.

"Because, you are my Queen."

"And that's it?' she pressed, eager to know why he cared so much.

Marcus balked and then replied, "Commander Sykes has been like a father to me and you are very important to him. Therefore, I need to do my best to protect you."

"I appreciate that very much," she said and then placed her hand on his shoulder affectionately. "I'll let him know when he awakens."

"That's not necessary, my Queen. It's my duty as well."

"Very well, then."

Marcus was relieved. He didn't care to get caught up in matters pertaining to Marina and Britt. He bowed and exited the ship.

"Kat will be here shortly," Dora mentioned. "She accessed some of the former allies' databases and found out some things."

Marina informed them that they would be staying down at the temple until she returned. The women were surprised to learn that there was an underground facility.

Kat arrived with a small carry bag, followed by her body guards. They boarded her ship and were surprised to see the girls on board. Kat immediately inquired, "Marina, are they...?"

"Yes, they are."

Kat ogled them and became excited. "This is all of them?" she asked anxiously. Marina nodded 'yes' to her.

"That's great!" Kat exclaimed. "You don't know what this means for us."

Marina replied, "It means that we have a great responsibility to protect them at all costs." Kat was flustered with Marina's response.

"You don't get it. They're the key to the future! They're here to protect us!"

Marina reached for the girls and put her arms around them. "Right now, we're going to train them to be the best that they can be and to look after our people."

Ginna looked up at Marina and remarked confidently, "Your Highness, these powers we have; they grow with us. We don't train for them."

Kara then startled Marina with something else. "You went to the IDC and saw those who seek to harm you," she informed her. "We took you there and you saw what you needed to know."

Marina was stunned by her revelation. Kat folded her arms and smiled at Marina. The girls were very powerful, especially when they concentrated together.

"So, you girls are telepathic as well?" Marina asked.

"We are," they answered in unison.

"I don't understand how you can project me into other places like you did," remarked Marina. "It was so real."

Kat suggested to the girls, "What you do need to be trained in is how to control your emotions."

"We may need to teach the two of you about self-control," kidded Kara. "You both harbor much anger and frustration."

The two girls faced each other and held hands, concentrating with closed eyes. An oblong ball of light formed between them. The ball grew to the size of a bowling ball and solidified into the crystal ball that Marina destroyed months ago. Marina and Kat gazed in awe at the object. Marcus and the bodyguards watched in astonishment, wondering what would happen next.

The girls released their handhold and backed away from the crystal. A bright flash filled the cabin, followed by Charisse's voice. "You are now one with the Eye of Icarus. You will serve it with your life for the good of all."

"We shall serve the Eye," the girls replied in unison. Kara took the crystal ball and set it on the table.

"But I smashed that crystal after I killed Victor! How …?"

Kara approached Marina and took her hands in hers. "The crystal is for the Seers, my Queen."

"So why was it my job to protect it?" she asked, stumped by its reappearance.

"It was there to guide you. Everything you did brought you to what you have in front of you today."

Kat beamed at Marina and remarked, "It's about them, not us."

"Holy shit!" blurted Marina playfully. "The sisters of pain!"

The girls giggled at her quip.

"We will always be there to help you, my Queen," Kara informed her, "in some way or form, wherever you are."

Marina glanced at Kat and back at the girls proudly. "Wow!" she exclaimed. "We do have a lot to think about, Kat."

Marina then discussed the use of the Temple of Icarus to protect and train the girls. Then she considered that someone should stay to protect the girls in case their location is discovered.

"Now that we know all about the girls," she mentioned to Kat, "perhaps you should stay with them."

Kat was reluctant to agree but knew that they could do more to help Marina from the temple than anywhere else. When Kat requested that Marcus accompany them to the temple, Marina sensed something peculiar about her request.

"Why Marcus?" Marina whispered in her ear.

Kat grinned deviously and replied, "You have Britt. I could use someone as well."

"Be good to him. He's a fine officer and gentleman." "Even better," remarked Kat giddily.

"There's that one stipulation for allowing you to help train the girls," added Marina sternly in a surprise change of tone.

Kat knew Marina was still apprehensive about her access to the girls. She smiled and waited patiently for her to speak.

"No black magic," Marina reminded her. "I would monitor their training myself but right now I have my hands full."

"You have my word," Kat assured her. "I will keep you apprised of their progress."

"Look, Kat, I don't want to involve the girls in warfare. They're too young for that."

"There may not be a choice," responded Kat stubbornly. "If it comes down to our survival, we will need to be united as one."

"Let's hope it doesn't come to that," she replied uneasily.

"You promised me that you would not hesitate to take action," Kat reminded her. "I expect you to hold true to your commitment."

Marina became annoyed by her reminder. "The bitch is back," she announced with determination in her voice, "and I'm more dangerous now than I was before."

"And so are we," added Kat. "We have your back."

Marina led them from the ship into the ruins of the palace and through the wine cellar to the secret passage. Her confidence in Kat grew after their conversation. Despite her warning to Kat about black magic, she considered that maybe she should learn a little black magic from Kat.

As they walked, Kat revealed to her that the former alien allies were uniting whatever forces they have left for a counter attack against the Fleet. It was unclear what their strength was though.

★ ★ ★

The next day, Marcus arranged for his men to execute a training drill away from the palace grounds.

Marina remained in the palace in the meditation room, hoping that Charisse or even her parents would appear and give her guidance. Wearing her former battle garb, black leather pants and vest, with leather boots, she donned the helmet with dreadlocks and silver flash grenades. After admiring it momentarily, she contemplated how to repay Drago for his kindness. Attached to her thighs were thick black straps, which each holstered four of the jeweled daggers. She felt secure as she ran her fingers across the hilts.

Kat's guards remained in the hallway, three at the top of the stairs and two by the window at the end of the hall.

Faust remained in the room with her. He watched with admiration as Marina delicately inspected each grenade. When she finished, she fitted the wig onto her head. She felt a surge of power as she recalled how many enemies she defeated in her past. Part of her craved a return to the Stardust that gave her the feeling of invincibility but she was clean for several months now and preferred to stay that way. Her attitude more than made up for confidence.

Faust went to the balcony and studied the shadows along the damaged palace walls. "It's getting dark, your Highness. I expect your foes will make their move soon."

"And we'll be ready when they do," she assured him. After stowing a pulse pistol behind her in her pants, she holstered two others to her hip.

"Dismiss your men to the wine cellar," Marina instructed Faust, "I want you on the balcony with me. When these assassins come, remain there as if you are abandoning me."

"But your Highness," Faust replied, confused by her request.

"You'll know if I need you to intercede."

Faust reluctantly relayed Marina's orders to his men. They left the area, baffled by Marina's plan.

Marina sat on the balcony with a bottle of wine and sipped from a half-full glass, waiting patiently. The sky darkened, but two full moons illuminated the palace grounds. Her temper rose as she stared at the damage inflicted on her palace. Then she considered that she didn't really care for the palace anyhow. It was her parents' home, though, and she felt an obligation to protect it. Now it lay in shambles. "Someone will pay," she repeated several times to herself.

Faust stood by Marina until she ordered him to sit. "You are a target out here with me."

"As are you, my Queen."

"It's personal with these assassins, Faust. It always is. They'll want face time with me."

"You know your enemies well," he remarked.

"The universe is a predictable place," she explained. "There are things that will always be: war, love, hate, envy, greed."

"And those who choose to follow those sins," he added.

Marina enjoyed the conversation with Faust. She felt a rapport with him and pressed for more personal information on Kat.

"What does Kat think about all this business with new Seers and the war?"

Faust hesitated as he pondered how to answer. Finally, he revealed, "Kat believes that all of you will form a sisterhood to battle the forces of evil. She fears that you will not be able to reign because of the evil in men."

"And she thinks I'll give up?" Marina countered curiously.

"No, my Queen. Katarina believes you will seek revenge on all who have defied you, even if it means your death."

"That's a really negative view of the future and a lack of confidence in my ability to rule, don't you think, Faust?"

"No, not at all, your Highness. At some point, as you know, you have to adapt to your enemies. An attempt to rule as a queen may become useless. Another position of leadership may be required."

Marina considered what it would take for her to resort to extreme means against her enemies with the Seers. She appreciated Faust's honesty and found comfort in Kat's earlier words.

As midnight approached, seven lines with grappling hooks flew over the palace rear wall and latched onto trees and statues. Seven figures dressed in black scurried over the wall and hurried toward the palace.

"Here they come," announced Marina. "Let the party begin."

Faust grew uneasy as they waited impatiently for the enemy to appear. Two of the figures barged into the room and spread out to the corners. Faust reluctantly remained seated on the balcony with Marina.

The other assassins entered one by one, alertly watching them. When the last figure entered, the assassins removed their hoods.

The leader, Willow, strutted to the center of the room. She eyed Faust curiously. He made no attempt to defend Marina. She turned her attention to Marina. "So much for your loyal forces, Marina," she taunted.

"I knew it would be you," Marina replied and sipped calmly from her glass. "You failed in your first mission and you've come back to save face."

Willow ignored her remark and walked halfway to the balcony. She was wary of a trap as she took note of Marina's attire. "Dressed for a costume party, I see," she commented, mocking Marina's attire.

"I wear this when I'm pissed off. I'd offer you a drink but I don't drink with hired help. You understand that, since I am the queen and you're just ...," she hesitated for a few seconds and then finished, "Let's just leave it at that."

Faust bit his lip to suppress a smile. He was impressed with Marina's coolness and intimidation, but still feared for her safety. Kat would be angry with him if anything happened to her. He witnessed, at one time or another, what Kat could do with her magic to those who failed her.

Marina stood and set her glass down. She paused a few feet from Willow and studied her with an amused expression.

"What's so funny?" asked Willow defensively.

"I told you what I'd do to you if I ever saw you again."

"You talk tough, Marina. Let's find out how tough you are."

Two of Willow's assassins approached Marina. She offered no resistance as each grabbed an arm securely.

"What, no fight in you tonight?" Willow inquired disappointedly.

"I have to know first," Marina started innocently. "Do we have a past?"

Willow drew a dagger and pointed it at Marina. She stepped toward her and shouted, "Oh, yes, we have a past! We have an ugly past."

Willow head-butted Marina and busted her forehead open. Marina's face turned red with rage. Still held by the assassins, she retaliated with a head-butt of her own against Willow and staggered her backwards. Before the two assassins could react, she jumped up and planted her boots behind each assassin's knee. Her weight coming down on each one's leg caused them to buckle and fall, while clutching at their damaged knees.

Marina drew a dagger in each hand, while kneeling over them, and stabbed the two assassins in the chest. With a coy grin, she assumed a defensive position toward Willow. "Then pray tell; spit it out," she urged Willow playfully. "Don't leave me hanging."

The remaining assassins listened curiously while awaiting Willow's orders. Marina distracted her from them, leaving another opportunity. Before Willow could answer, Marina fired her daggers at two other assassins. They both clutched frantically at the wounds in their throats and dropped to the floor, each in a pool of blood.

The remaining two assassins became nervous. As they assumed defensive positions, Marina yanked two of the silver balls from her dreadlocks and tossed them to the remaining assassins. Instinctively they backed away.

Willow lunged at Marina, knowing the silver balls were a trap. The ensuing flashes at eye level blinded the assassins and left them writhing with burns to their faces.

Marina wrestled with Willow, followed by a series of wild punches by both women, before they locked together tightly. They fell to the ground and broke apart. Both women got to their feet immediately, ready to charge at each other again.

Faust watched from the balcony, nervously sipping from his glass of wine. He felt helpless as he waited anxiously for a reason to interfere.

"You killed someone close to me," Willow cried out in anger. "You left her headless body on a barren planet!"

Marina was surprised when she realized Willow was referring to Fiona. "That's not totally correct," chided Marina. "I also took an eye from her as well." Then she mocked her, "Like you, she was in over her head."

Willow screamed in a rage and lunged, leading with her dagger. Marina deflected the dagger away again but Willow's impact sent them both tumbling across the floor. The two engaged in an all-out brawl, rolling across the floor. Each woman took turns pounding on the other. Their battle continued until Willow lay dazed on the floor, panting heavily.

Faust finally stepped forward with his sword and offered, "Would you like me to finish her off, your Highness?"

Marina gestured for him to back away. Exhausted and bruised with several cuts to her face, she knelt on top Willow and stared defiantly into her eyes. "You're mine now," she declared.

"Kill me," Willow pleaded. "Let me go with dignity."

"But you have no dignity. You're just hired help." Marina slapped her several times and humiliated her. "You're nobody, Willow" she mocked as she stood and stowed her daggers in her thigh belts. Faust was shocked at how much anger Marina displayed toward Willow.

"The next time I see you, I'll be on top and you'll beg me for mercy," warned Willow as she struggled to stand.

Marina offered her hand as if to shake. When Willow made the mistake of taking it, Marina clothes-lined her and left her flat on her back, gasping for air.

Nonchalantly, Marina went to the balcony and retrieved her glass of wine. She returned to the room and stood over Willow, debating how much more pain to inflict.

When Willow struggled to her feet, Marina nodded for Faust to arrest her. Willow rushed to the balcony, vowing to kill Marina next time. Faust pursued her, but she stepped onto the railing.

"That's enough, Faust," ordered Marina. He reluctantly backed away from Willow.

Marina approached her, grinning with satisfaction. "Don't leave so soon, Willow. I'm sure Faust has some friends who would enjoy the company of a skank like you."

Faust smiled fiendishly as he considered what his men would do with her.

"You haven't seen the last of me, Marina," she cried and turned to jump. Marina dove and grabbed one of Willow's ankles but Willow lost her balance. She fell two stories below and lay unconscious on the ground.

"Hang her by her wrists in the courtyard stripped bare," Marina ordered Faust. "Consider her a treat for the men."

Faust beamed with admiration for Marina. He remarked, "You were right about her, your Highness. It was personal."

"I showed mercy on her twice now when she threatened my life. The next time, her death will be quick." Marina staggered to the balcony and poured another glass of wine. She gazed out at the palace grounds and was amused by the sight.

Two of Faust's men arrived and whispered to him. He gave them Marina's instructions and then sent them after Willow.

"My Queen, are you alright?" he inquired, turning his attention to her.

Marina sipped from her glass. "I'm fine. Won't you join me?"

Faust stepped out onto the balcony and stared at her in disbelief. "Why do you have to be so difficult?"

Marina set the glass down and stood up. "You sound like Britt," she joked.

"You look like hell," he chided.

"Get used to it," she countered. "You should know by now: I like it rough."

Marcus barged into the room and was stunned by the sight of the dead assassins. Faust related how Marina defeated them, while she looked down from the balcony at Willow as Faust's men dragged her away. She returned to the room to hear Marcus' news. Faust excused himself to allow her a private discussion with Marcus.

Marcus informed her that arrangements had been made to set up a blockade of Witty's forces using militia warships. He was concerned that it wouldn't be enough if Witty summoned the remainder of his forces from across the galaxy. "They sustained heavy losses but they still have a number of ships left," he fretted.

"I appreciate your concern in handling this," Marina remarked. "I learned a long time ago, 'never underestimate your enemies'."

"That's funny," replied Marcus. "Britt says the same thing."

After some thought, Marina suggested, "I need to meet with former alliance members about what our intentions are. I'm really uneasy about it, but I have to do this."

"Don't worry," Marcus assured her. "I'll be there to assist in any way."

"I know you will."

Marcus left and she sat on the balcony alone to finish her glass of wine.

★ ★ ★

Marcus' guards took watch over the palace entrance while the militia patrolled the town, searching for any additional threats.

Marina took the stairs down to the wine cellar and then the underground base. When she reached the entrance to the temple, she was surprised to see Kat and Marcus engaged in a romantic kiss, leaning against a pillar.

"Now I see why you requested Marcus' accompaniment earlier, you sly Kat," Marina teased.

Kat and Marcus were embarrassed and quickly ceased their affection toward each other. "Why Marina, I didn't expect to see you down here," replied Kat sheepishly.

Marcus gestured with his hands and shoulders that he had no choice in the matter. Marina was amused and winked to show her approval.

Marcus was relieved that she understood. He worked hard to become a rising star in the militia and knew he was destined for bigger things. To risk it now would be foolish. Unfortunately, Kat had a powerful influence over him that he couldn't resist.

VI
FAILED ALLIANCES

Marina stood in front of *The Reaper* and wondered if she made a mistake in leaving without any backup. Faust insisted on going with her but she trusted him to keep Yord secure while she went to her allies for help. Without Britt there to handle things, there were few others she could trust.

As she stepped inside the ship and placed her hand on the knob to close the hatch, Kat and Faust approached the ship.

"What are you doing here?" Marina asked curiously.

"You're not going alone," replied Kat adamantly. "We're here to back you up."

"That would be nice," replied Marina, "but this is something I have to do myself."

Kat placed her hands on Marina's arms and smiled as if there wasn't a worry in the world. "You'll never be alone. No matter where you are, we'll be with you."

"I guess you won't take 'no' for an answer, will you?" she kidded.

"What do you say?" Kat pressed, hoping she'd relent.

"You two drive a hard bargain. Shall we go then?" Marina stepped aside and her friends boarded the ship.

Once they were underway, Kat raised her concerns to Marina over how her combative attitude would drive her back to her dark ways. Marina confessed that it felt good to fight Willow; inflicting pain and humiliation on her. She also revealed how she could have done more but refrained. Once Marina convinced Kat that she was in control of her emotions, they moved on to another topic - Yord's former allies.

Together, they studied the files on the disk Britt obtained for Marina. The files held a detailed description of how Marina's father won over each species and formed the alliance with them. She found it difficult to understand how her father was violent, yet restrained, in dealing with his enemies. In some ways, it mirrored her approach, but he had Shanna, Marina's mother, while she had no one. Even with Britt, it wasn't like family. They shared love out of necessity more than love itself and it showed by their decisions to place business first.

When they approached the first planet, Urthos, Marina noticed an unusual amount of debris drifting just outside the planet's atmosphere. She summoned Kat and Faust to the flight deck for their thoughts on the situation. With the help of short-range scanners, they determined that the debris was from both Fleet and Urthonian vessels.

"Why would the Fleet attack Urthos?" questioned Kat. "It's pretty far out of their way."

"And a lousy plan, if you ask me," remarked Faust. "They lost quite a few ships out here."

"Perhaps to keep the aliens from interfering with their plan," suggested Marina.

"Maybe Kronos' plan is to bait the aliens into retaliation for a trap," Kat surmised. "It would force them to reveal their remaining forces and, if defeated, they would know that that there is nothing to stop them in their endeavor."

"It's a very risky tactic, if that's the case," Marina commented.

"Or arrogant," added Faust. "Like you said, my Queen: sometimes things are personal."

Three Urthonian fighters darted toward *The Reaper*. The 'collision' alarm sounded as the vessels came straight at them. Marina immediately attempted to contact the leadership on Urthos but with no success.

"I hope you have a plan for this," Kat uttered nervously.

"Watch and learn," Marina instructed them. Their eyes were fixated on the monitor as the fighters appeared via the short-range sensors. Marina started a right break and then veered down and left away from the fighters. Before they could react, Marina was behind them. The fighters made several maneuvers to take away her advantage but she was relentless in her pursuit.

"I'm impressed," commented Faust, amused and wide-eyed. "Is there anything you can't do, my Queen?" he inquired, still with eyes glued to the monitor.

"A quiet evening with a chilled glass of red wine," she complained. "What I'd give for one of those."

After repeated attempts at contact, an Urthonian officer responded and warned them to stay away. Marina persisted in meeting with the emperor, reminding them of who she was. Finally, they relented and granted her permission to land. The coordinates brought them to a small landing area on top of a gothic stone castle. Marina ordered Kat and Faust to remain inside.

Nervously, she exited the ship, fearing what the aliens would look like and how she would be received. Promptly, she was met by three Urthonian guards and the three pilots of the fighters she embarrassed. Each was at least seven feet tall with long, sickle-shaped arms. Their bodies had distinct muscular tones with skin that consisted of shades of dark green and black, appearing more like a shell than skin.

The guards led her inside the castle and down several halls. They emerged from the last hall into a large chamber. Torches lit the walls around them, creating an eerie ambiance on the walls and floor. Ahead of them on a raised stone platform were two banana-shaped thrones, extending almost to the ceiling. Mist clouded her vision as she tried to determine if the Urthonian leaders were camouflaged on the throne or if it was an illusion. One of the guards placed his arm on her shoulder and spoke through telepathy to her. "Kneel before the Emperor Rethus and Empress Attilena."

Marina reluctantly knelt down and soon felt a strange sensation overcome her. Then she realized they were probing her thoughts. She attempted to communicate with them telepathically.

"Greetings Emperor Rethus and Empress Attilena. I am Marina of Yord, daughter of Will and Shanna."

"How dare you come here!" boomed a loud voice.

"And why do you mock our pilots?" a female voice blared at her.

So much for telepathy, thought Marina.

"I have come to seek your help. The Fleet and a group called Kronos have turned on all of us for reasons I do not yet know."

The empress replied, "Your Fleet has attacked us and the casualties were devastating. Why should we help you?"

"Because," Marina replied sternly, "they won't stop after one battle. Whatever they're planning, this is just the beginning."

The emperor challenged her, "How do we know you aren't here to spy on us? Perhaps you will leave here and report to them what our state is."

Marina had enough and stood up. The sentry placed his arm on her again and she took exception to it. She gripped the arm and used a leg-sweep to floor the sentry. Quickly, she drew two daggers and fired them at the two leaders. Each dagger struck the throne behind them, inches from their heads.

A second sentry slammed Marina in the side of her head with its long arm and sent her sprawling across the stone floor. Marina scurried to her feet and drew two more daggers. The third sentry slammed her in the back and knocked her face down in front of the emperor and empress.

Marina quickly rolled sideways as the sentry's claw struck the stone next to her. She leaped up and swung behind the sentry, using its long limb for leverage. Her weight and balance drove the creature to the ground. With both her daggers pressed against the sentry's head, she announced defiantly, "If you won't help me then I will walk out of here alive. Be it known that, if you don't help me, I will never grant you entry into the new alliance when it is formed."

"There is no alliance," responded Rethus sarcastically. "It died with your parents."

"And as their daughter, I will rebuild that alliance and make it stronger. One thing I am not is weak. Those who seek to do me and my allies harm will pay dearly. I have neither the patience nor the heart that my parents had."

Empress Attilena stood and approached her. In a more sympathetic voice, she remarked, "I first met your mother when she carried you. I sensed your strength and determination before you were even born."

Marina stood and warily stowed two of her daggers. She stared into Attilena's dark soulless eyes. "I've lived a long and lonely life, wondering what happened to my parents. Once I learned their fate, justice was quickly dispensed. Her murderers live no more."

Rethos stood next to Attilena and studied Marina for a moment. He then spoke, "You have nerve coming here with no one to protect you. That was foolish."

"I could have killed you both but that was not my intention," Marina remarked arrogantly. She stepped closer to Rethos and stared into his eyes undaunted. "I do not fear death. I would rather die for what I believe in than to live as a coward, afraid to fight for what I've earned."

The two leaders turned toward each other and communicated telepathically in their language. Marina was surprised she could hear them so clearly, although she couldn't comprehend their words.

When they ceased their telepathic conversation, Rethos informed Marina that they couldn't support her due to the casualties from the Fleet attack. He also revealed that the other allies Marina sought to join forces with were also attacked and suffered heavy casualties.

"How much damage has been inflicted on the Fleet, Emperor?" Marina inquired.

"Thus far, each battle has been a standoff. More than half of their attacking force has been destroyed and many of ours have been badly damaged or destroyed as well."

"Then an attack on the Fleet isn't realistic," she surmised disappointedly. "Can I count on you to rally the other races that supported my parents?"

"And what do we tell them is your intention?" asked the empress.

"Be prepared, for I will cut off the head of the snake. When the last of the Fleet forces are in disarray from their traitorous act, I want a show of force to suppress the remainder."

"What assets do you have at your disposal?"

"I have the militia forces and one Fleet battle ship," she announced proudly. "I don't wish to engage in a full-scale war if I can defeat them from within."

The empress turned to her husband and remarked, "She has all the tact and determination of her father."

Rethus responded, "And she has the fire of her mother."

"Go, Marina, daughter of Will and Shanna," instructed Rethos. "We will speak with old allies, but we make no promises."

"Be safe, Marina," said Attilena compassionately. "We will do our best."

Marina went to their thrones and retrieved her daggers. She bowed before them and replied humbly, "Thank you, Empress Attilena. I will."

The Urthonian leaders disappeared, again leaving her wondering if their presence was an illusion or real. Marina followed the sentries back to the ship. She glanced back at them before boarding. The sentries showed no emotion whatsoever. Even in battle, their facial expressions never changed.

Kat and Faust waited nervously as she stepped onto the flight deck. They immediately noticed her bruises and swollen ear.

Marina was amused by their rigid facial expressions and anxiousness. "I'm fine, in case you were wondering," she joked.

"What happened?" asked Faust uneasily.

"You didn't kill them, did you?" Kat added. "They're supposed to be our allies."

Marina sat down in the co-pilot's seat and sighed. "They don't have enough forces left to support us."

"What do you mean 'enough'?" Faust pressed uneasily for an explanation.

"The Fleet has launched attacks on all our former allies," she explained. "Both sides have sustained heavy casualties."

Kat grew disappointed and responded, "Then we don't have much of a force to fight with, do we?"

Marina considered what other allies she might gain sway with. "We're not done yet," she replied determinedly. "Let's try Calamaar. Perhaps their forces are still intact."

They departed the Urthonian atmosphere and headed for Calamaar. Kat had a bad feeling about the Calamaarians and urged Marina to let the Urthonians handle the other allies. Marina insisted that she needed to make her presence known to them so they realize she's in charge.

When they drew close to Calamaar, five fighters immediately raced out to intercept them. Faust cringed and placed his hand on her shoulder for support.

Marina contacted the leadership on Calamaar and requested a meeting with their leader. She recalled from the disk Britt obtained for her that the Calamaarians were a violent race, who only understood battle. She warned Kat about the dangers that could lie ahead on Calamaar.

"Then why are you going there?" questioned Kat.

"Because they will be the toughest challenge," she replied confidently. "If I can win their support, the others will follow."

Kat and Faust glanced uneasily at each other, wondering if Marina had lost her mind. The two did their best to show their support for her, although Marina was well aware of their lack of confidence in her decision.

The fighters approached in attack formation. Marina took a deep breath and navigated around them. Each time the fighters attempted to trap her in a crossfire, she eluded them. She had many opportunities to target the fighters but chose not to, despite the repeated cannon fire at her vessel.

"You have to do something, Marina!" exclaimed Kat. "They're trying to kill us."

"Just be patient," she responded coolly.

The transmitter beeped and the fighters peeled off, returning to Calamaar. Marina responded to the transmission and waited anxiously.

"This is Golgar, King of Calamaar. How dare you taunt my forces!"

"Just proving my identity," she replied confidently.

"There was only one person who could outfly the Calamaari and he had that same fighter. Unfortunately, he's gone."

"I am the daughter of that man, Will Saris. I am Marina, Queen of Yord, and I will gladly explain everything to you when we meet.

Marina smiled at Kat when Golgar granted her permission to land at the palace. She then questioned Kat about why they didn't have any telepathic contact with the girls. Kat replied that the distance may have something to do with it or the girls just chose not to.

"I could sure use one of those premonitions so I can see what's ahead," Marina complained.

Kat responded, "The power of the Eye only reveals itself to satisfy fate. It isn't for your amusement."

"Well, thank you, mother," Marina chided. The three of them stood by the hatch and waited anxiously as it opened.

"I never saw a Calamaarian before," Faust remarked.

"Me neither," added Kat.

"But you have seen aliens before?" asked Marina, surprised by their remarks.

"We have," she replied. "Several as a matter of fact."

When the hatch was fully open, six muscular creatures with a reptilian appearance and sharp, pointed teeth awaited their exit.

"Follow us," ordered one of the creatures through an interpreter box on his neck.

As Marina, Kat and Faust followed, the creatures circled around them. Three had pulse pistols, while the others were armed with clubs and maces. The Calamaarians led them to a stone chamber, much like the one in the

Urthonian palace. This time there were no illusions. Golgar sat on his sculptured granite throne with a large club in his hand.

When they knelt before Golgar, he stepped down from his throne and approached Marina. "How did you obtain one of our ships?"

"It belonged to my father," Marina replied. "I understand your people traded for it."

"He tricked us and left some of our troops stranded on a crippled ship," Golgar barked out angrily. "I find that quite offensive."

"Well, Golgar, you weren't the leader back then. Your uncle and my father obviously got along quite well after that."

"You know what it took to earn my uncle's trust, don't you?"

"I do," replied Marina as she knew what was coming next.

"If you gain my trust, we will speak."

"Very well, then. When do we start?"

Kat panicked and asked, "Start what?"

"Relax," Marina ordered her.

"I will fight for you, my Queen," volunteered Faust, knowing it was suicide for him to fight a Calamaarian.

"Faust, please don't interfere. I have to do this."

Golgar turned away from Marina set his club down next to a large rubber block beside the throne.

Marina gestured for Kat and Faust to step back. She knelt down and drew two daggers. Before she could stand, Golgar fired the block at her midsection. She was knocked backward against the wall and lay gasping for air. Faust was concerned and about to interfere when Kat grabbed him by the wrist and ordered him to stand pat.

Golgar laughed as Marina struggled to get to her feet. Her daggers lay on the ground a short distance away. The Calamaari leader then charged at her, determined to crush her against the wall. Marina's eyes widened with fear and she dove aside, barely avoiding him. Golgar crashed into the wall and injured his shoulder.

Marina staggered to her feet and retreated toward the throne. Golgar stood up, snarling at her. He picked up the rubber block and hurled it at her. The block caught her arm. She clutched at it, grimacing in pain.

One of the Calamaari guards reached for Marina's neck. Golgar shouted for the guard to stay back, but Marina already retrieved another dagger. She drove it under the guard's chin and into his head. The guard wailed and fell backwards, mortally wounded.

"Sorry, Golgar, but he wasn't part of the deal," she replied mockingly.

"That's the price of disobedience," he replied sternly. "He was told not to interfere."

Golgar picked up her daggers from the floor. Marina sensed that he would hurl them, just like the rubber block. He quickly raised his clawed hands to throw the daggers. Marina dove on the wounded guard and spun him on top of her. The two daggers struck the guard and killed him.

Marina shoved the body away and retrieved her daggers. Golgar rushed at her again. She jumped onto the arm of the throne and then leaped at him. Golgar, prepared for her move, clothes-lined her and left her spitting blood on the stone floor.

"Had enough, Marina?" he taunted.

"I'm just warming up," she uttered weakly. Marina struggled to her feet and again retreated toward the throne. He rushed at her again. This time, she leaped over him and latched her arms around his neck. Her momentum spun him around and she wrestled him to the ground. She bent his head sideways and pressed the blade of one dagger against his throat.

The guards raised their weapons, prepared to attack. Faust drew his pistol and sword. Kat fretted and attempted to use her mind control to handle the situation. Unfortunately, it didn't work on the Calamaarians.

"Enough!" barked Golgar. "You have made your point, Marina."

Marina released him and stepped back. Golgar stood and faked as if he would charge at her. Marina quickly stepped sideways, prepared to encounter him again.

Golgar laughed at her. "I haven't had that much fun in a long time," he remarked playfully. "My guards are reluctant to engage me in physical tests of courage."

"I wish I had that problem," blurted Marina as she painfully stowed her daggers. Her arm and shoulder throbbed and her head pounded from the impact of the clothes line.

The guards lowered their weapons, as did Faust. He glanced at Kat and both exhaled in a sigh of relief.

"You obviously fight a lot," remarked Golgar. "You are very adept at it."

"Thank you," Marina said, forcing a smile but reeling from the pain.

"Now we will talk," he announced.

Golgar led her into a conference room with a long, rectangular table and large chairs positioned neatly around it. He politely pulled a chair out and nodded for Marina to sit. She graciously accepted, pleased to be done with the fighting.

After relating the details of her parents' fate, Marina and Golgar discussed everything that happened with Kronos, IDC and the Fleet. Golgar informed her that their casualties were light due to his forces participating in an exercise at the far end of the sector.

"Would that happen to be sector five?" she asked curiously.

"It is," he replied.

"I have a friend whose vessel's mission was to go out to the fifth sector where 'nothing' was happening. Obviously, someone knew your forces were there."

"Why didn't the Fleet vessels make the trip there?" he questioned her suspiciously.

"As I said, I have a friend who is the commander in charge of that mission. She suspected something wasn't right about all this and took alternate actions."

Golgar stood and paced about the chamber. "So, you want me to support you in battle against these groups as part of the new alliance."

"I do," she replied sincerely.

"And you would like me to speak with the other races as well."

"I do. The Urthonians already offered to meet with some of the leaders and present my offer."

"I will consider it. Now I have other matters to tend to." Golgar replied abruptly and walked toward the entryway.

Marina grew frustrated from his lack of commitment. "How will I know if I have your support?"

Golgar paused and replied, "You will know, I assure you." He left the chamber, leaving Marina irritated. The guards prodded her back to the main chamber, where Kat and Faust followed them to the ship.

Once they departed the Calamaarian planet, Kat treated Marina's wounds. She cautioned Marina that the alliance she hoped for wasn't likely to materialize. The alien races wanted nothing to do with the humans right now.

"We don't have enough forces to fight them," complained Faust. "We need to reconsider our options."

"We don't need much... until the end," Marina declared confidently. "It's time to take the battle to Witty and Kronos."

★ ★ ★

Interim Commander Kannel contacted the commanders of the *Hydra* and the *Mantis*, using the secure communication equipment in Sheena's office. He warned each of them about the fate of Commander Brice and how he had concerns about the Fleet's new role in a mercenary coup for Kronos. The commanders pledged to support him if he could provide proof that General Witty was using the Fleet for such mercenary purposes.

Kannel debated between returning to rescue Sheena and continuing on to sector five. Either way, he disliked his choices. He ordered his communications officer to continue monitoring transmissions for any word from Sheena and inform him immediately of anything unusual.

The crew was on edge, concerned that they were participating in a mutiny against the Fleet or risking their lives against an enemy they had no proof of. Despite their concerns, Kannel ordered all three vessels to hold their position on the rim of the Fleet's territory until further instructed.

★ ★ ★

Marina piloted *The Reaper* to other former allies' planets and was firmly denied meetings with the leaders. Their position was clear that the humans could not be trusted and those races had engaged in costly battles with Fleet ships that she should have had control of.

Marina was silent as she set a course for Yord. Kat was right with her doubts about the formation of the alliance. Marina failed at her first real diplomatic test and now would have to take on Kronos alone. *If only I knew who the head of the snake was,* she questioned herself. She had no idea where to start with Kronos' forces, other than the mercenaries and assassins who made attempts on her life.

Kat attempted to console her and restore her confidence but to no avail. When she left Marina alone on the flight deck, Faust entered and sat with her. He recognized her depression and pointed out how tough she was in the face of adversity. She earned his respect when she took on Willow's assassins alone, using him for a minor distraction. *How could she not believe in herself?* he thought.

Marina pondered her situation and realized that she needed a wild card to get the upper hand on Kronos. She considered everything that happened since the agent appeared in town and harassed her people. Then she contemplated how Tulley and Rock fit into the scheme of things. "That damned chip," she mumbled to herself. "It's the root of all our problems."

When she recalled how Severin took the time to discuss her parents with her on the day she turned over the chip, she realized that it must still be on Orpheus-2. The chip was her answer and she had to find it.

Faust discussed several possible scenarios for the Fleet's actions with Marina and how a corporation like Kronos could benefit from a destructive plan like the one that ravaged both Fleet and alien forces alike. After several productive discussions, Faust left her alone to consider her options.

Kat checked in on her and was pleased with her upbeat attitude. When she questioned her change of heart, Marina revealed what she believed about the chip's location.

"Then we're going to Orpheus-2?" inquired Kat.

"No, we're re returning home first to meet with the militia leaders. After that, we're going to Orpheus-2 to find that chip."

"That's a big station to search for a tiny chip," Kat remarked. "I hope you have something a little more concrete to go on than a hunch."

Marina explained, "When I asked Tulley how he escaped from capture on Orpheus-2, he replied 'the same way I did'."

"And how was that?" asked Kat curiously.

"Through the ductwork," she answered confidently. "What better place to hide a chip."

"You're kidding!" Kat remarked in disbelief.

"It's got to be attached to one of the ductwork walls somehow. All I need to do is find it."

"Well, if I was going to hide it," remarked Kat cynically, "I sure wouldn't make it easy to find."

"And I know of two such places," she replied confidently.

★ ★ ★

Witty entered his office as his computer beeped, signaling a high priority message. "Kiss my ass!" he grumbled. "I ain't even had a coffee yet and they're callin' already."

Witty sat down and logged into his ALQ-19 multi-purpose computer system. When he accepted the message, a hologram formed in the middle of the room. An illusion of Klingman appeared before him with a scowl on his face.

"What the hell is going on, Witty?" he demanded to know. "Your Fleet is getting their ass handed to them all over the galaxy!"

Witty rubbed his eyes to mitigate a growing headache and sipped from his coffee. He leaned forward and stared down the hologram, knowing it was projected back to Klingman as a message response. "Listen here, you little shit, when this is over, the Fleet will have won," he declared. "You worry about that damn weapon and let me take care of the freaks. Got it?"

The hologram vanished momentarily, giving Witty a chance to check his reports. Losses were much heavier than he projected in the alien assaults. Then he considered that maybe Brice could be of some value.

The computer beeped and a live hologram of Klingman appeared this time. "My people reported that you lost Lilith. Is that true?"

"We didn't 'lose' Lilith," he answered sarcastically. "Let's get that straight right off the bat."

"Then what do you call it?"

Witty stood and leaned on his desk. He appeared demonic in his expression and replied, "Your butchers were ineffective. As a result, I've taken control of the situation."

"And how is that?" inquired Klingman.

"Lilith is out in the field with some of my people. We are making arrangements with someone who knows where the chip is and how to recover it."

"Then why did you release Lilith?"

"Because she is the only one who can validate the data and activate it," Witty informed him.

"You don't need to concern yourself with the chip, Witty," chided Klingman. "Just do your damn job!"

"I do need the chip! Your butchers damaged Lilith's memory. She can't provide the data we need. She can only validate it."

"Don't screw this up, Witty," Klingman warned. "You don't want me coming down on you over this."

"You just make sure the weapon is ready and I'll get you the friggin' chip." Witty ended the conversation and shut down the connection. "Damn beaurocrats!" he shouted angrily.

He sat down and sipped from his coffee again. As he contemplated his next move, Col. Lennox entered. "Good morning, sir."

Witty gestured with his hand for her to sit. He set his coffee down and focused on her. "What the hell happened to our fleet?"

"The alien numbers were greater than we anticipated," she replied disappointedly. "We didn't expect such resistance."

"And why not?" he barked at her.

"They were supposed to be involved in a multi-force exercise in sector five. That's why we ordered Brice to report there."

"If someone invaded us, we'd throw everything we had at them, don't you think?" he challenged her. "We should have anticipated this was a possibility."

"I have another problem, sir. Did you see what they did to Jeffries?"

"Screw that little pussy!" shouted Witty. "He was useless to me. I don't need kiss-asses."

"Maybe so, but he had value to me, sir."

Witty stared into her eyes and then burst into laughter. "He was your boy toy, huh Lennox?"

Offended by his disrespect for her, she replied coldly, "Sir, he had value to me."

"Well, he screwed up royally on this one. Get me Commander Brice now."

"But, sir?" she responded, fearing that he would turn to Brice for answers.

"Lennox, did you hear me?"

"Yes, sir." Lennox mumbled and reluctantly left the general's office.

Witty's computer beeped again. "What the...!" he groaned and pressed 'accept'. A hologram of Sexton appeared in front of him.

"What do you want, Sexton?" he inquired irritably. "I'm very busy right now."

"You're jeopardizing our plans, Witty. Kronos isn't very happy with your progress right now."

"You tell Kronos to go screw themselves," he responded angrily. "I'm in the middle of cleaning up their mess."

"Well, I hope your plan is viable. You have five days to get results."

"Get the hell out!" he blurted. "Five days wasn't part of the deal!"

"Several alien races are amassing their forces at the edge of the sector as we speak. We no longer have the luxury of time or surprise on our side, thanks to you."

"You son-of-a-bitch! Don't put this on me."

"Just get those results or else," warned Sexton. The message ended and the hologram vanished.

"I'm gonna kill that mother!" he shouted and spilled his coffee. "Damn it!"

★ ★ ★

Inside one of the holding cells, Sheena sat despondently while Rock lay across the floor mumbling incoherently. She wondered how her career went so wrong so quickly. The oath she took was to protect humanity, not enslave it. After several years of hard work and training, she finally made commander and received her own ship, The *S.F. Argo*. In less than two weeks, it was all gone and here she sat a prisoner, about to be charged with treason. "What the hell are you mumbling about?" she asked Rock irritably.

"I'm counting all the times that Marina outwitted everyone, including me," he answered.

"Why would you care about that now?"

"Because she'll do it again to these guys before they know what hit them," he explained. "They know her history and that's why they have to stop her before they continue with this plan of theirs."

"If only you were right," she uttered dejectedly.

Rock sat up and became defensive. "You underestimate Marina. She is capable of almost anything."

Sheena backed down and relented, "Maybe she is as good as the stories I've heard. But that doesn't mean she can help us in here."

Rock stood up and leaned on the bars, facing the door to the corridor. "You're right, Commander. We need to get out of here somehow to where she can help us."

Lennox peered in at them through the window. She activated the lock and released the latch. Rock immediately noticed her sinister stare and cringed. "Yikes!" he shouted. "Here comes the devil's spawn herself."

Lennox opened the cell gate and approached them. "Which one of you attacked Jeffries?" she demanded to know.

Sheena was surprised by the question. "Why do you care about a traitor?" she replied.

"Personal reasons. Now who fucked him up like that?"

Neither Sheena nor Rock replied. Lennox grew angry and clenched her fists. "We can do this the hard way," she remarked coldly. "I do prefer hard."

"I'll bet you didn't get that from Jeffries," Sheena taunted.

When she shoved Sheena against the wall, Rock immediately attacked her. Lennox easily subdued him with a shot to his head and an arm bar that left him on his knees, begging for mercy. She shoved him to the ground and stomped on his hand until he cried.

Sheena stood face-to-face with Lennox and inquired, "How much are they paying you to sell your people out?"

"It was you who attacked Jeffries, wasn't it?" she replied.

"Maybe," Sheena responded. "You didn't answer the question. How much does it take for a Colonel with as many years in the Fleet as you to sell out?"

Lennox lost control and decked Sheena with a punch to the mouth. Sheena lay on the floor, rubbing her mouth. Blood seeped from her busted bottom lip. She was stunned by the force of Lennox's punch, but maintained her defiance.

"Just as I thought," Sheena continued. "You did it for free. What else do you do for free?"

Lennox grabbed her by her collar and yanked her to her feet. Sheena grinned, evoking more anger from Lennox. Lennox slammed her against the wall several times before Sheena finally retaliated.

Sheena surprised Lennox with a thumb to her eye, followed by a knee to the midsection. She grabbed Lennox's arm and slung her against the bars. Before Lennox could recover, Sheena pulled her arm through the bars and bent it back, applying as much pressure as possible.

"When I get loose, I'm gonna kill you, Brice," Lennox shouted, grimacing in pain.

Rock got up slowly and smiled; impressed by Sheena's aggression toward Lennox. "Hold her still," he instructed Sheena and removed Lennox's belt from around her waist.

Sheena removed one of the gloves from Lennox's hands and was shocked to see a metallic prosthetic hand. "Rock, look at this!"

"She's a Frankenslut!" Rock joked. "Would you look at that?"

"Stay behind the bars. She can't touch us there," Sheena instructed him.

Lennox tried to wriggle free from Sheena's grasp but Sheena's leverage on her arm through the bars made it impossible. "You no good bitch!" shouted Lennox. "I'll gut you like a pig."

Sheena smiled at her and again taunted, "Seems like you know all about pigs. I'm sure your mother was quite the 'ho', I mean sow."

Lennox screamed in a rage at them with an outburst of obscenities.

Rock stepped outside the cell and, reaching through the bars for her other arm, strapped her wrists tightly together outside the cell. Lennox was bound to the bars, humiliated by the turn of events.

Sheena admired Rock's handiwork. "I see you've had experience at this."

Rock wasn't done though. "I'm just warming up," he replied giddily.

He knelt down and pulled each of Lennox's legs through the bars and pulled her feet back far enough to hook them behind the lower bars. Without her legs to support her, all of Lennox's weight was on her shoulders and arms.

"Let me go!" she screamed at them.

Rock stood in front of her and cocked his arm to punch her through the bars. Sheena stepped between them and grabbed his arm. "No!" she shouted at him. "That's enough." She pointed to the door and glared at him. Rock lowered his arm disappointedly.

"I'm warning you, Brice: you'll pay for what you did to Jeffries," Lennox spoke in a low-pitched voice that sounded more like a growl.

Sheena sneered at her and replied, "I guess you'll just have to play with yourself from now on. I'm sure it won't be the first time."

Rock was upset that she prevented him from beating up on Lennox. "I want her to bear my child, Brice," he announced, almost rubbing noses with Lennox as he opened the zipper on his pants. "I want to give it to her good!"

Finally, she explained, "If Witty catches us, we're gonna need her to get out of here. If you hurt her, there's no deal - only punishment."

"How's he gonna know?" countered Rock. "Look what they did to me."

"Fine," relented Sheena. "You've got five minutes to put a smile on her face."

"A quickie, huh?" Rock commented. "I'll do you proud, Commander," he promised.

Sheena stared at him suspiciously as she pondered his sanity and then left the cell. She waited in the hall, wondering if she did the right thing.

Then she heard Lennox's shouts. "Is that all you got, you little prick! Stop it. Don't! Please stop!" Then her threats became moans and she cried.

Rock emerged from the cell, fixing his pants and wearing a contented smile.

"Feel better?" asked Sheena condescendingly as they walked down the hall. "That changed everything, didn't it?"

"I could have driven a semi through that pussy, it's so worn out."

"But you rode it anyway, didn't you?"

"Of course - prison style."

"That's disgusting," she complained. "I thought you were better than that."

Rock got on the elevator, beaming with satisfaction. There was silence as they rode to the main floor. The door slid open and Witty stood there with arms folded.

"I knew you were up to something, Brice," he remarked sarcastically and then stepped aside for them to exit. Sheena and Rock watched him carefully as they stepped off the elevator.

"I'm afraid Col. Lennox isn't as sharp as she used to be," Sheena responded.

"I hope for your sake, she's okay," he warned her. "Where is she?"

"She's hanging out down in the holding cell," interrupted Rock. "Don't worry, General, only her pride is hurt."

Witty eyed him suspiciously. "Then we're ready to proceed with negotiations."

Sheena glanced at Rock with a puzzled expression. They both realized this was too easy. Since he didn't summon his security detail and made no threats to them, they followed him down the corridor to his office under the assumption that he needed them.

"What made you reconsider, sir?" Sheena asked curiously.

"I don't want to get bogged down on trivial matters now that we're nearing a pivotal part of the formation of the New Order."

"Would you care to explain this 'New Order' to me? I have no idea what's going on and, yet, you're holding me accountable."

Witty led them inside his office and directed them to sit. He contacted security on his speaker phone and requested they release Lennox from her cell.

Rock bit his lip to keep from laughing. Sheena noticed and kicked his shin, drawing a glare from him.

Witty folded his hands and stared at them for a moment. He explained, "I need to put an end to this feud between the Fleet and the militia which means I have to make nice with that stubborn little bitch."

"And why would Marina be interested in a truce, if that's who you're referring to, sir?"

"I want that missing data chip. I know that someone knows where it is and I have to have it before Kronos gets their hands on it."

"I thought you were working with Kronos, General," commented Rock. "They'd be very upset if they knew you went end around on them."

Witty pointed a finger in Rock's face and replied, "Kronos doesn't need to know about this and they won't. Understand?"

Sheena and Rock both nodded in agreement.

"So, here's the deal," he began calmly, "Marina and her people get me the chip and call off the militia ships. I, in turn, will spare Yord from any further aggression. I will also forgive her for what she did to Lennox. She's never been the same since that incident."

Rock joked, "I've taught her to see things differently."

Sheena glared at him and then countered, "How do I know you'll honor that agreement, sir?"

Witty grew angry at her for questioning him. Before he could respond, she continued, "Marina's going to ask me that and I'll need a good answer if you expect her cooperation."

Witty tapped his fingers on the table and considered a response. Rock took advantage of his hesitation and suggested they leave Fleet Headquarters and meet up with Marina. "With no threat from the Fleet and our freedom, she'll know you're serious."

Witty stared at the two of them, wondering if they planned to screw him over the first chance they got. "What happened to Lilith?" he inquired. "I know you had something to do with her escape."

Sheena looked disappointedly at him and answered, "Lilith fled to safety with the other prisoner, Willow."

Witty chuckled at her and then explained, "You do know that Willow was an assassin sent by Kronos to kill Marina."

Sheena was shocked by his revelation. She and Rock glanced at each other, horrified that they turned her loose on the *Argo*.

Col. Lennox entered the room, leaving two security officers outside the door. Witty was appalled by her condition. Her uniform and sports bra were torn revealing her large, shapely breasts with hickeys across them. She held her tattered pants over her arm and her underpants were stretched out of shape, barely clinging to her hips. Her lip was busted open and her left cheek was swollen.

General Witty looked at her disappointedly. She fumed as she glared at Sheena and Rock. Witty pointed to a chair and nodded for her to sit. She reluctantly obeyed.

Sheena and Rock enjoyed seeing Lennox play the role of lap dog. Witty noticed and grew irritated with them. He pointed to the transmitter on his table. "Do whatever you have to do to make this happen," he instructed them.

Sheena used the transmitter to contact the palace on Yord. After waiting several minutes for her transmission to pass through many relay stations, she was directed to *The Reaper* and waited for a response.

On board *The Reaper*, the transmitter beeped, signaling an incoming message. "This is Marina," she responded and waited.

"Marina, this is Sheena. We need to talk."

Marina was surprised and immediately suspected a trap. "I thought you were taken prisoner, Sheena?"

"I was. General Witty wants to make a deal with you."

Marina glanced at Kat uneasily. "Go ahead. I'm listening."

"Witty wants to cut his losses before it's too late. He'll spare Yord and make a truce with you if you can get him the chip."

"Why does he want the chip so bad?"

"Betrayal. Greed," answered Sheena.

Witty glared at her, unhappy with her response.

"What about Kronos?" inquired Marina.

"I don't think Witty is enjoying his relationship with Kronos."

"So how do we proceed?" Marina asked.

"We can meet somewhere and put together a plan."

"Where are you now?" asked Marina.

"Fleet Headquarters."

"Witty's bitch will be with you, I assume," remarked Marina.

Lennox sneered at Sheena, wanting to assault her so badly.

"Of course," replied Sheena, smiling at Lennox. "He's not taking any chances."

Marina pondered for a moment and then responded, "We'll meet you on Orpheus-2. I want your ship, the *Argo* there as well."

"I'll do what I can," responded Sheena. "Do you have any idea where the chip could be?"

"Not yet, but I'm sure with all the right people in place, we'll figure it out," she answered confidently. "Tell Witty he's got a deal but he and I have something to settle when this is over." Marina waited patiently for a response.

Finally, Col. Lennox couldn't take any more. She rushed to the transmitter and blurted, "I'm sure the general will be more than happy to grant you some face time if you get past me. I look so forward to settling whatever issues you have with us."

"Well, Ms. Lennox, I'm sure we can arrange that soon," taunted Marina.

"It's Colonel Lennox!" she shouted over the transmitter.

"Whatever," Marina mocked and toggled the transmitter off. She turned and faced Kat with a somber expression and then burst into laughter.

Kat was concerned about Marina's arrangements. "You don't have to take on Witty and Lennox, Marina. That's going to get you killed."

"People like that don't back down with a peace treaty," she explained. "They're just saving their vengeance for another day."

At Kat's urging, she left the flight deck and rested. Not realizing how tired she was, she slept for two days. Kat was unnerved by Marina's relentless disregard for safety. She and Faust would do anything to protect her but, when she became reckless, they had doubts. She felt ashamed for feeling this way but Marina was a wrecking ball that no one could control.

Witty paced the room, eying Sheena and Rock. "Here's how it's going to work," he began. "Commander Brice, you will stay here in my custody."

Sheena was shocked. "But sir!"

"You heard me," he replied callously. "Lennox will escort your friend here to Orpheus-2."

Rock grew uneasy as he feared what retribution Lennox might seek against him. Lennox noticed and smiled at him. "What a beautiful reunion we'll have," she taunted. "I'll be sure to make you ever so comfortable."

Witty walked behind her and slapped the side of her head. "If you touch him just once before I get that chip, you'll have me to deal with."

Lennox frowned as she touched her ear gingerly.

"Did you hear me, Lennox?" he barked and slapped her again.

"Sir, yes, sir!" she answered, with a pained expression on her face.

"Good. Now get the hell out of here and take that fruitcake Jeffries with you. I want him off my base."

Lennox was appalled at how little loyalty he showed for them. She cowered as she walked past him and left the office.

"And you, Commander, are my insurance policy that nothing happens to Lennox. Understand?"

"Yes, sir," she replied despondently. This wasn't how she planned for things to go.

"We'll need to let the *Argo* know what's going on, sir."

"And why is that?" Witty asked arrogantly.

"Because they will join forces with the militia against you if they don't hear from me soon."

Witty laughed hysterically. "Now why would they do such a traitorous act?"

Sheena stood and spoke confidently, "Because they're my crew and they're loyal."

Witty laughed half-heartedly as his doubts began to show.

"And," she continued, "because we will not be fooled into turning on our allies. Once the other ships learn of our actions, they will question your motives."

Witty became red-faced with anger. "And you think they'll all leave based on your word?"

Sheena smiled at him and replied, "All I need is half of them. You've already lost most of your fleet. What an honor that must be for you."

"I have all of the Fleet at my disposal, so don't threaten me, Brice!"

"Is that so?" she chided. "Then why are you even talking to me. I know you wanted the *Argo* in sector five to backdoor the alien races in case your casualties were too high during your initial attack."

"And you disobeyed those orders, Brice. You will be tried for treason."

Sheena laughed at him. "I'm the only chance you have. Cut the shit, General. You played your hand and lost. Kronos beat you at your own game."

"How dare you, Brice? Kronos did nothing to me!"

"They fed on your ego. With the Fleet in shambles, you have no leverage and you did it to yourself. It couldn't have been any easier for them." Sheena smiled and left his office.

"Where are you going?" he shouted at her.

"To Orpheus-2," she replied confidently. "You want this to work; this is how it must go down."

Witty picked up the phone to call security but then realized Sheena was right. He needed her if there was any chance of getting that chip.

Later, Col. Lennox boarded a shuttle, followed by two men carrying Jeffries on a stretcher. Rock was escorted by two others with handcuffs, securing his wrists in front of him.

Once inside, the men laid Jeffries down on the left side bench. The other two shoved Rock down on the right-side bench. Lennox thanked the men and they departed.

"I will have my day with you, you bastard," she threatened him.

Rock forced a smile and remarked, "I was really disappointed in you, Lennox. You were a lousy lay."

Lennox balled her fists and stomped toward him. He shook his head at her and warned, "Don't do it! You know what Witty said."

Lennox punched the wall next to him and stared him down. "I could rip your head off right now," she threatened him.

"What's the warranty on those pleasure puppies?" he antagonized her again as he eyed her breasts. "I guess you like it cold - just like Jeffries."

Lennox grabbed his chin and squeezed until Rock was nearly in tears. "Don't push your luck," she warned as she flexed her metallic hand. "I'm going to remove your balls when this is over."

"You're gonna hurt somebody, robo," he responded sarcastically. "Cut it out."

"Oh, I'm gonna cut something out all right," she warned.

Sheena boarded the shuttle and closed the hatch. Lennox was startled to see her. "Get on the floor now," ordered Sheena as she drew her pistol and aimed at Lennox's face.

Rock scurried to his feet and grabbed Lennox from behind. With the chain from the handcuffs against her neck, he rammed his thumb into her eye and pressed as hard as he could. Lennox screamed until Sheena fired at both of them with her pistol set to 'stun'.

Sheena changed the setting from 'stun' to 'kill' and then warned that her next shot would be permanent.

Lennox lay paralyzed but shouted, "What the hell is this? Witty told you to stay!"

"Things have changed," replied Sheena.

"Boy, am I glad to see you!" exclaimed Rock giddily as he tried to stand.

Sheena smiled at him and suggested, "Check her pocket for the key and you might want to tie her up before she gets that metal hand around your neck."

Rock dug into Lennox's pocket and retrieved the key. "I got it from here. You just get us to Orpheus-2."

Sheena glanced down at Lennox and back at Rock. "Try to keep her clothes on, this time," she suggested to him. He grinned and cuffed Lennox' hands to the hull.

Sheena piloted the shuttle away from Fleet Headquarters. Once underway, she contacted the *Argo*. Kannel was ecstatic to hear from her. Sheena instructed him to head for Orpheus-2 and rally whatever support he could get from other vessels in the area.

As she navigated the ship toward Orpheus-2, she worried that Marina's plan would fail and they'd all perish.

VII
ORPHEUS - 2

When *The Reaper* drew near to Orpheus-2, Marina returned to the flight deck and took a seat next to Kat. Pleased to see her, Kat inquired as to what Marina's plans were for the damaged palace.

Marina looked down sadly and pondered the recent events. The palace could be rebuilt but the lost lives could not be replaced. Her people already lost patience with her and became angry mobs. *They have every right to hate me*, Marina thought. *I failed to protect them.*

"What is it?" asked Kat, sensing Marina's sorrow.

"I don't want to rule Yord anymore," she replied sadly.

"What?" exclaimed Kat. "You're the Queen!"

"They don't need a queen," she uttered dejectedly. "They need a leader."

"But you are their leader!" Kat reminded her.

"I can't lead from a palace. I have to be out here where shit happens."

"Then who will be their leader on Yord?"

Marina thought for a moment and then answered, "They don't need a single leader. Each region can rule itself."

"But who'll unite them when it counts?"

"We'll set up a council made up of the leaders of each group. The leaders will be held accountable by their own people."

Kat was surprised by Marina's decision and realized that her plan made sense. "So, what would you do if you weren't queen?" she inquired curiously.

Marina smiled and replied, "I'd like to go to Andros-5 with the girls and start our own colony."

"That's crazy!" exclaimed Kat. "These girls need people around them to develop their social skills."

Marina laughed at her and then remarked cynically, "Not like the secluded temple I was raised in. I'm talking about a rural atmosphere where there are limited distractions. I still have the responsibility of building the alliance and making treaties with the other races."

Kat realized that Marina was right. The young Seers would be away from the evils of greed and power until they became adults.

The transmitter beeped, interrupting their conversation. A female voice from the station commander requested they identify themselves and their ship. Kat gestured for Marina to be silent and then responded to the transmission.

Kat identified herself and used the name of her former ship, the *Galactic Witch*. She then informed the officer that she was there to meet with some very important people, noting that Col. Lennox was one of them. The commander immediately granted them permission to dock.

"What do you think you're doing?" Marina questioned Kat. "They're expecting to see me."

"I'm buying you time to do your thing," Kat responded. "You have the advantage right now since the others haven't arrived."

"Why the high and mighty look?" inquired Marina curiously.

Kat explained giddily, "I always wanted to be a queen, even if it's only for show."

"They won't buy it," Marina chastised her. "Besides, I've been here before. They know my face."

Kat waved her hands in front of her face and became the mirror image of Marina.

"What the hell did you just do?" Marina asked, stunned by the image.

"It's an illusion. That's what they'll see when I want them to." Kat waved her hands again in front of her face and the image cleared, leaving her true face.

Marina shook her head in disbelief and remarked, "That's some crazy shit right there."

"I told you; I'll do whatever it takes to support you," Kat reminded her.

"Damn, girl!" Marina exclaimed, chuckling to herself. "You weren't kidding."

The ship docked and several security officers waited at the hatch. When it opened, Kat emerged, using her magic to create the illusion of Marina's face.

A middle-aged, bearded captain named Mallon inquired, "You're the queen?"

"I am," Kat answered. "Has Colonel Lennox arrived yet?"

"Not yet," he replied coldly. "Follow me."

The officers glanced at each other, baffled by her appearance at the station. They weren't sure whether she was an ally or a foe. Mallon instructed Kat (Marina) to follow him to her quarters. As they walked through the station, Mallon inquired, "Why have you turned everyone against us?"

Kat (Marina) laughed at his ignorance. "Is that what they've told you?" she replied.

He stopped and stood face-to-face with her. "My brother was killed during an attack by the Calamaarians. Don't question me on what happened out there."

"By whose orders did the Fleet attack the Calamaarians?" countered Kat.

Mallon didn't answer. "I thought so," Kat remarked snidely.

They arrived at the first cabin on one of the lower floors. Mallon opened the door and stepped aside. "I suggest you remain in here for your own safety."

Kat stared into his eyes with billowing flames in hers. Mallon felt something evil reach into his soul and twist his thoughts. "Are you sure it's my safety you're worried about?" Kat asked.

Mallon backed away nervously and pointed inside the cabin. "Stay here until we come for you," he ordered, his voice shaking.

Kat entered the room and sat on the cot, staring out at Mallon. He quickly slammed the door shut and returned to the bridge.

★ ★ ★

Marina, dressed in a hooded cloak, left the ship and hurried to the elevator. She rode it up to the fifth floor, but was immediately intercepted by three sentries.

They drew their pulse pistols and targeted her. She kept her head down and remained still.

"You're Marina!" exclaimed one of the sentries.

"How many of you were loyal to Severin?"

The sentry responded, "Most of us were. Why do you ask?"

"How did that piece of crap Jeffries get promoted to her position?"

The sentries lowered their pistols sensing that their encounter would remain civil. The lead sentry, Ensign Jay Harville, answered, "Colonel Lennox came here and announced that he was the new commander. Did you know Commander Severin?"

"I did. She was a close friend," replied Marina, still with her head down, avoiding eye contact.

"What are you doing here?" Harville asked. "How did you get on this station?"

"I stowed away on a ship and waited for the opportunity to seek out someone with honor and dignity," she explained.

"Follow us," instructed Harville.

They took Marina down a series of corridors and then through a steel door, requiring retinal scan. Harville led Marina into a conference room with an oval table and thirteen chairs spaced evenly around it. High-tech surveillance equipment was stacked along the end wall. The other two sentries waited outside.

"You can remove your cover now, your Highness," Harville directed her. "If we're going to talk, I'd like to see your face."

Marina removed the cloak and responded, "What is this room?"

"It's the 'ComSec Room'. There is complete security in here."

Marina laid the cloak across a chair and inspected the surveillance equipment. "I don't remember this being here before."

Harville stood beside her and explained, "Kronos technicians installed it a short time ago."

"That doesn't sound like good security to me when your security system is entrusted to strangers."

"We wondered why they were given access to a Fleet facility like this," he commented.

"Why would they install this kind of equipment here?" Marina pondered aloud. "They already took control of the GSS for their base of operations."

"All I know is that they expect to assume control in the next few days when the quantum computer is activated."

"And you have no idea why, I assume."

"No. Jeffries had little interaction with us since Kronos' reps showed up. He was like one of them."

Marina and Harville discussed all the events that occurred and what they might mean to the Fleet and to her. Harville agreed to help her search for the chip if she would help him to take over the role of commander on the station. The men were unhappy with Jeffries and Mallon but had no power to alter the station's leadership. Marina was more than happy to accommodate him, if they succeeded in defeating Kronos.

A sentry's voice came across the wall speaker, "Sir, the *Argo* is on its way and its commander is eager to speak with the queen."

Harville acknowledged the information and waited for an answer from Marina, who declined to respond for now. She instructed him to assist Kat, however necessary. Harville agreed and ordered the sentries in the corridor to report to Kat.

"I need to know if Commander Brice has been heard from. Can you help me with that?" Marina asked.

Harville replied, "She's on her way here in a shuttle with Colonel Lennox and a passenger named Rock."

Harville then questioned Marina about the logic of attacking all the alien races and decimating much of the Fleet. Marina explained that greed and power have driven people like General Witty, Colonel Lennox, the IDC and Kronos to do incredibly risky things.

Marina placed the cloak on and covered her face. "I must go make preparations for our visitors. I'll be in touch."

"Be careful, your Highness," Harville advised her.

"Thank you, Harville," she replied appreciatively. Marina opened the door, peering left and right. No one was in sight so she hurried off down the series of corridors to the elevator. As she turned the last corner, she recognized the HVAC room that she used to escape six months earlier.

Marina again peered up and down the corridor. It was still deserted. She used one of her daggers to pry the locked door open. Once inside, she removed the ductwork panel and slid through the access hatch with only a flashlight to guide her. *"This is freakin' de ja vu,"* she thought to herself.

For hours she slid her hands along the ductwork, searching for any sign of the data chip. Frustration overcame her and her patience wore thin as she reached the vent over her ship in the transportation hub. She sat for a few moments and considered that maybe she was missing something and the chip wasn't there at all.

QUEEN OF PAIN

★ ★ ★

Marcus stood over Britt and prayed for his recovery. He feared taking control of the militia at such a young age along with the resentment that the elder commanders might have. He squeezed Britt's hand and wished him well. As he tried to release his hold, Britt's grip remained tight. "What the heck?" blurted Marcus.

Britt opened his eyes and kidded, "You nearly jumped out of your skin!"

Marcus was elated. "Damn, sir! It is so good to see you awake! How do you feel?"

Britt tried to sit up but the half cast on his leg made it difficult. "Where is Marina?"

"Orpheus-2, sir. She's made some arrangement to obtain the chip and trade it for a treaty."

Britt scoffed at the idea. "They won't honor any treaty! We have to get to Orpheus-2 right away."

A loud explosion caught their attention. "What the hell was that?" Britt shouted.

"Wait here, sir. I'll find out." Marcus rushed from the infirmary to the palace.

The remainder of the palace was in flames. Several men already fought the fire with hoses, spraying water and foam on the burning edifice.

Marcus panicked as he feared for the Seers in the temple below. He climbed through the debris, choking violently from the smoke. When he reached the wine cellar, the secret entrance was blocked by the collapsed wall. Flames made it impossible to get closer.

Drago crawled out of the wreckage nearby and pleaded for help. Marcus lifted him to his feet and ushered him back to the ship for medical attention. As they stumbled through the smoldering debris, Drago informed him that he overheard a man named Haney communicating with someone by transmitter. He mentioned that he was going to Orpheus-2 to kill Marina.

"Have you seen the girls?" Marcus asked anxiously.

"No, I haven't."

Fearing the worst, Marcus returned to the ship with Drago. They would have to access the temple through the cliffs. When the two men boarded the *Wasp*, Britt was standing at the entrance with crutches accompanied by the doctor and the young Seers. Kara and Ginna had tear-streaked faces.

"I'm so happy you girls are okay?" Marcus blurted. "Where are your guardians?"

Kara revealed that an Oriental man killed Dora and Magdalena to get information about where Marina was. "We slipped away to the cliffs before the explosions went off," explained Ginna.

"Is the temple intact?" asked Britt.

"No," replied Kara sadly. "Everything is destroyed."

"And the palace?"

"It's gone," added Drago somberly.

"Marcus, they're coming with us," ordered Britt. "Marina needs us now."

Marcus was surprised by his determination, despite his injuries. "Are you sure about that, sir?"

"It's too dangerous here and we need to pool our resources together."

Marcus informed the other commanders of their course of action.

★ ★ ★

Kat and Faust stepped out of the cabin and were immediately approached by Ensign Harville. "I know you aren't Marina," he challenged. "I just spoke with her."

Faust interceded, anticipating a battle. Harville held his hands out for Faust to stand down. He gestured for them to return to the cabin and followed. Once the cabin door was closed, he related the details of his meeting with Marina. Kat requested that she meet the IDC personnel when they arrive. Harville agreed and suggested they follow him. When they exited the cabin, they were met by Captain Mallon.

"What the hell is going on here, Harville?" he demanded to know.

"They are here to help, sir."

"Like hell!" he shouted. "That one's a witch!"

Kat grinned at him and extended her hands to him. He tried to resist but she had control of him and made him take her hands. She explained, "If I wanted to harm you, I'd have done so already."

He looked embarrassed and replied, "I'm sorry, ma'am. It's just that I thought..."

"Relax, Captain. We're on your side," Kat assured him.

Mallon led them to his office on the third floor where her safety could be assured. After Kat shared her information on what the Fleet, IDC and Kronos had done thus far, Mallon agreed to join them in their attempt to stop Kronos, including Witty.

★ ★ ★

The shuttle from Fleet Headquarters arrived and docked inside the space station. Sheena shut down the engines and left the flight deck. When she entered the main cabin, she was appalled to see Rock mounting Lennox from behind on the floor for what likely was one of many times he raped her. Before she could respond, Lennox broke free of the bench supports that bound her wrists.

Rock had a sadistic grin on his face as he pumped himself into her once more. But then his luck changed for the worst. Col. Lennox reached around and caught him in a headlock. In one quick motion, she rolled on top of him and ripped his throat out with her prosthetic hand. Rock lay across the floor with his arms out, his life quickly leaving him as his blood spurted onto the floor.

Sheena pounced on Lennox and smashed her head several times with her pistol until she was unconscious and barely breathing. She backed away, unsure of whom she should support in this case. Rock had raped the woman multiple times and Lennox was determined to kill her anyway, once her mission to obtain the chip was complete.

Sheena fretted how she'd find the chip now that Rock was dead. She also wondered how she would explain to Witty how the situation got out of hand under her control. Her ire got the better of her as she kicked Lennox several times in the ribs. It didn't matter to her if she killed her or not.

After binding Lennox securely, she exited the ship and met the security detail on the dock.

Sheena requested the sentries take Lennox into custody for Rock's murder and provide her with medical treatment as well. In addition, she had Jeffries' body moved to a hospice where he would be terminated peacefully. She was relieved when she noticed *The Reaper* docked a short distance away with its hatch open and hurried toward it. There were four sentries guarding it from a distance but they recognized her and allowed her to pass.

"Marina," Sheena called out. "Are you in there?"

She waited but there was no reply. As she peered inside the hatch, a noise from above startled her. Marina slid off the top of the ship and pushed Sheena inside. Quickly, she closed it behind them.

Sheena was shocked by the bruises on Marina's neck and arm. "Marina, what the hell happened to you?" she asked in a concerned tone.

"Just making friends with the alien races," Marina kidded. "They see things a little differently than we do."

The two women embraced in a long hug before engaging in a lengthy discussion about what happened. Then Sheena inquired curiously, "What were you doing on top of the ship?"

Marina grinned and answered, "I was looking for something." "On top of the ship?"

"No," she replied giddily. "In the duct work. I came out through the vent over the ship."

Sheena grew even more confused by Marina's explanation but decided to let it go. "I'm so glad you're alright," she replied excitedly. "So much was going on and I couldn't get in touch with you."

Marina appreciated her friend's concern and the risks she took for her. Then Marina recalled that Col. Lennox and Rock were supposed to be with Sheena. "Didn't you have a couple of traveling companions?" she asked.

"Yeah, well, uh, that went to hell in a hurry." Sheena explained the encounters with Lennox and Rock and how she killed him. Then Sheena warned, "Lennox has a metal prosthetic hand. If you and she go at it, be careful."

"Oh, I'm sure we'll go at it very soon," Marina replied cockily, looking forward to fighting Lennox.

The women discussed the *S.F. Argo* and Lilith's presence on board. Then Sheena informed Marina about her encounter with Willow and how she let her escape unknowingly.

Marina inquired as to why Jeffries didn't make the trip. Sheena explained, "He did, but he was moved to a hospice. We had a disagreement and, thanks to Rock, he's more of a vegetable than a man."

Marina beamed with pride. "You and I are so much alike. It's great to see you again." The two women again exchanged hugs.

"What's our plan?" Sheena asked anxiously. "Witty is expecting to hear from Lennox about procuring the chip."

"When the *Argo* gets here, you and I need to meet with Lilith about this damned chip." The transmitter beeped, catching Marina's attention. "I'd better get that."

Marina responded and nearly fell over the chair with surprise when she heard Britt's voice. He informed her of the explosion caused by an IDC agent and the deaths of Dora and Magdalena. Then Britt questioned her about what her intentions were.

"Just winging it, my love," she replied excitedly. "I can't wait to see you."

Ignoring her pleasantries, Britt was less than enthusiastic about her approach and warned her against taking unnecessary risks. When the transmission ended, Marina was ecstatic. She told Sheena of Britt's misfortune and how the palace was destroyed by mercenaries from IDC, most likely Dr. Haney and a few friends.

"I'm so sorry, Marina," Sheena repeated several times.

Marina responded callously, "Don't be. I never liked that palace anyway."

"But your parents built it," Sheena reminded her.

"The only concern I have is revenge for those who disrespected them. Everyone who had anything to do with those attacks will suffer. I promise you that."

When their discussion was finished, Sheena received a message that the *Argo* just docked and Lt. Kannel was anxious to meet with her. As soon as she informed Marina of the *Argo's* arrival, they left the ship. Marina wore the cloak with the hood and used Sheena as her Fleet escort.

Once on board the *Argo*, everyone cheered Sheena's appearance. Marina was impressed with the degree of respect Sheena's crew had for her. Sheena immediately requested that Lt. Kannel take them to Lilith.

Lt. Kannel notified her that the two accompanying ships on their mission, the *Hydra* and the *Mantis,* were standing by for orders near the fifth sector. Marina was pleased by the news and ordered Lt. Kannel to inform both the Urthonians and the Calamaarians that the ships were friendlies and would leave shortly to avoid any more hostilities.

Kannel led them into a secure room at the infirmary where Lilith slept. The women were appalled by Lilith's wounds from her torture.

Lt. Kannel spoke softly to her, "Lilith, you have visitors."

Lilith opened her eyes and smiled at Sheena. "You were the one who rescued me," she whispered weakly.

"I am," replied Sheena, "and I need your help."

Lilith stared at Marina and remarked, "You look like the Queen of Yord."

Marina held her hand and replied, "I am she. Do you feel well enough to speak with us?"

Lilith nodded to her affirmatively.

Marina explained everything she learned about Kronos, IDC and the Fleet. Then she mentioned the surveillance system installed on the station.

Lilith looked frightened by the news and shuddered. "This is really bad."

"How does all this tie together, Lilith?"

"There are thirty satellites programmed to interact with a single control system. IDC is responsible to operate the control system from GSS."

"What's the big deal with this system?" inquired Marina, somewhat confused.

"It was supposed to be used to heat and cool atmospheres on various planets to make them conducive for agriculture," explained Lilith. "Kronos and the Fleet want to use it for a targeting system of immense proportions."

"Where does the data chip come in?" Marina pressed her.

"It has the formula necessary for the data installed in the control system to convert the energy from each satellite into a more powerful laser. It also has the program for the targeting device to function."

Marina paced the room, absorbing everything Lilith just told her.

"If what you say is true about Fleet Headquarters and the hi-tech surveillance equipment," Lilith continued, "it sounds like someone wants to take control of the system once IDC makes it operational."

Sheena inquired, "Do you know from memory the information that's on the chip?"

Lilith smiled at her weakly. "I do not. The program on the chip, when installed, does all the work. I just programmed it to collect the data, analyze it, and then perform the necessary actions on the target. The power conversion is controlled by the operating system on GSS."

Lt. Kannel was lost by the conversation. "This is well over my head," he commented.

"A low level of power," explained Lilith, "will alter the atmosphere of a planet to create rain when needed. A concentrated level of power, in this case an immense level of power, will superheat the atmosphere and destroy every living thing on the planet."

"If I can find the chip, can you change the programming on it?" Marina requested. "Perhaps we can alter its instructions."

"Of course. If we only had it."

"So, what about the surveillance equipment here?" inquired Lt. Kannel. "How does Fleet stand to gain from this?"

"If Kronos is going to override IDC, then the Fleet will try to take control of the operating system from Kronos. They'll have the ability to target anything they chose."

"And what about IDC?" continued Marina. "What's their gain in this?"

"I'm sure IDC doesn't know that Kronos installed their equipment here," revealed Lilith nervously. "They think they're the only ones who will have control of the system. You see, Kronos couldn't build it, but they can override control of it."

"And that explains why Witty wants the chip so bad," remarked Sheena. "He wants control of Kronos once they take it from IDC."

"Like a pack of thieves scheming against each other," Marina commented sourly. "Let's go find that chip, Sheena."

Marina and Sheena hurried out of the *Argo*'s infirmary and returned to the station.

★ ★ ★

At the space station's infirmary, the doctor stitched up a cut in the back of Col. Lennox's head. When he finished, Lennox awoke and sat up. The doctor instructed her to lie down but, overcome with rage, she slid off the gurney and shouted, "Where are they?"

The doctor shrugged his shoulders and answered wryly, "I fix people. I don't track them."

Lennox reeled as she tried to regain her senses. When the doctor placed his hands on her arms and attempted to push her back down on the gurney, she grabbed him by the throat and warned him to back off. He quickly complied and left her alone. Lennox stumbled into the corridor and sought out Captain Mallon.

⋆ ⋆ ⋆

Kat and Faust waited for the elevator door to open. Harville and Mallon stood by her as escorts. Mallon was still uneasy around Kat and resented the fact that she had occult powers. When the elevator arrived and the door opened, they were surprised to encounter Marina and Sheena.

Marina gestured for them to enter and then locked the elevator with the doors closed. She warned Harville and Mallon that Kronos cannot be allowed to activate their surveillance equipment under any circumstances.

Harville suggested that one of his techs could disable the system outputs while the rest of the system functioned normally. That would delay any suspicions by Kronos.

"You can guarantee me that no signal will be sent," Marina pressed him sternly.

"I know a bit about systems like that and I'm sure we can turn off the outputs," Harville assured her. "At the least, it'll buy us a week before they figure it out."

"Then do it." Marina unlocked the elevator and pressed 'five'.

Harville made a call to one of his tech's and ordered him to meet them at the elevator.

Marina then instructed Mallon, "I need you to detain the Kronos techs for security reasons as long as possible."

"For what?" he asked, confused by his role.

"Make something up," answered Marina tersely. "Just don't give them access to their equipment until Harville and his tech finish their job."

Marina turned to Kat and Faust. "Kat, I need you to wait for Britt's arrival. Get him on board *The Reaper* immediately. Faust, stay with her, no matter what."

When the elevator door opened, Marina and Sheena took the left corridor toward the HVAC room. Harville went to the right and met his tech in the corridor.

Mallon pressed 'one' on the elevator and grumbled. He wasn't happy about Marina ordering him around like this. When the door opened on the first floor, Mallon was startled to see Colonel Lennox standing there. As he attempted to leave, she grabbed him by the arm and slung him back inside.

"Where are they?" she shouted at him.

"Where's who, sir?" he replied nervously.

"That damned queen and her traitor friend Commander Brice!"

Mallon wanted no part of Lennox's issues with the women. "They got off on the fifth floor, sir," he replied timidly.

Lennox pressed 'five' and glared at him.

"What's this about, sir?" he asked. "I'm sure I can be of assistance to you in resolving any issues you have with the station."

Lennox grabbed him by the throat with her steel hand and lifted him in the air. He kicked wildly as he gasped for breath. "You let that bitch Marina and her traitor friend on your station without any authorization. Now, what assistance do you have for that?"

Mallon turned blue as he struggled to get free. Lennox released him and he fell to his knees just as the elevator doors opened. She pulled him by his collar down the corridor until they reached the HVAC room. Lennox studied the broken door handle and frowned.

"See that, Mallon!" she chastised him angrily. "That's a security breach." She slammed his head into the door several times and then kicked it open. Immediately she noticed the vent cover was removed. Determined to get her revenge on Marina, she shoved Mallon to the ground. "You stay right here and if anyone but me comes out of that vent, you kill them. Understand?"

Mallon nodded, looking like a frightened child. Blood streamed from cuts on his forehead from the door. Lennox threw him against the wall and sneered at him in disdain. This wasn't the way she expected Fleet officers to behave.

Lennox peered inside the vent shaft and listened to the scuffling sounds from below. She retrieved a flashlight from the bench drawer and climbed inside. Looking out once more, she warned Mallon in a threatening tone, "You kill them or else. Got it?"

Mallon nodded and cradled his pistol against his chest.

Lennox knew they wouldn't be coming out, but she enjoyed making him suffer in humiliation.

Marina and Sheena crept along the lower duct until they reached a vertical drop off. They paused and listened carefully. The sound of Lennox in the upper shaft caught their attention.

Marina whispered, "You go ahead. Wait on the other side of the modulator."

Sheena nodded and scurried ahead. Marina slid down into the vertical shaft and dangled from the rim. While waiting, she felt something against her arm. A small metal box with a magnet was attached to the side of the duct. *How about that shit!* She waited patiently, knowing that the box probably contained the chip.

A few minutes later, Lennox came upon the opening. "You mother...!" she groaned. Without further hesitation, she rushed at the opening and leaped across. Falling short, she hung on the opposite rim with her back to Marina.

A loud rumbling filled the vents as the air handlers activated. The noise was almost deafening. Unaware that in the darkness Marina was right behind her, Lennox pulled herself up and continued forward.

Marina climbed out of the vertical shaft and retrieved the magnetic box. Eagerly, she opened it, hoping that it was the elusive chip. Adding to the suspense, she found a second box wrapped in foil inside. Content that it was the chip, she returned the box to the shaft's side and then leaped across, using the lip on the right side of the duct as leverage to push off to the other side.

Further ahead, Sheena slid through the large vanes of the modulator, covering her face to protect it from the powerful force of the air. Suddenly, Lennox's steel hand reached through the vanes and grabbed her by the shoulder. Sheena struggled to break free but couldn't. Her flashlight fell to the floor and rolled away. The light shined back at the women; its brightness blinding them.

"Now you'll pay for what you did to Jeffries," Lennox shouted at her sadistically. She squeezed Sheena's shoulder tighter as she slid through the vanes. Sheena crumbled to her knees as she struggled against Lennox's grip.

Marina crept closer to the vanes and saw the rough outline of the two women beyond the vanes in the glow of the light. She reached through and wrapped one arm around Lennox's neck. Once she had a firm grip, she yanked her backwards through the vanes. Sheena fell on her back, lying between the vanes, but she was free of Lennox's grip.

Marina pounded Lennox's face with several punches until her mouth was bloody and swollen. Lennox rolled out and stunned Marina with a roundhouse right to the side of her face. The prosthetic hand nearly dislocated her jaw.

"This is where you meet your end, Marina," taunted Lennox. "How fitting?"

She dropped down toward Marina, driving her fist at Marina's face. Marina curled her body just in time and a loud bang echoed through the ductwork. Lennox's hand left a deep indentation in the duct floor.

Instinctively, Marina shoved both her thumbs into Lennox's eyes and gouged. Lennox screamed and slapped Marina with both hands to the side of her head. Marina was stunned by the impact of the slap and lay hurting.

Sheena got to her feet and retrieved her flashlight. She shined it on Lennox as she choked Marina. Sheena struck Lennox in the back of the head from behind and staggered her. Lennox fell to one knee with blood streaming down her neck from the cut Sheena reopened.

Sheena helped Marina to her feet. The two hurried through the vanes, but again Lennox was right behind them. Once they cleared the vanes, Marina lunged at Lennox and grabbed her in a head lock. She tried to keep her body close to Lennox to limit the range of her prosthetic hand.

"I'll kill you, you little bitch!" shouted Lennox as she pounded on Marina's back.

Marina landed a series of punches to Lennox's rib cage and shoved her into the wall. Lennox pushed off and shoved Marina into the opposite wall.

Sheena stepped through the vanes again, covering her face from the blast of the air. She jumped on Lennox's back and attempted to choke her. Lennox backed away from Marina and pulled Sheena over her shoulder, slamming her on the floor next to the vertical shaft. Sheena's momentum carried her over the edge of the vertical shaft and she fell over the side. Hanging by one hand, she frantically tried to pull herself up.

"No!" shouted Marina, fearing that Sheena fell to the bottom. Full of rage, she pounded Lennox's face with a series of punches and chops that staggered her. Then she followed up with three kicks to the face and knocked her against the vanes. Another series of punches and a kick sent Lennox through the vanes and on her back.

Marina breathed a sigh of relief, expecting Lennox to stay down. Before she could step away, Lennox reached through the vanes with both hands and grabbed her in a choke hold.

Sheena crawled out of the vertical shaft and rushed to Marina's aid. She tried to pry open Lennox's grip on Marina's throat but the strength of her steel hand was too much to overcome.

The air handlers shut down and the shaft became eerily quiet. The vanes closed slowly on Lennox's wrists as she desperately tried to pull Marina into them. Sheena held on tightly to Marina with enough leverage to keep her away from the vanes. Lennox pulled her prosthetic hand free but the other was crushed and severed in the vanes. Lennox's ear-piercing screams echoed through the ducts as they sealed shut.

Marina and Sheena sat on the ground against the duct wall, exhausted from the encounter. They heard Lennox' cries from the other side but couldn't care less.

"Thanks for saving my ass, Sheena."

"Anytime," she replied. "Is she finished?"

"I doubt it," replied Marina smugly. "But she's short-handed now so we have an edge."

Sheena laughed at her joke and kidded, "You really are messed up. You know that?"

"Yeah, pretty much," Marina answered. The two embraced, grateful for their friendship. Lennox' cries ceased and they wondered if she was finished.

After they leaped across the open vertical shaft, Marina knelt down and retrieved the magnetic box from the side of the duct wall. She held it up proudly for Sheena to see.

"So that's the chip that everyone's dying over," Sheena remarked.

"Sure is and I have an idea."

They backtracked through the ducts toward the HVAC room. Mallon sat in a chair with his pulse pistol in hand, muttering to himself. He preferred the boring routine of the station with Jeffries compared to the drama and chaos that the women brought with them.

When Marina peered from the duct, Mallon stood and aimed his pistol at her. "I'm sorry but Colonel Lennox gave me orders to shoot you," he whimpered.

Marina ignored him and climbed out of the duct. She reached in and pulled Sheena out as well. The two women stared at him, neither one believing he had the courage to shoot.

"Put that pistol away, you fool," ordered Marina.

"I'm serious," he stammered. "I will shoot."

Marina stood in front of him, the barrel of the pistol against her chest. "You go ahead and pull that trigger and you will have doomed the Fleet." Mallon considered her warning, but still targeted her with the pistol.

Sheena stepped in and explained, "We've been sold out by Witty and Lennox. Unless you want to answer to Kronos, I suggest you listen to her."

Mallon slowly lowered the pistol. "Where's Lennox?" he asked nervously.

"She's wounded badly and trapped behind the modulator. I don't think you have anything to fear from her," answered Marina.

Mallon stowed the pistol and followed them into the hall. Marina instructed him to assist Harville with the surveillance system. She had to explain in detail to convince him how the new equipment wasn't for surveillance but for Kronos to override the GSS control system and take over the galaxy.

Captain Mallon, still concerned about Colonel Lennox, reluctantly agreed to help but left them. Marina and Sheena then hurried back to the *Argo* with the magnetic box containing the chip.

Kat sat on the flight deck of *The Reaper* and spoke to Marcus on board the *Wasp*. She was elated to learn that he was coming with Britt but was concerned when she learned that the Seers were with them. She warned of the unnecessary risks Marina was taking and hoped they could rein her in. Marcus informed her that Drago was with them as well, hoping it would help with Lilith's cooperation. Kat decided to save that piece of information as a surprise for Lilith.

Marina barged onto the flight deck, followed by Sheena. Kat, despite being startled, was pleased to see them. "I have good news, Marina!"

"And so do we," she replied, displaying the small box with the chip. "We're in business."

"The militia warship *Wasp* is on the way here with Britt and Marcus."

"What about the rest of the officers on the station? Can we count on them?" she questioned Kat eagerly.

"Harville says that most were staunch supporters of Severin so he thinks we're good."

"Then our next action is to get Lilith moved on board. Whatever we do with the chip, we can't trust anyone right now."

Sheena explained in detail the arrangement she had with General Witty and then offered to contact him to discuss the situation with Lennox. Sheena then volunteered to arrange for Lilith's transfer to *The Reaper*. Marina agreed and reiterated her concern for caution and not to trust anyone despite Harville's assurances. Sheena left them and sought out the communications officer.

Marina and Kat discussed possible strategies for the chip. They were concerned with how to manipulate the Fleet, IDC and Kronos against each other. Marina feared Kronos the most since they had the financial backing to acquire any resources necessary to achieve their goal. The Fleet suffered heavy casualties in disabling the alien forces so they weren't the threat they once were. IDC still believed they had control of the targeting system which was to her advantage. Unfortunately for them, Kronos planned to override their control from the station and dispose of them, using the system on GSS as they pleased from Orpheus-2.

Harville approached *The Reaper* and requested permission to board. Marina and Kat were leery of his intentions, but opened the hatch and permitted him entry.

"I have some disconcerting news, ladies," he began. "A shuttle arrived here a short while ago with Dr. Haney from IDC."

"What's he doing here?" blurted Kat uneasily.

"He didn't respond to our requests after he landed," Harville explained.

"Track that bastard wherever he goes," ordered Marina. "He and I have something to settle, but now's not the time."

"Perhaps he suspects Kronos' plan to undermine their control of the targeting system," he suggested.

Marina realized that was also a key issue that would bring Haney to the station. "Let him know that I'd like a meeting with him tomorrow."

"Are you sure that's a wise decision after your last encounter?" questioned Kat.

"I don't have a choice. I'm just hoping to buy some time."

"All the rats are assembling in one place," remarked Kat.

"Including us," quipped Marina. "Perhaps we can use that to our advantage." Harville understood the importance of her request and promptly left.

★ ★ ★

The *Wasp* arrived and docked on Orpheus-2 on schedule.

Harville contacted Marina and announced their arrival. She and Kat departed *The Reaper* and waited at the dock for their friends to exit the militia ship.

When Marcus and Britt emerged, the women rushed to them. After sharing their moments of affection, they were interrupted by the appearance of Drago and the young girls.

Marcus reiterated everything that happened on Yord and how someone named Haney was responsible for the deaths of Magdalena and Dora. Marina hugged the girls and swore she'd have her revenge on Haney.

"You already know this man?" inquired Marcus.

"I do," replied Marina. "He's very dangerous... and he's here."

Drago interrupted and reminded her that he had some new things for her that she'd find useful in dealing with Haney. Marina recalled that she was supposed to meet with him before departing and forgot.

"I must apologize, Drago, for missing our appointment. I was greatly distracted at the time."

"No worries, my Queen."

The group moved their reunion to *The Reaper* where Marina related the details of their previous encounter with IDC and Haney, in particular.

Drago set a brief case on the table in front of Marina and assured her that she'd be better prepared the next time she met Haney. He opened the brief case and removed two steel wrist bands. Everyone watched curiously as he strapped them on his wrists and held them up.

"When you tap the two devices together...," he began and tapped them together. Two serrated blades instantly protruded vertically. "...these blades will cut through nearly any material." He tapped them again and the blades retracted.

Marina was impressed and eagerly accepted them from Drago. Britt and Marcus glanced at each other, amazed at Drago's cleverness.

Drago reached inside the briefcase again and removed what appeared to be an amulet, subtle and gothic. The amulet was made of an elastic band with a skull, shaped from darkened titanium and two red eyes made of rubies. He donned it on his head and grinned at Marina.

"I don't know about that, Drago," she said somewhat confused by its relevance. "I'm not the type to wear trinkets."

Drago remarked, "You'll wear this one, I'm sure." He head-butted the oak table and when he raised his head, there was a neat hole about an inch deep. "I know you have a penchant for head-butting, my Queen." He pressed the sides while removing it and the spike retracted.

Marina was excited and anxiously took the device from him. "These will come to good use, I assure you, Drago," she responded jubilantly.

"Ah, but I'm not done yet," he continued and removed a set of leather ankle straps. Each was long enough to cover her legs from the bottom of her knee to the top of her foot and was studded with short, razor-like studs. "For your karate kicks, my Queen. Now your quarry will have something to remember you by."

Marina beamed as she donned the new equipment. She announced confidently, "The first thing I'm going to do is find Haney and make him pay for what he did on Yord." She opened the glass cabinet and removed the conical helmet with the dreadlocks. Underneath, she wore the amulet. She eyed the jewel-encrusted daggers and then replaced hers with them. "Drago, I can never thank you enough," she said, feeling invincible in the new armament,

"You already have, my Queen," he replied proudly.

Kara and Ginna approached and knelt down in front of her. Kara warned, "Haney is here to kill you, Queen Marina. He has no interest in the targeting system."

"And, at this point, neither do I," she replied. Marina was surprised that Kara mentioned the targeting system. "What do you know of this weapon?" she asked curiously.

The girls held hands and closed their eyes. A light formed between them. As it grew, it took the shape of the universe and then narrowed to a galaxy. Everyone watched in amazement. Marina glanced at Kat, wondering if she knew about their surprising capabilities. Kat returned a confident smile to her. Britt and Marcus watched with their jaws agape in amazement.

The Galactic Space Station (GSS) came into view. Numerous purple laser beams shot from a turret on the top through space until they struck satellites far away in a circular array. Once all thirty satellites were contacted, the beams were redirected at one planet and engulfed it in fire.

The looks changed from awe to sheer horror as they realized the planet was Yord. The girls opened their eyes and let go of each other. The image vanished.

"Holy shit!" blurted Marina. "The weapon has that much power?"

Britt exclaimed, "They'd be unstoppable!"

"No wonder Kronos wants control of the whole system."

"We can't let them get away with something like this," Marcus commented uneasily.

Drago added, "Lilith's plan was to use the new lasers at a much lower power to create moisture in the atmosphere of planets where needed to help with their agriculture. It was meant for peaceful purposes."

"Something this valuable can't be destroyed," replied Marina, "but it can be implemented with safeguards, can't it, Drago?"

"I'd have to speak with Lilith on that, my Queen, but I believe it could be."

Marina tossed the cloak aside and eyed her new tools of war. Britt became nervous as he knew what she was thinking. Marina noticed and suggested, "Perhaps you should go to GSS and discuss the situation with Ford and Janus, Kat."

"What makes you think that's a good idea?" Kat responded.

"They seemed reasonable when we were there and expressed displeasure with Haney's hostility toward us. Find out what they want out of this - agriculture or destruction."

"Take Marcus and Faust with you, Kat. They'll watch your back."

"I'd like that," replied Kat appreciatively.

"Would it benefit you to take the girls with you, Kat?" she asked. "I'm concerned about their safety here at the station."

Kat studied the girls' faces briefly and considered the consequences of leaving them. Kara stepped forward and informed them, "Our powers will be more than adequate for both missions if required."

"Damn!" responded Marina. "And you're how old, Kara?"

"Twelve."

"You girls are more mature than some of the people I work with," she joked, glancing at Britt and Kat.

"I could say the same about certain others," kidded Britt.

The girls giggled and appreciated Marina's compliment.

"Britt, you'll stay here and guard the ship," Marina ordered.

"From what?" he asked defensively.

Before she could respond, Sheena entered, pushing Lilith in a wheelchair.

"Lilith!" cried Drago as he rushed to her. He knelt in front of her and they embraced.

Sheena did a double-take when she saw Marina, donning the new armament. "The warrior queen has arrived," she remarked giddily.

"No, this is more like the *Grim Reaper* preparing to dispense justice."

Everyone but Britt laughed at her remark. He feared letting her fight without him. Sooner or later, her aggression would get her killed.

Sheena informed them that she spoke with Witty about the problem with Lennox. Witty agreed that Lennox had outlived her usefulness and needed to be dealt with by Marina.

Marina smirked and replied, "Of course. He doesn't have the balls to do it himself."

"He also said to remind you that 'we have a deal'," added Sheena. "I'm sure we can find a way to accommodate him our way."

"Oh, we will," assured Marina.

Drago returned to the table and removed an electronic box from his briefcase, the last item he brought with him.

"Is that for me, too?" asked Marina excitedly.

Drago smiled and replied, "No. This is for Lilith. It's the key to fixing our little problem." He handed the box to Lilith, who eyed it anxiously.

"Can I have the chip?" requested Lilith.

Marina took the small box from inside her bodice and handed it to her. "Do you have a plan?" she asked.

"I think so," answered Lilith. "It will take time but I think we can turn this into a positive situation."

"Then I'm going after Haney. Kat, do your thing and Britt, keep these two (Lilith and Drago) safe."

"I'm going with you," Sheena said sternly. "You need someone to watch your back."

"I'd like that," she responded. "Let's go get some." Marina kissed Britt on the cheek and departed the ship with Sheena.

"Some things never change," complained Britt.

"She loves you," Kat reminded him. "We'll be in touch." She took Marcus by the hand and the two left the ship.

Britt sighed as he watched Drago and Lilith embrace, kissing passionately for several minutes. He wished it was Marina with him but, as usual, they were business first. It used to be him that chose business first. Now the shoe was on the other foot and Marina was all business. He only had himself to blame for this. Marina warned him that things would be like this if she took the throne.

★ ★ ★

Marina and Sheena went to the cafeteria, assuming that newcomers would be taken there first for a drink or a quick meal. When they entered, it was dinner time. The cafeteria was full of Fleet personnel and security specialists. They became quiet when they noticed Marina in her battle attire. The women scanned the rows of tables and over one hundred faces in search of Haney.

Marina suddenly felt a premonition come to her and became lightheaded. A vision appeared and showed Haney in the corridor, eying her with a metallic silver star with blackened poisoned tips in his hand. He raised his arm to fire the star-shaped object at her from behind. The vision cleared and her focus returned.

"He's not in here," uttered Marina disappointedly. "I was hoping to put on a show and humiliate the bastard."

Sheena chuckled at her. "You have the strangest sense of humor of anyone I ever met," she remarked.

"You ain't seen nothing yet," Marina remarked sarcastically and left the cafeteria. Sheena followed her, wondering how Marina knew Haney wasn't there in a crowded area like that.

They walked down the corridor toward the elevator, discussing Sheena's captivity. When they reached the elevator, the floor numbers cascaded from eleven down toward five as the elevator descended. Marina pushed Sheena gently against the wall next to the doors and then moved to the other side. Holding her finger to her lips for silence, she stepped back and took a defensive stance. The doors slid open and Haney emerged.

"Looking for me," Marina questioned him.

Haney stared down Sheena and warned her, "You should have stayed out of this." Then he turned to face Marina. "This time, I'll finish you off, you little bitch," he announced scornfully.

Marina heard a voice in her head; Kara's voice that said, "Fight defensively and wait for your chance."

"Rodents never go away easily," Marina taunted. "Let's finish this, Heeney."

"It's Haney, although it won't matter to you in a few minutes," he responded arrogantly.

Sheena stepped back and placed her hand on her pistol. She knew better than to interfere in Marina's fights.

Haney grew impatient as Marina smiled but held her ground. He stepped slowly toward her, raising his hands to chest level and balling his fists.

Marina was anxious to go at him but after her last encounter and now the warning from the girls to be defensive, she had to show self-control. Haney lunged at her, striking at her with multiple punches. Marina's patience paid off as she deflected each one.

Haney backed off and grew angrier as Marina remained cool, even smiling briefly. He discreetly reached into a leather sack attached to his belt and removed the silver star she saw in the premonition. Chuckling at her, he fired the star at her head. She deflected it with the wrist band. Angrily, he fired two more. Marina easily deflected them as well.

Haney rushed again at her and attempted a karate kick at her head. Marina ducked and swept his standing leg out from under him. Haney fell to the ground with a thud, but quickly rolled away from her and stood up.

"What's wrong, Haney - losing your touch?" she taunted.

Haney glanced down at his leg and saw splotches of blood. Then he noticed Marina's studded ankle wear. He snarled and rushed at her again. Marina tapped the two wrist braces together and the blades protruded.

Haney delivered three punches toward her face. She deflected each one, leaving him baffled by his now bloody wrists. His anger got the worst of him as he rushed again. This time, he dove feet first at Marina's midsection and floored her. He scrambled to his feet and leaped on top of her, pinning her wrists to the ground.

Marina struggled to get free but he positioned his body on top of her chest where he could use his legs to pin her arms. With her legs now free, Marina had an opportunity to counter his position. Haney punched her in the face three times and as he prepared to deliver a chop to her throat, Marina swung her legs up and locked them around his neck.

Haney howled in pain as the studs cut into his neck and chin. He struggled to break the leg lock she had on him. Marina pulled with her legs until he fell backwards and she could sit up between his legs. Now it was her turn to go on the offensive. She delivered three blows to his groin and left him gasping. She released her hold on him and stood up.

"Had enough, Heeney?" she taunted.

Haney stood up in obvious pain. Blood was smeared across his neck and chin area. The pants covering his left leg now had bloodstains from her studs. Feeling desperation set in, he charged at Marina again. This time he shoved her against the wall and engaged her in a bear hug. Both of them took turns slamming the other into the walls until fatigue set in and slowed them down. Then Haney made the fatal mistake: he head-butted Marina. She was dazed but knew what happened to him.

When Haney backed away, blood streamed from his forehead. He felt the hole made by her amulet and became dazed. Marina struck him in both sides of his neck with her wrists. The blades left lethal cuts in Haney's neck.

"Nice knowing you, Heeney," she taunted once more and kicked him in his ribs.

"It's Han..." he tried to say but then fell to the ground in a pool of blood.

Marina felt her swollen lip and wiped the blood off with her hand. Sheena placed an arm around her shoulder. "Let's get you back to the ship," she said sternly. "That lip's gonna need stitching."

Marina gently rubbed her cheek and eye. Both were swollen as well. "That piece of shit can sure hit hard," she complained.

Sheena contacted Harville and informed him of Haney's attack on Marina and the outcome. She and Marina then returned to *The Reaper*.

When Britt saw Marina, he was distressed by her facial bruises and busted lip. "Couldn't you just shoot him?" he asked sarcastically.

"No, I had to try out my new weaponry," she replied, holding up her arms.

Britt noticed the blood particularly on her amulet over her forehead. "I take it, your new toys worked well," he remarked cynically.

"Very well, indeed."

Marina and Sheena proceeded to the flight deck where Drago and Lilith worked diligently, using the electronic box and the data chip with *The Reaper's* computer system.

Drago and Lilith looked up at Marina with concerned expressions. "Are you alright?" Drago asked.

"I am, thanks to you."

Lilith then explained that she created a copy of the original program and modified it to backfire on Kronos.

"We're making significant progress thus far," Drago informed them.

Lilith added, "When this is over, I believe we'll still be able to use the technology for the good I intended it for."

"I hope so," Marina replied weakly and then staggered.

Britt and Marcus were quick to assist her to a seat. "What's wrong?" Britt asked uneasily.

Marina shook her head briefly and closed her eyes. Britt and Marcus both turned to Sheena for an explanation.

"She took some pretty good shots to the head from Haney before she put him down."

Britt lifted her in his arms and carried her back to her cabin.

Sheena explained to Marcus, "She ordered me to stay out of her fight. I wouldn't let her die but I couldn't interfere unless it came to that."

"We all know Marina is stubborn," he replied. "Let's just hope her injuries aren't too severe."

"I have faith in her," Sheena responded confidently.

Kat whispered in Marcus' ear and the two left the ship. Sheena returned to the *Argo* to meet with her people while Drago and Lilith continued their work on the duplicate data chip.

VIII
A SETUP

Marina awoke and sat up in her cabin. She was surprised to see Kara and Ginna standing on either side of her.

"Good morning, Queen Marina," said Ginna politely. "We're glad to see you are safe."

"Thank you for your advice," Marina said appreciatively. "You saved my life."

The girls smiled at her. Kara then warned Marina about taking chances and the extent of her injuries. Marina insisted she could handle it but Kara frowned at her and reminded her, "We can only help so much."

Ginna inquired, "With the palace and temple in ruins, what plans do you have for us, Queen Marina?"

Marina sighed and then recalled how she wanted to flee to Andros-5. She related the stories of her father and how he hid from the aliens there for a time. The girls were very interested and willing to go if that's what Marina wanted.

"What about Yord?" asked Kara. "What will become of it?"

"Yord doesn't need a queen. I can do much more from a distance."

"But you are the queen," replied Ginna.

"Yes, but I'm not very good at it. My parents knew how to rule much better than I do."

Ginna placed her hand on Marina's shoulder and responded, "These are different times with different adversaries."

"And you are taking them down, one at a time," added Kara.

"But there is still a long way to go before we accomplish our goals," countered Marina. The girls urged her to be patient.

Britt entered the cabin to check on Marina's condition. The girls, sensing their need for intimacy, left them to their privacy.

"So, you have your medical team tending to you," he kidded.

"They know so much, Britt," she replied proudly. "They saved my life when I fought Haney." She went on to explain how she heard their voices and they warned her to remain defensive in the fight. Britt was impressed but feared that the girls' youth would somehow jeopardize their mission.

Marina removed her battle gear and her bodice. Britt became aroused as he watched. She kicked off her boots and unfastened her pants. Pointing toward her ankles, she requested, "Would you do the honors?"

Britt eagerly tugged on her pants until he removed them. Marina was a sight to see; her shapely body in black lace bra and panties. Britt secured the cabin door and slowly removed his shirt. The cast on his leg and fractured ribs restricted his motions but he refused to let that interfere with their encounter. He slid next to her and Marina took it from there, eagerly maneuvering herself on top of him. She was overcome with lust and love at the same time. Both felt a renewed sense of self-worth over their encounter; something they dearly missed.

When they finished, both were fast asleep. Britt lay with his arm wrapped tightly around Marina; his head nestled against her neck. Marina embraced him as well, her legs locked around his hips. In a dream, Marina found herself sitting in a field with a picnic basket. Kara and Ginna played nearby, tossing a ball back and forth. Marina enjoyed their laughter and wondered how they enjoyed life without their real families. She missed her childhood so much since she learned the truth about her parents' fate. Then Kara approached her and asked a startling question, "Why did you let Kat die?"

Marina thought that was odd. "I don't know. Why did I?" she countered, hoping for an explanation. Their conversation was interrupted by a loud banging sound. The field shook and the girls fled, leaving Marina alone. She searched for the source of the sound but couldn't locate it. The sound grew louder. Suddenly she felt herself falling and panicked.

Britt awoke to the sound of banging on the cabin door and then heard Marina gasp. He shook her until she awoke. "Honey, are you okay?" he asked anxiously.

Marina regained her bearings and responded, "Yeah, I just had the weirdest dream." She got out of bed and dressed.

Britt ogled her as she went to the door and opened it. Drago stood there with arms folded. "Kat is waiting patiently to speak with you, my Queen."

"I'm sorry, Drago. I didn't hear you knock," she replied humbly. "I must have been in a deep sleep." Marina glanced back at Britt and winked, before leaving him.

"Apparently, Kat has some important information from GSS," he informed her. "She's been anxious to tell you for quite a while."

Marina glanced disappointedly back at Britt and then followed Drago to the flight deck. "How are things with Lilith?" she asked.

"We're so happy to be back together," he replied appreciatively. "I owe you for that."

"I'm glad it worked out," Marina said as she patted his shoulder.

"Regarding the data chip; I think we're close," he revealed to her.

"That's great! I can't wait to spring this one on Kronos. I can see their faces now."

Marina entered the flight deck alone and pressed the receiver for the transmitter. "Kat, how are you?"

Kast responded, "Very well. I see you and Britt are catching up on things."

"Yeah, that and I had a few bumps and bruises to deal with."

Kat informed Marina that Drs. Janus and Ford were interested in Lilith's technology for peaceful purposes and that Haney was the one who pursued the Fleet and Kronos for a weapons system. Marina warned her not to trust them despite their apparent interest in a peaceful application of the advanced laser system. Then Marina requested, "Can you look into what happened to the Galleans?"

"Of course," replied Kat. "Why do you ask?"

"Because that will tell you how much we can trust Ford and Janus."

Kat agreed to investigate and report back. Marina considered speaking with her about the dream, but thought better of it for now. When she returned to the main cabin, Drago and Lilith beamed with pride as they admired not one, but two data chips.

Marina pulled up a chair and sat next to them. She waited anxiously for an explanation, sensing that they accomplished something exciting. Lilith nodded to Drago who spoke for her. "We've created a fantastic scenario for you, my Queen," he remarked eagerly and displayed the chips for her. One was marked 417Q-1B, the other 417-3B.

Marina took one and studied it. She recalled the original chip was numbered 417Q-1B so one of these was a modified version. "The suspense is killing me, Drago," Marina responded. "What's the deal?"

"Version 3B is our collateral."

"And the original?" she inquired.

Lilith held it up and explained, "This one stays with us until the system can be controlled by responsible beings."

"That's a wise decision," Marina commented. "Please, keep it safe," she instructed her. "When Kronos is defeated, we'll discuss how to proceed, using the new laser system and the satellite network for the benefit of all."

"We are in your debt, my Queen," said Lilith humbly and handed the original chip to Marina for her inspection.

"Nonsense. You have done much for me as well," Marina responded gratefully as she examined the chip. "What happens when the other chip is used?" she continued curiously and returned it to Lilith.

"If installed, it targets the user," replied Drago. "It's a one-way ticket for those bastards."

"I'll take care of IDC and the Fleet," Marina assured her. "We'll make sure someone uses the fake chip at the right time."

Lilith stowed the altered chip in a small box and marked it '3B'. She handed it to Marina and wished her well in distributing it at the appropriate time. Their task completed, Lilith and Drago left her and returned to the *Argo*.

★ ★ ★

Kat, Faust and Marcus returned to the main control center of the Galactic Space Station where Dr. Janus and Dr. Ford ran system tests. Dr. Ford acknowledged them with a wave of her hand for them to join her. When they were seated, Dr. Janus inquired, "You still don't trust us, do you?"

"I'm not sure," replied Kat. "I do remember our last visit here that you weren't supportive of Dr. Haney's behavior toward us. That counts for something."

Dr. Janus frowned at her and then responded, "Haney was an asshole. We never got along."

"So, you don't have any remorse that he was killed?" questioned Marcus.

Dr. Janus, with a look of surprise on her face, responded, "You're serious? Haney's dead?"

"Marina took him out in their rematch. She's not known for being a good loser."

Drs. Janus and Ford were pleased by the news.

"I have to ask about something else," Kat informed them on a more serious note. Noting her somberness, they became attentive again. "What happened to the Gallean population on this station?" Kat inquired. "There were over seven hundred of them before IDC came in."

Dr. Janus grew nervous and hesitated in her response. Kat and Marcus both took notice of her and then saw that Dr. Ford became uneasy as well. "Kronos sent their people in first to negotiate the turnover of control of the station to us," explained Dr. Janus. "I understand the Galleans refused and the situation was handled."

"What do you mean 'handled'?" Kat asked uneasily.

"I believe they were killed. When we arrived, the station was vacant except for Kronos security personnel."

Marcus interjected, "Could Kronos have affected the station's systems in any way?"

"What are you surmising," asked Dr. Ford.

"I mean once the weapons system is operable," replied Marcus, "is it possible that Kronos has the capability of taking control from a remote location like their headquarters?"

"We never considered that," responded Dr. Janus. "Perhaps we should look into it."

Sexton and Klingman both appeared in the entrance, accompanied by three sentries, clapping their hands mockingly. "Well, Tripp, I guess the secrets out. I didn't think our friends were smart enough to figure out our little plan."

Drs. Janus and Ford were horrified. Kat and Marcus appeared unconcerned by their appearance and were anxious to learn more.

"You know what we have to do with you now," Jack Klingman announced mockingly.

"That's probably not a good idea," Kat informed him. "If you want the chip, then you need us."

Sexton walked behind her and massaged her shoulders. "You see, Ms. Tosci, the way it works is this: if your friends want to see you alive, they'll give me the damned chip." When Sexton began to choke her, Marcus and Faust lunged from their seats at him. They were intercepted by the sentries and, after a brief battle, both stood wounded over the dead sentries.

Faust looked down at the blood stain forming on his abdomen and fell to his knees. Marcus grabbed onto Klingman and threw him against the wall. The two traded punches and spun wildly around the room in an all-out brawl. As Marcus was about to punch Klingman in the face, Sexton drew his pistol and fired at him. Marcus staggered backward with a hole in his side. His uniform was quickly stained with blood.

"No!" screamed Kat.

Marcus fell to the floor next to Faust. Both men were helpless and fading from blood loss. Sexton punched Kat in the head and knocked her out.

"Thank you, Tripp," said Klingman as he straightened his suit. "I had hoped for something more civil from our visitors but I see they only understand pain."

Sexton grinned and slapped Kat's face despite her unconsciousness.

"That wasn't necessary," chided Dr. Janus.

"You know, Marjorie, I think we're done with you and your partner. You're fired!" Before she or Ford could reply or act, Klingman fired his pistol several times and killed both of them. Their bodies fell to the floor with multiple splotches of blood across their chests.

Klingman called in his security detail to imprison Kat and dispose of the other bodies.

"Not bad," remarked Sexton. "I think we just moved up our time table."

"I believe that, with our leverage, Marina is now a non-factor."

The two men chuckled and shook hands.

★ ★ ★

As Marina considered how she would negotiate the altered chip to the Fleet and IDC, Col. Lennox boarded the ship. Her wrist was a bandaged stump thanks to the louvers in the HVAC system. Marina was acutely aware that her hand on the other arm was the prosthetic one and gave her a significant advantage. She was red-faced as she stared Marina down.

"Well, well. Look who showed," taunted Marina. "I thought you retired to spend time with your boy toy Jeffries."

"You and I have a debt to settle," replied Lennox hoarsely, "but not today."

"I'm disappointed. I so looked forward to another date with you. We're so compatible."

Lennox charged at her and grabbed her by the throat, "Where is Brice?"

Marina tapped her wrists together by her knees and the blades shot out from the devices Drago gave her. "If you don't let go of me right now, I'll slice that pretty face of yours into pieces," she warned.

Lennox glanced down, surprised by Marina's new armament. She feigned a smile and released her hold. Again, she asked, "Where is Brice?"

"Why do you care?" countered Marina. "Your business is with me."

"Jeffries died this morning and she is responsible."

Marina held out the box with the altered chip. "I think this is more important than that worthless dog," she remarked arrogantly.

"Is that the chip?" inquired Lennox eagerly as she ogled it.

"Sure is. Rock hid it in the HVAC duct."

Lennox reached for it anxiously but Marina pulled it back. "I want you to contact Witty and let him know I'm ready to deal," Marina instructed her. "Then we'll come up with an arrangement that's amicable for both of us."

Lennox was more than agreeable and sat down at the comm/nav station. She made several attempts to reach Witty and had to direct her signal through several satellites to reach Fleet Headquarters. When she finally made contact, Witty's course voice erupted through static, "I hope you have something worthwhile for me, Marina."

"Lennox looked disappointed that he expected to hear from Marina. "It's Colonel Lennox, sir. I'm onboard Marina's ship and I have the data chip."

"Are you sure that's the real chip?"

"It appears so, sir. The numerical identifier is 417Q-3B."

Witty recalled that the chip was a 417Q but couldn't remember more than that. "Let me speak with Marina," he ordered her.

Marina slid her chair up to the comm/nav station. "Greetings, General. Are you prepared to honor our deal?"

"Not yet," he replied cynically. "There's something, I mean someone you were supposed to take care of."

Marina glanced over at Lennox with a sadistic smile. She drew one of her daggers and held it to Lennox's throat. "That can easily be arranged."

"Sorry Lennox," he taunted over the speaker. "You've become a liability and I can't afford that."

"But, sir!" Lennox exclaimed. "I've always been there for you."

Marina interrupted her plea and informed him, "Commander Brice will bring the chip to you on the *Argo*."

"I don't think so, Marina," he informed her. "I want you to deliver it personally."

Marina frowned and considered his demand. "I'd be happy to send you an autographed picture, General," she joked. "I have a busy schedule, you know."

"Bring it to me or else!" he shouted.

"Very well. I'll be in touch." Marina terminated the transmission.

Colonel Lennox complained, "This isn't what I had in mind for us."

Marina stowed her dagger and stood up. "I'm sure we can work something out between us girls," Marina said coyly. "After all, Witty did sell you out."

Lennox smiled and eyed her distrustfully. "I'm sure we can. Witty will pay for his betrayal."

Marina knew it was only a matter of time before the two of them go at it and the next time would be the last time. The two women did not take well to losing and would go to any lengths to come out on top.

"So, what are we going to do?" Lennox inquired suspiciously.

"We're going to IDC to deliver the chip."

"What?" Lennox blurted in disbelief. "What the hell's wrong with you?"

Marina pointed to the chair and waited patiently for Lennox to sit. Lennox realized she wasn't going to get an explanation until she obeyed, so she reluctantly sat down. Marina was pleased to see that she had some control over the volatile officer.

"IDC wants the chip to complete the system," she began.

"Gee, what a surprise," mocked Lennox.

"Kronos knows that and when they learn that the chip is going to IDC, they'll do anything to get it."

"Including killing us!" Lennox chided. "That's the stupidest plan I ever heard."

Marina grinned at her and waited for her to press for more details. Finally, Lennox asked to know more.

"The chip we're taking has been altered. When Kronos sends their people to take over the station, we're going to take them out. If we fail, the chip will program the targeting system to destroy them for us"

Lennox seemed a little more comfortable with the plan but was still baffled by the logic. Marina explained further, "The real chip will be delivered to the Fleet through you. If you choose to terminate Witty and take over the Fleet, you'll have the chip and the ability to take control of the system."

"I'll make sure that happens," replied Lennox contentedly as she now understood the potential of Marina's plan. She stared at Marina, wondering why she would trust her with the chip at all.

Marina noticed and glanced back. "What?" she asked curiously.

"Why would you trust me, especially after our past?"

"I try to keep things business, not personal," explained Marina. "This is for all our benefit."

"That doesn't work for me," responded Lennox stoically. "Everything is personal."

Britt emerged from Marina's cabin wearing pants and no shirt. He was surprised to see Colonel Lennox sitting with Marina. "Excuse me," he said politely. "I didn't know we had company." He retreated into the cabin and dressed.

"Quite a catch you have there," remarked Lennox. "Better hold on to him."

Marina looked at her defensively and replied sternly, "Oh, I will."

Lennox grinned and left the ship. Marina attempted to contact Kat several times to inform her that they were coming. When she received no reply, she then tried to contact IDC at GSS directly. Still there was no response. "What the hell is going on there?" she grumbled.

Britt emerged from her cabin, now fully dressed, and stood behind her. He rubbed her shoulders gently and asked, "Is everything alright?"

"Is it ever?" she replied despondently. "I can't reach Kat."

★ ★ ★

On the bridge of the *S.F. Argo*, Sheena questioned Lilith about what she knew of Kronos and IDC. Although vague, the answers did give her a better idea what they were dealing with - mercenaries and corporate greed.

Sheena's communications officer entered and announced, "Commander, General Witty would like to know where his merchandise is."

Sheena smiled and replied, "Is he waiting for a response?"

"Of course, ma'am."

Sheena went to the communications room and sat down at the console. "General Witty, I understand you're growing impatient over our agreement."

Witty responded sarcastically, "That and I have a problem with Lennox. I want to make sure it's been handled."

"I'm sure Marina has Lennox under control," she replied confidently.

"Well, I know her a lot better than you or Marina and she will stab you both in the back if you don't put her down," he warned.

"I believe that Marina has already dealt with that."

"And what of my merchandise?"

"We have a few obstacles to overcome right now, one of them being Kronos. I assure you," Sheena promised, "once these are behind us, we will deliver your data chip."

"That's nice of you," he remarked cynically, "but right now, alien forces are amassing at the edge of the fifth sector. If I don't have that chip soon, there's going to be a blood bath. You understand?"

Sheena became concerned over his remark. "I do, sir. I will pass that on to Marina." The short crackle told her the transmission was terminated. She considered what the alien forces might be planning and summoned Lt. Kannel.

The two of them discussed the possibilities and then decided it was best to recall the *Hydra* and the *Mantis* from the edge of the sector and relocate them at Orpheus-2 to put the alien leaderships at ease.

Sheena contacted Marina to inform her of the growing tensions in sector five and what actions she should take. Marina agreed that removing the Fleet ships would show good faith toward the aliens and then revealed her mission at the Galactic Space Station. Meanwhile, Sheena's objective was to secure the space station. When the subject of Col. Lennox came up, Marina decided it was best to keep her close where she could control her.

Once preparations were made, Marina departed Orpheus-2 with only Colonel Lennox to accompany her. What she didn't know was that Kara and Ginna stowed away on board *The Reaper*.

Once they departed, Col. Lennox elected to sleep in Marina's cabin rather than the couch or floor. While uncomfortable with the idea, Marina relented. As she set the auto-pilot on the control console, Kara and Ginna emerged from the shower stall at the rear of the ship and entered the flight deck. Marina was shocked to see them.

"What are you two doing here?" she asked frantically.

"You need us to rescue Kat," explained Ginna. "She is in grave danger."

"What do you know of IDC and the space station?" inquired Marina curiously. "And how do you know she's in danger?"

"There are bad people there," answered Kara. "These are not the people you met before."

Marina contemplated what could have happened. "And you say Kat is in danger."

"Yes, these people mean to harm her," replied Kara nervously. "And they will harm you as well."

Marina pondered what turn of events could have happened to endanger Kat, Faust and Marcus. She never imagined that Kronos would involve themselves so soon with IDC at the station since no one had the chip yet.

Ginna explained, "The IDC scientists are dead. Marcus and Faust are dying."

Marina was horrified by her revelation. Ginna continued, "I see two men in suits, escorted by ten men and women in uniforms."

"And what of Kat?" asked Marina anxiously. "Where is she?"

"She is captive in a cell," answered Ginna. "Likely unconscious."

"Damn it!" blurted Marina. "They're gonna pay for this!"

"You must remain calm, Marina," Ginna advised her. "These people will test your resolve."

"Well, I'm going to test their ability to survive a good ass-kicking!" she replied determinedly. "You both will remain on this ship no matter what. Do you understand?"

"We will do what needs to be done," Kara responded.

"No, you won't," countered Marina. "You stay on this ship."

Ginna explained, "There are things that need to be. It is destiny."

"And what if you get hurt or killed?" Marina challenged.

"Then it is our fate," answered Ginna stoically.

"You are my girls and I won't have you in harm's way," she declared. The girls glanced at each other and said no more.

When Col. Lennox returned to the flight deck, she was surprised to see the two girls with Marina. "So, you're baby-sitting now. Finally, a challenge you can handle."

Marina grew irritated and replied, "At least I still have my hands to handle things."

Lennox glanced down at the bandaged stump and the prosthetic hand. "No thanks to you," she replied sarcastically.

"Look, Sandra, the first time we met you tried to put on a show with me in front of my people. You left me no choice."

"I underestimated you. That won't happen again." Lennox hesitated and then commented, "You called me Sandra. I haven't heard that name in years."

"Well, I assume we can be civil toward each other since we're both getting screwed by Kronos, the Fleet and IDC."

"Perhaps we can, at least for now."

Ginna and Kara eyed Col. Lennox suspiciously. Marina noticed and suggested the girls move to the main cabin. When they left, Lennox took the co-pilot's seat next to Marina. "What's the deal with the girls?" she asked curiously. "Did you kill their parents or something?"

"No, nothing like that," Marina replied, careful not to reveal the girls' true purpose. "They're orphans, thanks to that little weasel Haney from IDC."

"The Oriental chap you killed back at the station," Lennox remarked.

"Yeah, he was quite a challenge when we met the first time at GSS," Marina related. "He was very adept at the martial arts."

"And you defeated him anyway," Lennox added arrogantly.

"No way," she answered humbly. "His associates, Janus and Ford, were much more open to discussion than Haney. They afforded me the opportunity to get away before he could kill me."

"So how did you handle him at the station?"

"I fought defensively," answered Marina.

"Huh?" Lennox uttered, baffled by her response.

"I forced him to come at me. It was much easier using his offensive moves against him as he did to me the first encounter."

Lennox was surprised by her revelation. She questioned Marina on her thoughts about being queen and what her intentions were with a new alliance. Marina was happy to share her feelings with someone for a change who could appreciate her position, even if they harbored bad feelings toward each other over their past.

Lennox suspected that the girls had much more importance to Marina than she let on. She considered that she might use them for payback, whether it be against Marina, Sheena or both. The physical detriment she received from Marina and the loss of Jeffries due to Sheena and her cohort was something she'd have to live with the rest of her life. *When the time comes, someone will pay,* she reminded herself.

When *The Reaper* approached the Galactic Space Station, Marina attempted to contact Drs. Janus or Ford. After several transmissions, there was still no response.

"Something's wrong," Lennox remarked coldly. "IDC had complete control of that station not so long ago."

"Who else would have access to the station?" Marina thought aloud. "They obviously were permitted to enter and dock."

"Perhaps they had an outbreak on board or an accident," Lennox suggested.

"No, this is something more."

"Then I suggest we go in armed," Lennox replied determinedly.

When they arrived at GSS, they found one of the outer bay doors open. Both women glanced at each other nervously, knowing it was a trap. Marina guided *The Reaper* inside the bay and secured the ship against the dock.

"It looks like we'll be suited up for this visit," Marina commented sourly.

Lennox kept her eyes on the outside monitor. The outer bay door closed and mist seeped from piping overhead, an indication that oxygen filled the bay. "I don't think that will be necessary. Look."

Marina watched the monitor and frowned. "Someone's waiting for us," she grumbled uneasily.

"I don't like this," complained Lennox. "It's a trap and we're at a big disadvantage."

Marina opened her weapons cabinet and took out two pistols. She eyed Lennox suspiciously and then tossed one to her. She hesitated and then returned the second pistol to the cabinet.

"Where's yours?" questioned Lennox.

"I don't need it."

"Damn, you have balls, Marina."

Marina responded coldly, "It comes with the territory." She donned her cloak and positioned the amulet on her head, ensuring it was placed in the center of her forehead.

"Ready, Colonel?"

"Sure am," Lennox replied confidently. "Lead on."

Ginna and Kara stepped in front of Marina, blocking her exit from the ship. "We're coming with you," Ginna informed the women.

Marina knelt down in front of them. "I explained this to you before. It's too dangerous."

The two girls glanced at each other and stepped back. Marina knew they weren't going to listen. Even if she locked the ship's hatch, the girls would use their powers to open it.

"Please, just trust me," Marina pleaded. The girls frowned and said nothing. Marina nodded to Lennox and they left the ship.

"They're stubborn, like you," quipped Lennox.

"That's not a good thing," Marina remarked cynically. "It'll probably be the death of me for what it's worth."

They exited the ship and walked across the dock to the interior station access hatch. When Marina reached for the lever, the water-tight door opened automatically. She glanced at Lennox nervously and stepped through first. Lennox checked her pistol and followed.

The long corridor to the elevator was empty with only the sound of ventilation humming to break the silence. They reached the elevator with its doors already opened. The women warily stepped on and waited as the doors slid closed.

"What floor?" asked Lennox curiously.

"It doesn't matter. They're controlling it, whoever 'they' are."

After ascending several floors, the elevator stopped and the door slid open. Marina and Col. Lennox each stood to the side and watched for an ambush. There was only silence.

Marina stepped off first into the corridor and listened for the sound of boots. There was none. She nodded to Lennox who followed. The two women crept down the corridor toward the control center.

Marina pressed the access knob and the door unlatched. She pulled the heavy steel door open and entered. Lennox peered behind them often, expecting an attack from behind.

Inside the control room, lights flashed on the console and the monitors displayed *The Reaper* in the transport bay. Suddenly, the hatch opened on the ship and the two girls exited. Marina was stunned as she watched. Her face grew taut with concern. "Damn it" she swore angrily. "I told them to stay."

"Forget about them," Lennox ordered her. "We have to focus here."

Marina approached the console and sat in one of four seats. The monitor in front of her went active and displayed several people in the control room earlier on a security recording. Marina took notice of the two men, Klingman and Sexton. "There," she said confidently as they watched the recording. "They are from Kronos."

Then the horror unfolded as Marcus, Janus and Ford were killed. Kat was beaten down and knocked unconscious. Then the screen went blank for several seconds. Finally, Sexton's face appeared.

"I wondered how long it would be before we finally met, Marina," he said pleasantly.

"And who are you?" she asked.

"I'm Tripp Sexton, Vice-president of Kronos Enterprises."

"Where's Kat?" she demanded.

"Come now, Marina. You know I'm a business man," he quipped. "A good businessman never gives anything away for free."

"You killed a friend of mine and you have another in your custody," Marina announced sarcastically. "It seems I owe you something."

"Ah, now you're learning."

Lennox warned her, "He's up to something."

Marina was well aware, but they had little opportunity to take action thus far. "You didn't answer my question, Sexless. Where's Kat?"

"My name is Tripp Sexton," Sexton chastised her. "I would appreciate it if you showed the proper respect."

"Then answer my question, asshole!" shouted Marina.

Lennox was impressed with Marina's boldness. She was anxious to see her in action when the fighting started.

"Sit back and relax. We'll be down with your friend shortly."

Lennox took a seat next to Marina and both women turned away from the console. Lennox watched the main entrance while Marina watched a side entrance. They waited impatiently for Sexton to arrive with Kat.

"You know your friend is probably in bad shape," Lennox mentioned, breaking the silence.

"Not as bad as he'll be when I get done with him," Marina uttered defiantly.

"I hope you're right."

The side access door opened and Jack Klingman entered, accompanied by three sentries. He looked quite pleased to see Marina. Marina, on the other hand, was anxious to beat him to death. The sentries targeted Marina with their pistols while Klingman paced about the room nonchalantly.

"Sexton can't make it, I presume," she said coldly as she stood with clenched fists.

"He'll be here," he replied. "I'm Jack Klingman and I'm hoping we can do business together."

Marina stepped toward him warily and demanded, "Where is Kat?"

Klingman extended his hand toward her in friendship without answering. Marina instinctively took it and twisted his arm behind his back. "Easy girl," he urged as he grimaced. "I'm your friend."

The sentries charged at her and placed the barrels of their guns against her head. "Stand down," he ordered and then gestured for his sentries to back off.

"That remains to be seen," Marina responded gruffly. "Now, where is Kat?"

"Sexton is bringing her down," he replied calmly, hiding his pain.

Marina released her hold on him and shoved him away. "Where are Janus and Ford?" she inquired. "I thought this was their show."

Klingman smiled at her and replied, "We had a layoff. Their services were no longer required."

"Like the Galleans," she countered.

"I see you've done your homework," he commented and pointed toward the main entrance. The hatch opened and Sexton entered with Kat and five more of his sentries. Kat's hands were bound behind her back and her mouth was gagged. Her eyes were puffy and she was bruised badly. Two of the sentries stepped outside the room and stood guard at the side hatch.

Lennox slipped quietly behind the group toward the side entrance with her eyes on the two men. As she neared the open hatch, watching Marina's captors, one of the sentries appeared from the corridor and struck her in the back of the head. Lennox fell to the floor unconscious.

Marina heard her groan and looked back. She was incensed by their treatment thus far. "This doesn't look like business to me," she responded, standing but a few steps from Klingman.

"Where's the chip?" he asked, suddenly in a somber tone. "I'll only ask once."

Marina pointed to Kat and responded coldly, "Release her first, then we'll talk."

Klingman nodded to Sexton to comply. He reluctantly untied her. Kat struggled with the gag until she removed it. "Don't give him the chip!" she shouted.

Sexton punched her in the stomach and doubled her over. Marina instinctively reached under her cloak for a dagger and fired it at Sexton. The dagger struck him in the shoulder.

Klingman struck her in the throat with a karate chop and floored her. He rushed to Sexton's side, but the wound was nonlethal.

A splotch of blood formed on his suit as he yanked Marina's dagger from his wound and tossed it aside. "I told you not to trust the bitch," Sexton uttered, wincing from the pain.

"Sorry, buddy," Klingman said sympathetically. "She'll pay for it, I assure you."

Marina gasped for air as she clutched at her throat. Klingman stood over her with a scornful look. "You shouldn't have done that," he said bitterly and stomped on her chest repeatedly. Marina's eyes bulged as she struggled to breath. Finally, Klingman backed off and took a seat nearby. He stared at Marina, wondering what it would take to break her.

The sentries dragged Lennox's still body across the floor and set her next to Marina. Kat uttered a spell and raised her hands in the air. Before she could finish, one of the sentries struck her in the back of the head and knocked her out.

Marina seethed as she struggled to regain her composure. When she did, the five sentries stood over her with their pistols trained on her head.

"I have the chip" she replied hoarsely.

"Now that's better," Klingman responded nonchalantly and held his hand out to her.

Lennox and Kat both stirred. Marina nodded for them to stay down.

"Are you ready to consummate a deal or should I remove the distractions?" he warned, while pointing at Kat and Col. Lennox.

"I have the chip here on the space station, but first, I want to know what this plan of yours is?"

Two sentries entered the control room with Kara and Ginna. Marina was horrified that they were now in the hands of madmen.

"I told you to stay on the ship!" she shouted at them angrily.

"Don't worry," Ginna assured her. "It's okay, Marina."

"Leave them out of this," Marina pleaded with Klingman.

Klingman warned her that the girls would die if she didn't turn over the chip immediately.

"Your friggin' plan probably won't work anyhow," she grumbled and reluctantly took the altered chip from under her cloak. "Here's the damned chip, now let them go." She tossed the chip to Klingman and waited for his response.

Klingman eyed the chip hungrily as he inspected it. Sexton hurried over to inspect it as well. The two men glanced at each other, wondering if it was the real thing.

"What do you think?" Klingman asked suspiciously.

Sexton took the chip from him and looked it over meticulously. "Well, the markings appear correct," he remarked. "The 417Q was the identifier for the chip that we were briefed on."

"And the suffix?" asked Klingman curiously.

Sexton stared at the suffix briefly and said, "Dash 3B -that's the revision level. Nothing unusual about it from what I can tell."

"You got your chip; now let the girls go," demanded Marina.

Klingman took the chip and stowed it in his pocket. "I think we'll keep the girls for insurance. If your chip works, then they'll go free. If it doesn't, well you know the deal."

"You piece of shit!" shouted Marina.

"Perhaps there is another way," suggested Sexton.

Marina glared at him, feeling the desire to rip both their throats out. Lennox saw the opportunity to escape and crept out of the control center while everyone's attention was on Marina.

Sexton stood in front of her, grinning. "You care a lot about your friends, I see," he remarked.

"Something you'd know nothing about," she replied.

Sexton turned to Kat and was shocked to see Lennox missing. Suddenly, his smug face became taut with anger. "Find the officer, now!" he screamed.

Four of the sentries hurried out the side access after Lennox. Klingman took out his own pulse pistol and aimed it at Marina's head. "Don't even think about it or I'll put a hole in your head so big..." he warned her. He then turned to Sexton and ordered him to make his point so they could leave.

Sexton removed a small case from his jacket pocket and opened it. Inside was a syringe with red contents. "I believe we need a little more insurance than the girls," he remarked while holding up one of the syringes, containing red fluid.

Marina feared what was in the syringe as he stowed the case in his pocket. The girls remained passive and silent through the whole ordeal which baffled Marina. She pondered why they were there at all.

"Look, you got your chip. Let us go," she pleaded. "I don't give a shit what you do with the damned thing."

"Here's the deal, Marina," Sexton began. "If you take the injection, your friend here lives. If she gets the injection, you'll have to wait for us to determine that the chip is authentic to get the cure for her."

Marina heard Kat's voice in her head. "Don't worry about me, Marina. You have to survive to save us."

Marina noticed the girls showed no reaction over her situation. She assumed Kat cloaked her thoughts from them. "Come near me and I'll kill you," she replied.

Sexton knelt over Kat and injected the red contents into her neck. Kat shivered as he pinned her to the ground with his knee in the middle of her back. Marina watched in horror as he emptied the contents of the syringe into her neck. Kat gasped and became motionless.

"Is she alive?" asked Klingman.

Sexton checked for a pulse. There was none. "Oh, well," he replied smugly, "Looks like you lost another friend, Marina," he taunted.

The girls were confused and looked hurt. "Why did you let her die?" Ginna asked Marina. Marina froze as she realized it was just like the premonition. Then she recalled the girls' responses to many of her questions. "It was fate," she replied. "It had to happen this way."

Both Klingman and Sexton retreated to the main entrance of the control center. The remaining four sentries nudged the girls to the entrance as well.

"Sexton!" Marina shouted. The men halted to hear her words. "The next time we meet, you'll pray for death," she warned. "What I do to you will be unfathomable."

Klingman laughed at her and said, "I'd consider killing you myself but I want to see you suffer."

Marina pointed at him and threatened, "What I do to you will be far worse; I swear."

The men laughed, while the girls stared pitifully at her. They left the control center, leaving Marina alone. The door closed and the sound of gas, streaming from jets in the wall, filled the room. Marina panicked as she searched for a way out. She crawled to Kat and attempted to move her. Whatever the gas was, it sapped her strength and left her reeling. She shook Kat and begged for her to respond. "Please, Kat, don't die on me," she pleaded. "I need you."

The rear door opened and Lennox staggered in. She was covered with blood and still dazed. Marina looked up from the floor and was stunned by the sight of her.

Lennox approached her and lifted her to her feet. "Gald to see me?" she uttered calmly.

Marina coughed a few times and replied, "You'd better believe it."

Lennox ushered her into the corridor and then returned for Kat. Marina was shocked that Lennox would help them like this. Sitting against the wall were Faust and Marcus. Both were unconscious.

When Lennox emerged from the control center with Kat in her arms, Marina quickly closed the hatch. Lennox fell to her knees and set Kat down. Marina dropped to her knees next to Lennox as well.

Lennox stared at her with sharp, piercing eyes. "You questioned my honor as an officer of the Fleet," she reminded Marina. "I hope this answers your question."

"It does, more than you'll ever know."

"Take your friends and get out of here," ordered Lennox. "I'll help you get her on board your ship."

"What about you?" Marina inquired, confused by Lennox's motive for staying.

"You tell that son of a bitch Witty, if he wants his chip, come get it. I'll be waiting here for him."

"Are you sure this is where you want to confront him?"

"What better place? It's abandoned and once those assholes leave. Witty won't be concerned about a trap."

Both women stood up. Marina placed her arm on Lennox's arm compassionately. "Are you sure you're okay?" she asked. "You're a mess."

"You should see the others," she joked half-heartedly. "They won't be a problem anymore."

"What about Klingman and Sexton and the girls?"

"They fled to their ship and left. I heard one of them say they're going to Kronos Headquarters."

Marina wondered why they would take the chip to Headquarters and not insert it here at the space station. She lifted Kat to her feet. Together, she and Lennox ushered Kat through the station to *The Reaper*.

Marina and Lennox stared briefly at each other and then Lennox left the ship. Marina felt as though she should say something, but knew that it was better this way. Urgently, she started the ship and pulled away from the dock. The outer doors opened automatically for departures but required someone inside to allow entrance to the station.

★ ★ ★

Britt and Sheena assembled all the officers and briefed them on the possible threats from Witty, IDC and from Kronos. Sheena ordered them to ignore any directives from Witty and that he would be brought to trial for treason against the Fleet.

Many of the officers were interested in the fate of their comrades on the attacking forces. Sheena reluctantly informed them that most of their ships had been destroyed as well as the alien forces. Despite their anger toward the aliens, Sheena convinced them that Witty was responsible for their losses and was on Kronos' payroll.

Britt warned them that the aliens may try to retaliate despite Marina's efforts to convince them that she would work with the Fleet to remove Witty and his accomplices from power.

Col. Lennox was on a mission with Marina to regain control of the Galactic Space Station and that she no longer supported General Witty. Sheena dispatched the remaining Fleet vessels into two groups: one to protect Fleet Headquarters and another to protect Orpheus-2. The militia fleet would protect Yord. Sheena also instructed them to take no action unless she gave them direct orders. The officers were uncomfortable with the situation, but obeyed her command.

"So now what do we do?" Britt questioned Sheena.

"The *Mantis* and the *Hydra* will remain here. We're going after Marina in the *Argo*."

Harville approached them and inquired, "Four techs arrived, claiming to be from IDC. We imprisoned them."

"On what grounds?" Sheena questioned him curiously.

"They were armed and attempted to secure the servers in the Red Room," he explained uneasily. "I'm afraid some of the servers were damaged in the attack."

Sheena glanced at Britt and then replied, "Let's hope we can salvage them. We may need them before this is over."

Harville informed her that his techs were working frantically to restore as many of the servers as possible. Sheena requested that he take charge of the station until she returned. Harville gladly accepted the responsibility and left.

Sheena and Britt promptly boarded the *Argo* and departed for GSS. Lt. Kannel met them in her quarters and discussed what to expect from GSS if their arrival turned hostile.

Shortly after their departure, the communications officer summoned Sheena from her quarters to the bridge for an incoming transmission. When Sheena entered the bridge, the officer informed her that Marina was waiting for her response. Sheena eagerly sat at the console and accepted the transmission.

Marina informed her of everything that took place and that she was pursuing Kronos' ship with the girls on board. She was pleased to hear that they were in route to back her up. She informed Sheena that she would contact Witty and relate to him that Lennox and the chip are waiting for him on GSS and that Lennox is helpless. Once they finished their

QUEEN OF PAIN

discussion, Sheena returned to her quarters to brief Britt and Lt. Kannel on the situation.

Britt mentioned, "I hope no one uses that dummy chip."

"Why is that?" inquired Sheena.

"Because Lilith programmed it to target the user of the chip."

"You've got to be kidding!"

"Nope. I was afraid something like this might happen."

"We've got to get word to Marina!" exclaimed Sheena.

Britt shook his head 'no'. "She already knows. If Kronos has the girls, she's going after them no matter what."

Sheena and Kannel stared at each other with concerned expressions, knowing they could be destroyed as well. Britt rubbed his eyes and stared blankly at the wall. All he could think was that Marina was taking risks alone and once again resorted to the hard way out - violence.

★ ★ ★

On board *The Reaper*, Marina sat teary-eyed at the controls of her ship. The girls were in danger. Kat was dying. She was no closer to defeating Kronos than before. Things couldn't get any worse until the transmitter beeped. She knew it was going to be bad news from someone. She pressed the 'accept' button and replied, "This is *The Reaper*. Go ahead."

"Marina, is that you?" inquired a strangely familiar voice.

Marina thought quickly before replying. Then she realized it was Emperor Rethus. "Emperor, it's good to hear from you. It is Marina."

"I attempted to rally the former alliance members and their neighbors on your behalf but failed."

Marina looked down dejectedly and then responded, "I appreciate that you tried. Perhaps later, they will reconsider."

That's not the worst of it," he said.

"What do you mean?"

"They are uniting their forces for a mass attack on the Fleet, the space station and then Yord. I tried to convince them that you were targeted as well but they refused to listen."

"Who is leading them?" she asked disappointedly.

"I believe Golgar is responsible for this," he revealed. "I will continue to communicate with them."

"I will try to reach him as well, but in the meantime, let them know that Kronos is behind all this. I'm tracking them to their headquarters as we speak."

"Can you handle them by yourself?"

"They have the data chip that controls the new weapons system but the chip has been modified."

"How so?" he asked curiously.

"It is programmed to destroy the location of the user, no matter where it is installed."

"But, if you are pursuing them, won't you be in danger?"

"Yeah, but that's part of the job," she answered cynically. "When am I not in danger?"

"I will let them know," he promised. "You won't reconsider going to Kronos, will you? You're risking your life without any support."

"No, I won't," Marina replied bluntly. "I have to do this for my parents, friends and allies. It's the only way we'll have peace."

"The next time we meet, I assure you that you'll be well respected by the Urthonians and many others for your valiant efforts. I will see to it."

"Thank you, Emperor. I must go now."

"Our prayers are with you, Queen Marina."

The transmission ended. Marina wiped tears from her eyes as she realized the likelihood that she would die, along with the girls. At times she felt as though Kat was trying to reach her telepathically and hoped that she was still alive. Their connection was weak if, in fact, it was a connection and then she wondered if it was just her emotions playing games with her mind.

As she considered her next move, she remembered that Lennox was waiting at GSS for Witty to appear. She sent a transmission to Fleet Headquarters and requested a response from him. After several minutes, Marina grew agitated and considered terminating the transmission. Just before depressing the switch to end the transmission, Witty's gruff voice crackled over the speaker.

"I hope you have something important to say to me," he grumbled. "I have my hands full with an alien attack right now."

Marina smiled, knowing he was desperate. "I wouldn't waste my time if it wasn't. Yours, I couldn't care less."

"Do you have the chip?" he asked anxiously.

"I did but I gave it to a colleague of yours," replied Marina giddily. "She's holding it at the GSS."

"What the hell good does that do me?" he shouted.

"The GSS station is abandoned except for Lennox."

"You were supposed to kill her, damn it!" he shouted angrily. "That was the deal."

"No it wasn't," Marina replied arrogantly. "You asked me to take care of her and I did. You'll find she's one bloody mess."

"So how does that help me here?" he inquired cynically.

"You go there and get the chip. Then you install it and operate the system. It doesn't take a genius to figure out that you need it to stop the alien attack."

"You couldn't just bring it to me, could you Marina?" he complained.

"I have my own problems!" she snapped at him. "That asshole Sexton poisoned my friend and they took my nieces for collateral! I'm going after them."

There was a moment of silence and then Witty asked, "Collateral for what?"

Marina realized she said too much and thought quickly. It was time to let him in on part of the plan. "I gave them a chip. It's not the real one."

"And what happens with this chip when they attempt to use it?" he inquired uneasily.

"You're quicker than I gave you credit for, General," she mocked. "The chip will operate the weapons system but it will target their headquarters and destroy it."

"Bravo!" shouted Witty with the sound of his clapping hands heard over the speaker. "But won't you be killed with them?"

"Most likely, although I'm sure you won't mind."

"I guess I underestimated you," he remarked.

"Everyone does," she replied cynically.

"For what it's worth, I hope you rescue your friends and escape in time," he said compassionately. "Our agreement will hold, regarding a truce with Yord."

"Thank you, General. And I hope you get your chip in time from Lennox." Marina terminated the transmission and sighed. She went to her cabin to check on Kat. She appeared dead, but Marina knew there was life in her. *What kind of poison is this?* Marina thought. Both Faust and Marcus were close to death. There was nothing she could do for them. As *The Reaper* gained on Kronos' ship, Klingman's navigator took notice and informed him. Klingman approached the console "Contact that ship," he ordered the officer. "I want to know who's on it."

The officer promptly tried to contact Marina but with no success. Klingman grew impatient and instructed him to keep trying. He then summoned Sexton to the bridge and informed him of their pursuer. Sexton arrived in a tee-shirt and dress pants with his shoulder bandaged.

Sexton pondered for a moment and considered the events on GSS. "I believe the pilot of that ship is Col. Lennox from the Fleet," he surmised.

Klingman fumed and shouted at him, "I thought you sent a team to kill her before we left!"

"I did," he replied disappointedly. "But they didn't return."

"Why didn't you tell me about this?" he screamed. The surrounding crew evacuated the bridge, except for the pilot. He placed headsets on and pretended to be occupied with his duties.

Sexton placed his hands on his hips and stared at the ground as he considered what motive Lennox would have for coming after them. "Let me speak with her," he requested. "I'm sure I can solve this little misunderstanding."

Klingman glared at him and warned, "You'd better. I don't need any distractions right now."

Sexton nodded and took a seat at the communications console. Klingman folded his arms and paced the bridge.

★ ★ ★

Witty sat at his desk and tapped his fingers. He was annoyed that he never considered a duplicate chip or a dummy. Then he wondered if Lennox's chip wasn't fake as well. *Perhaps,* he thought, *my chip will destroy Fleet Headquarters.* He knew Marina was conniving and couldn't be trusted. Then he had an idea. He attempted to contact Klingman at Kronos Headquarters. The agent informed him that they hadn't returned,

Growing more frustrated, Witty ordered him to give Klingman a message. "I believe our business relationship is over. I have the real chip. Contact me or else."

Witty ended the transmission and grinned. He reached into his drawer and took out a bottle of Cognac. "I believe I deserve a victory drink," he stated as he poured a glass. Just as he was about to sip from it, his personal communication unit beeped for an incoming transmission. With a smile, he sipped from his drink and then responded. "This is General Witty," he announced confidently. "What can I do for you?"

"Witty, this is Klingman. What the hell's going on?"

"Ah, Klingman. It's good to hear from my ex-boss so soon."

"Cut the shit, Witty. What's going on?" demanded Klingman.

"Well, it seems that the remaining alien forces have amassed with plans to destroy what's left of the Fleet, not that you would care."

"What do you want, backup?" Klingman offered.

"Hell, no. You see, I have the real chip for the laser targeting system."

"That's bullshit!" shouted Klingman.

"Nope. I already tested it on two alien vessels," he lied. "It works like a champ."

"Then what do you want?" Klingman asked suspiciously.

"The alien forces were so impressed with the weapon that they were willing to forge an alliance with the Fleet. We're coming after you and the rest of your Kronos bigots."

"That's a stupid idea. We're so close to achieving our goal, Witty."

"No, Klingman. We're so close to achieving your goal. And now, well, it's not gonna happen."

"Why are you doing this?" Klingman asked uneasily.

"You set me up. You made sure I lost most of my Fleet to weaken everyone for your benefit. There would be no one left to oppose Kronos."

"We had a deal," Klingman reminded him. "You are part of us."

"Am I?" he inquired. "Where is my officer, Colonel Lennox?"

"I don't know," Klingman lied.

"And how about the queen? I'm sure you know where she is?"

"Why do you care?" countered Klingman.

"Because I had a deal with the Queen and Lennox was sent to execute it. If anything happened to either of them, I'll personally take care of you."

Witty waited patiently for a response. Klingman was stunned by the turn of events, unaware that Witty was bluffing, and frantically considered a possible response to deter Witty from attacking. "I last saw the queen and Col. Lennox on the space hub. We had a negotiation with them that proved fruitless and we left."

"So, you're telling me that they're both alive?" he questioned.

"Of course, they are!" Klingman responded emphatically.

"I sent a ship to GSS and they tell me there are no life signs at all," Witty lied. "The station is abandoned."

"That can't be," he replied nervously. "If they're dead, then they must have killed each other."

"Then I guess there's nothing left to talk about. Nice doing business with you, Klingman," said Witty stoically and he terminated the transmission. He wondered how long it would take Klingman to assemble his force of mercenaries and send them after the alien fleet. He would do to Kronos what they did to him. He reached into the lower drawer in his desk and took a cigar from a small humidor. He sipped again from his cognac and then lit the cigar. Leaning back in his chair, he looked relaxed as he took a puff from the cigar.

Klingman then contacted Kronos headquarters and dispatched every armed ship to take on the alien and Fleet forces before they came to Kronos. Meanwhile, Witty contacted Golgar, who led the alien forces, and informed him that Kronos was sending a fleet of armed ships to finish them off. He proposed a truce until Kronos was defeated. Golgar agreed to hold back until they validated Witty's claim, but vowed to destroy the Fleet if Witty's claim was a lie.

Witty summoned one of his aides into the office and instructed her to set up a conference call with all Fleet commanders. The aide nodded and left the office. Witty considered contacting Marina but decided to let things play out with her. Either way, he was in control now.

IX
THE TRAP UNFOLDS

Lt. Kannel entered Sheena's quarters and requested permission to speak with her. Sheena invited him to sit at the conference table and listened intently.

"Things are under control on the space station, Commander," he announced. "Harville's techs have disabled all outputs from the servers associated with the weapons system."

"That's good news. Thank you, Ensign Harville."

"I have additional information from Fleet Headquarters."

Sheena folded her hands together and waited for him to continue. Lt. Kannel looked disturbed as he began to speak. "The aliens have amassed all their remaining forces for an assault on Fleet Headquarters."

Unaware of Witty's recent agreement with the aliens, Sheena leaned closer with grave concern. "Do we know why?"

"Unfortunately, we do," he answered uneasily. "The Fleet launched a major attack on the aliens earlier. Casualties were high on both sides. This is payback."

"Damn!" shouted Sheena as she stood and paced the room. "Make contact with General Witty for me."

"Yes, Commander," he replied and left her quarters.

Sheena fretted as she realized the two sides could annihilate each other, leaving Kronos to take over the sector uncontested. Then she considered the danger Marina could be in. If something happened to her, there was no one capable of restoring peace between the humans and the alien races.

Lt. Kannel's voice rang out from the intercom, "General Witty is ready to speak with you."

Sheena frowned and left her quarters. When she appeared on the bridge, Kannel looked concerned as he stepped aside from the communications panel. Sheena sat down in front of the console and spoke nervously, "General, are you there?"

"What do you want, Brice?"

"I just received word that alien forces are preparing to attack the Fleet. I've dispatched the *Hydra* and the *Mantis* to support you."

"No, need, Commander," he replied smugly. "Everything is under control."

"But, sir," she responded, baffled by his lack of concern.

"It's under control," he repeated irritably. "Now where is my chip?"

Sheena was caught without a response and admitted that he had to speak with Marina.

"You don't know what her intentions are?" he questioned.

"No, sir. She went to GSS with Colonel Lennox and I haven't heard from them since."

"Then I suggest you get in touch with her about our arrangement before you become expendable," he warned.

"Yes, sir," she replied obediently and terminated the transmission. "That no good son-of-a-bitch!" she shouted angrily.

Lt. Kannel waited nervously for direction from her. She clenched her fists and instructed him to follow her. Once inside her quarters, she closed the door and sat across from him at the oval conference table. "We have a problem," she stated angrily. "That pompous asshole is going to destroy us all!"

"I agree, Commander," replied Kannel. "What do you think we should do about it?"

"Send the *Mantis* and the *Hydra* to Fleet Headquarters," she replied. "Order them to abstain from the battle for now and keep me apprised of the situation there."

"Is that wise?" questioned Kannel. "I mean the General did instruct us to stay away."

Sheena stared at Kannel with a surprised expression. "How long have we known each other, Lars?"

Kannel was surprised by her switch to informal titles. "Six years, sir," he answered.

"Right now, I'm Sheena, your friend. Haven't you learned to question motives yet?"

"Yes, and you taught me well. I just assumed..."

Sheena held her hand up for him to stop. "Witty has something up his sleeve. Why else would he refuse support in the face of a pending attack?"

Kannel considered her question and then posed, "What if he had a trick up his sleeve to convince the alien force not to attack?" she continued. Kannel thought for a moment but had no answer.

"And why would the aliens listen to the man who just launched a galactic invasion against them that resulted in mass casualties?" He continued to ponder the question and replied, "He's convinced them that they have more to fear from Kronos!"

"Exactly!" she responded excitedly. "Now, could the data chip give him this kind of leverage if he somehow obtained it?"

"I don't see how," replied Kannel as he considered her question. "The alien forces don't know anything about it. As far as they'd be concerned, it's propaganda to sway them from continuing with their attack."

"So, what else do we know that could influence them like this?" she queried.

"Who else is out there that could tilt the odds in his favor?"

"It has to be Kronos," she announced confidently. "Witty still wants the chip and is bluffing that he has it."

"If that's true, what is the advantage of keeping the *Mantis* and *Hydra* from engaging?"

Sheena smiled and replied, "We don't know what Kronos' military capability is. The *Mantis* and *Hydra* are our aces against them. Send out probes to search for their forces and interpolate their point of origin. I want to know where that base is."

Kannel now understood the big picture and agreed with her assessment. "What do we tell the commanders of our ships?" he inquired.

"Inform them of our suspicions and to be alert for Kronos' force, a force of undetermined size as of yet."

"Very well, Sheena," he remarked. "I learn something new from you every day."

Sheena smiled at him and replied, "It's all about motive. When you know the motive, you can predict your opponent's actions, almost every time."

Kannel smiled and left Sheena's quarters. Sheena pounded the table gently and uttered to herself, "I've got you now, you son-of-a-bitch!"

Britt entered the bridge, looking much better and with improved mobility. Sheena was surprised to see him. "Good afternoon, Commander," she greeted him.

"Good afternoon," he replied pleasantly. "Have you heard from Marina?"

"We're pursuing her to Kronos' headquarters. Kannel will try and contact her shortly. There is much going on right now that we need to talk about."

Britt recognized the severity in the tone of her voice. He pulled up a chair and sat. "Go ahead, Commander Brice."

Sheena glanced around the bridge at the personnel that were present. Feeling comfortable discussing the recent events, she related to Britt all that had happened from Witty to IDC that she knew of.

"I should return to my men," Britt decided. "Someone will need to make the decision whether or not my forces need to engage."

"That would be wise," replied Sheena. "We're still basing our decisions on presumptions, although I don't see how this could play out any other way."

"I will coordinate with your ships against Kronos and we'll figure out what to do with Witty later."

Britt left the bridge dejectedly and returned to the *Wasp*. He had to restore order to the militia and sway some of the traitors back to his side if possible.

★ ★ ★

Marina sat in the pilot's seat and studied the monitors. Her long-range sensors showed the distance between Klingman's ship and hers decreasing. She attempted to channel her thoughts to Kara and Ginna for several moments. As she became frustrated, Kara's voice startled her. "It's alright, Marina."

"Kara, where are you?" she projected her thoughts outward.

"I'm with you," she replied. "We're both with you."

"Are you safe?"

"We are well," Kara answered. "We are working to save Kat right now."

Stunned by her remark, Marina realized that she was right. Kat still had life in her. "Can you help me?" Marina asked frantically.

'What do you require of us?'

"I need to know where Kronos' base is."

Kara informed her, "I don't know the location."

"I have to find a way to get on board that ship if there's any chance of rescuing you girls."

"Your ship will soon be masked from the evil ones so you can follow," Ginna informed her.

"I'm going to rescue you both; I promise," Marina assured her between tears and sobs.

"There are twenty sentries at Kronos Headquarters, well-armed and well-trained," Kara informed her.

"I can handle them," Marina replied confidently.

"Don't be foolish," warned Kara. "You must be smarter than them or you will perish with the others."

Marina was about to make an arrogant remark about what she'd do to them but then realized the lives of Kara and Ginna were in her hands. Then there was the possibility that Klingman would use the chip and destroy all of them. "What of Kat's fate?" Marina asked.

"Trust that Kat's fate has been determined. We cannot change that."

"But she's dying!" Marina exclaimed, fearing that she was alone on the ship with three friends who were dying or dead."

"We cannot change fate," Kara repeated to Marina. "Be safe, my Queen."

"What of Faust and Marcus?" Marina pleaded. "Can we do anything for them?"

"It's about fate, Marina. Believe in your fate." Kara's voice vanished, leaving Marina frustrated. She knelt over Kat's still body and hugged her tightly. "Who'd have thought it would come to this?" she muttered to herself. "I'm so sorry, Kat." Marina kissed her forehead and then knelt between the two men. Clutching their hands in hers, she cried out, "Alright, you win!" Marina stood and looked down sadly at the two men who would give anything to protect her. She again cried out, "What do you want from me? They didn't deserve this; I did!"

A familiar voice filled the room. It was Charisse's voice. "You have much ahead of you, Marina. You must focus."

"Damn it, Charisse!" she shouted angrily. "I need help."

"You will do what needs to be done. We have faith in you," her soothing voice replied.

"That's just fucking great because I sure don't!" she uttered sarcastically and returned to the flight deck. "Fuck those ghosts! I don't need them anyway."

As soon as she sat down, the transmitter beeped twice. Marina acknowledged the signal and responded, "Go ahead. I'm listening."

"Marina!" exclaimed Sheena. "Where are you?"

"On the way to Kronos Headquarters," she replied stoically.

"Kronos dispatched a large fleet of ships toward Fleet Headquarters. I sent two warships to help defend it."

Marina knew immediately that something was wrong. "It's a trap, Sheena. You'd best warn them," she advised.

"But we already know it's a trap. I suspect Witty will use the alien forces to turn on Kronos using a temporary truce."

"Kronos won't send all their forces in one direction," Marina explained.

"Look for them to split up and go after Orpheus-2 as well."

"How do you know?" Sheena inquired, baffled by Marina's remark.

"They'll attempt to use the station's servers to operate the weapons system," Marina revealed. "They don't care about GSS since the IDC techs were terminated and the station is functional. It can be operated from a remote location, likely Orpheus-2."

"Who has the chip?" Sheena asked anxiously.

"Klingman took the altered one. He'll try to operate the servers remotely."

"Then we'll return to Orpheus-2 with the *Argo* and defend it. I sure hope you're right about this."

"I know what these assholes are up to. Have Britt summon the militia to support you."

"Understood," Sheena responded. "What about you?"

"I'm fine," she replied sarcastically. "I always am."

"Be careful. I can't do this alone."

"You won't be alone, Sheena. We have friends."

Marina ended the transmission and sighed. There was no easy way out of this. The transmitter beeped and another transmission came in. She toggled the switch and accepted it.

"I know you're out there," said Klingman defiantly. "It doesn't matter where you are, I win."

Marina clenched her fists, but refrained from losing her temper. "I don't have time for games, Klingman," she said calmly. "I have an alien assault to deal with and I hear that a large force left your headquarters. That tells me we're in the last stage of your little plan."

"And what of your girls?" he taunted. "Surely you won't let them die like your friend Kat."

Marina again clenched her fists. She warned, "If anything happens to them, I will hunt you down and when I do…"

"So, you really aren't coming after them?" he asked with mock surprise. "I'm so disappointed."

"Don't worry," she replied confidently, realizing that the girls cloaked her ship. "You and I have a date with destiny."

"I'll be waiting for you, if you make it past my ships," he said, followed by a taunting laugh.

"Count on it," she replied confidently and terminated the transmission. The monitor showed that she was close behind Klingman's vessel. Smiling, she eyed her armament. "I'm gonna enjoy this like never before," she uttered aloud.

Marina considered contacting Lennox at GSS but thought better of it. If Witty was on his way, the two can have each other any which way they want. As she again glanced at the monitor, she saw something large on the perimeter of the screen. "What the hell is that?" she blurted to herself.

A monstrous space station loomed ahead of her. If that was Klingman's headquarters, there would surely be a contingent of soldiers there, just as Kara said. She knew this wasn't going to be easy.

★ ★ ★

Sheena relayed Marina's orders to Britt. He felt the same doubt that Sheena did upon hearing the news. When Britt contacted the other commanders, he expected to hear that they were based at Yord. Instead, he was horrified to learn that half of his militia had defected and were attacking Fleet headquarters. Those commanders who were still loyal to Britt, seven in all, fled the battle and headed for Orpheus-2. Britt went into a rage and smashed his fist against the wall. "I never saw this coming!" he shouted angrily. "Kronos bought them out from right under my nose!"

On the bridge of the *Wasp*, Britt stared dejectedly at the floor, wondering if he should be impressed with Marina's insight or concerned. If she was wrong, they sacrificed Fleet Headquarters and possibly Yord for nothing. But, if she was right, then this was the only way to survive Kronos' attack.

"How many vessels are still loyal?" inquired Sheena uneasily through the transmission.

"Seven," he answered somberly. "That means twenty-four of my friends betrayed me."

Sheena reminded him that they had tough decisions to make and ended the transmission. She gestured for Kannel to follow her.

When Kannel was seated, Sheena leaned on the table with her palms and stared at him. "What is the likelihood that Marina is right?"

"She has great deductive reasoning," answered Kannel. "While I wouldn't expect such a move by Kronos, she may have reason to."

Kannel rubbed his chin as he mentally analyzed the information. Sheena noticed his devious expression and waited anxiously for him to respond. Finally, he spoke. "If the deserting militia commanders didn't back Kronos, then they would require their entire fleet of vessels to take on the Fleet and the alien forces. It wouldn't make sense."

Sheena added, "That's why Kronos needs them."

"So why does Kronos divide their forces now and attack two targets?" challenged Britt.

"Opportunity. If Kronos believes they have the numbers with the militia traitors to take over Orpheus-2, then why stop? If they succeed, the galaxy is theirs."

"So, everyone was baited into this master plan of Kronos and crippled each other's forces," summarized Sheena. "These remaining forces are the last impediment to their reign."

"If this comes down to defending Orpheus-2, we will be fighting to the end," added Kannel. "No one will be left to defend anything."

"Kronos obviously thinks they can win if they only sent half of their vessels. We don't stand a chance."

"Then summon the *Hydra* and the *Mantis* to return," Sheena declared.

"But that means sacrificing Fleet Headquarters!" Kannel exclaimed.

"Yes, it does," she replied sadly. "We have no advantage there, even with the two warships to support them."

"Neither do we have an advantage at Orpheus-2," he pointed out.

"This is where we will make our stand," Sheena informed them. "That's my final decision."

"Then let's make it worth our while," responded Lt. Kannel. "I will not die in vain."

"And neither will I," she assured him.

"When my group arrives, I need to join them," Britt informed them. "I need to make sure there are no more traitors."

"Understood," answered Sheena. "Kannel, send out the probes. I want to know how many vessels are moving and where they are moving to."

"Yes, sir," he replied and left her quarters.

★ ★ ★

Col. Lennox sat at the control center of the Galactic Space Station, watching the destruction of Fleet Headquarters on the monitor in her blood-stained uniform. Despite several serious wounds from her battle with Klingman's sentries, she was ready to fight one more battle.

The short-range monitor revealed a small craft approaching the transport bay. Lennox was pleased, sensing that her revenge was close at hand, and operated the outer bay doors. She wondered, after all the time and money invested in the station, why would Kronos abandon it? Then she considered that it was programmed to operate without human interaction. She reminded herself abruptly that it wasn't her concern right now. Dealing with Witty was. Lennox left the control center, seeking an appropriate location to encounter him.

As Witty docked his ship, he was confident that he would soon have his chip and Lennox would be gone forever. Based on Marina's information, Lennox might already be dead and he was safely away from the battle at Fleet Headquarters. In his head, he believed that he would soon rule everyone and everything with the targeting system under his control. The Fleet was just collateral damage and Kronos would be at his beckoning.

Lennox slid a small, blood-stained knife from her boot and stared at the blade. A vision of her as a young girl filled her mind. She was with a young, handsome boy on a hill amid a forest of oak trees. They just finished lunch from a picnic basket. Everything was so beautiful and then it went so bad. The boy came on to her roughly and, when she resisted, he punched her in the face, knocking her out. When she awoke, she was face down in the grass, being violated. When he finished, he beat her until she was unconscious. Thinking she was dead, the boy left her, helpless and bleeding from her wounds.

Lennox summoned all her strength and crawled to a nearby creek to wash. She vowed that she would never be vulnerable again. A few years later, she graduated as an officer and a rising star in the Space Fleet. Cold-hearted and determined, she never backed down from anyone. The memory passed, but then her encounters with Rock rekindled that hatred. He paid, as far as she was concerned.

Lennox fumed as she dealt with the fact that Witty destroyed the Fleet, her Fleet, for his own greed. He took away the one thing that gave her life meaning. Now he would pay. She waited patiently until he finally reached the control center. When he arrived, he looked surprised to see her sitting upright and alert.

"I guess Marina exaggerated your frail condition to me," Witty chided.

"It doesn't matter what condition I'm in. You and I have business to settle."

"Give me the damned chip," he demanded.

Lennox stood and approached him. "Over my dead body," she responded arrogantly as she assumed a defensive position with her knife in hand.

"Oh, that can be arranged," he remarked and lunged at her. Lennox attempted to plunge the knife into his side but he grabbed her wrist and bent it behind her back. Before she could respond, he slammed her face-first into the hull.

Dazed, she dropped to her knees. The knife fell from her hand to the floor with a metallic clank that reminded her of a death knell. Witty kicked it away and slammed her head again into the wall.

As Lennox tried to balance herself on the floor, Witty unbuckled his pants. "I've dreamed of this for a long time, Sandra dear," he taunted.

Lennox regained some composure and tried to get up off her knees. Witty, sensing he had her at a disadvantage, grabbed her by the hair and slammed the back of her head into the hull. "Now, you'll do what you were meant to do," he declared emphatically.

Lennox recalled the vision of her experience as a girl. "This will never happen to me again," she swore that day. She reached up in desperation with her prosthetic hand and grabbed his genitals through his shorts. His eyes widened in horror.

"Let go, you bitch!" he shouted, but Lennox squeezed harder.

"This *is* what you dreamed about, General," she taunted. "I'm on my knees for you."

Tears streamed down Witty's cheeks as she twisted his manhood, savoring his unbearable pain. "I'll... kill... you," he muttered as the pain brought him to his knees.

"Kiss that chip goodbye," she taunted. Then, feeling the rush of vindication, she ripped his appendage and testicles from his body. He wailed like a wounded animal and fell backward as his shorts quickly became blood-soaked. His genitalia fell out of his shorts onto the floor by his side.

Lennox gazed sadistically at her prize and then at his feeble state. "Nothing to be proud of, General. I'm so disappointed in you."

Witty tried to speak but fear and shock left him motionless with a tortured expression on his face.

She took his pulse pistol from him and aimed at his head. His eyes seemed to beg for an end to his pain. Then, recalling how her life as a Fleet officer was over, her rage drove her to shove the bloody mass of flesh into his mouth. Witty gagged as she held his mouth shut. His body shuddered while he struggled to breath. Finally, his eyes rolled back and he passed.

Lennox got to her feet and staggered from the control center. If she made it to Witty's ship, she could program the auto-pilot and hope someone found her. Her head spun and she vomited several times but she finally reached the shuttle. Once inside, she strapped herself in the pilot's seat, but then passed out.

★ ★ ★

Sheena stood on the bridge, joined by Lt. Kannel and eyed the long-range monitors. Twenty-five ships headed in their direction from Fleet Headquarters.

"I assume the battle's over," Kannel remarked somberly.

"I'm afraid so," she replied dejectedly. "Have the *Mantis* and *Hydra* detour to the Ramses Asteroid field. I want them out of sight."

Kannel was stunned by her request. "Commander, we're already at a disadvantage."

"I'm aware of that. Perhaps we can lull them into early tactical mistakes."

Kannel was again confused by her tactic, but obeyed her orders. Sheena went to her quarters and contacted Ensign Harville on Orpheus-2. She requested a private conference with him to include Drago and Lilith.

An hour later, their images appeared on Sheena's wall monitor. After a brief update on the chilling events, Sheena directed her attention to Lilith and inquired, "Can you operate the targeting system from Orpheus-2?"

Everyone was surprised by her request. They believed the intent was to disable the weapons capability permanently. Lilith glanced at Harville.

"My people can restore the output connections and the main server functions, if that's what you want," he replied.

Lilith then replied, "I have to run a significant number of system checks and configurations to make the central computer system compatible with the satellite uplinks. Each connection has to be verified."

"So, it can be done?"

"Yes, it can."

"Lilith, your creation is the only salvation we have left. It's a shame it has to be in war."

"I understand. It has to be done."

"We'll support her in any way possible," added Harville.

"Kronos' force is already on the way," she informed them. "Please, do what you can. Time is of the essence." The video conference ended and Sheena returned to the bridge.

Lt. Kannel informed her that the *Mantis* and *Hydra* were redirected. Sheena seemed distant and only nodded in affirmation.

"The supporting militia ships have arrived," he continued. "Commander (Britt) Sykes has taken charge of them."

"Thank you, Lars."

★ ★ ★

Marina piloted her ship, *The Reaper*, which was much smaller than Klingman's, into the gigantic transport bay. As the large transport moored at one of many empty docks, Marina maneuvered her ship beneath the Kronos vessel and waited patiently for them to disembark.

The outer bay doors closed and a steady flow of oxygen soon made it breathable. While waiting, Marina scanned the transport bay and was stunned at how many ships it could house. She took notice of the ventilation for supply and exhaust of air. Perhaps, one of those would be her way in. The lights extinguished, leaving the bay engulfed in darkness.

Marina knew they had left the ship. She checked her arm and ankle armor, and then secured two pistols to her belt. As she donned her helmet with dreadlocks and prepared to leave the ship, Kat coughed and reached for her frantically. Marina fell to her knees next to Kat and lifted her into her arms.

"I'm here, Kat," she said compassionately. "What can I do for you?" Kat's breathing stabilized and she relaxed. "Help me up, please. My back is killing me," she complained.

"I thought you were dying, you bitch!" she shouted giddily as she lifted Kat to her feet. "I thought you were poisoned?"

Kat smiled at her and replied, "The girls helped me to control the poison in my body for a later use. Sexton is mine and it's my turn to return the favor."

Marina hugged her tightly and inquired, "Are you sure you're up for this?"

"I will be shortly."

Marina escorted Kat to the flight deck and related the recent events. Kat then inquired about the girls and what interaction Marina had with them. She revealed how Kara and Ginna cloaked her ship while she trailed them.

Kat was determined to pursue Sexton alone and then rendezvous with Marina at the control room. Marina was reluctant to let her friend venture off without support, especially after just recovering from near death from Sexton's toxin. After a brief argument, Marina relented. Kat instructed her to go ahead and she would join her later.

When Marina was out of sight, Kat knelt between Faust and Marcus. She uttered several spells as she held their hands tightly. After a number of repetitions of the spells, she left the ship.

Marina paused at the end of the corridor and wondered if she made a mistake by not staying with Kat. As she proceeded down the straight corridor toward the elevator, she saw a premonition. The vision showed her getting off the elevator on the fifth floor and facing ten men with pistols. Before she could react, they fired a barrage of shots at her and left her bleeding profusely on the floor. The vision cleared and she stopped at the elevator. Once again, the girls had saved her life.

The elevator door slid open. There were three hand rails along the walls and a maintenance hatch in the ceiling that she considered using for her attack. *How did the girls know I was here?* she wondered. Their never-ending run of surprises made her nervous as she considered that they should mentor her instead.

Her stubbornness got the best of her. She entered the elevator despite the warning and pressed 'five' then 'six'. As the doors closed, she climbed up on two of the handrails in the corner and opened the hatch. The elevator jerked a little as it began its ascent.

At the top of the elevator was a series of servos. Along the walls were energized buss bars which provided power to the elevator servos through sliding contacts.

Marina pulled herself through the hatch and perched on one knee, balancing herself carefully. The elevator lurched as it came to a stop. She closed the hatch and latched it.

Next to her were the smaller servos that operated the doors and in front of her were the light sensors aimed at a mirrored lens along the entrance and sides of the elevator to prevent inadvertent closing. The voices of several men entering the elevator alarmed her as it shifted. Fortunately, they weren't there for her, just a ride from 'four' to another floor.

"Who pressed 'six?" asked one of the men. "We're going to five."

"The station should be secured on all floors except the 'sixth' and 'tenth', replied another.

"I'll call it in," he announced.

"Don't sweat it," a third responded. "The motion sensors will tell us if there's an intruder."

A woman's voice among them spoke cynically, "Look where we're at, goofballs. How in the hell are intruders going to get in here?"

"She has a point," said the first man.

The elevator doors closed and the elevator ascended one floor. Marina eyed the servos and the sensor as the doors opened once again. Two of the sentries stepped halfway out and peered both ways down the hall, thus blocking the sensor.

Marina took her dagger and placed the blade in front of the sensor. After three attempts, the blade reflected the signal back to the sensor and the doors immediately closed on the two sentries. One of them fell outside the elevator but the second wasn't so lucky. The doors slammed on him, crushing his rib cage.

The other sentries tried frantically to pull the doors open. Marina took a second dagger and placed the blade in front of the middle sensor that acknowledged the doors were closed completely. She reflected that signal back to its origin and the elevator moved upward toward the sixth floor.

The trapped sentry screamed briefly as his body was ripped in half. His comrades backed away, horrified by the spectacle. "What the hell is going on?" shouted one of the men.

"Calm down," ordered the woman. "It's a malfunction."

"Tell that to Roo's old lady when she sees him in pieces," he replied sarcastically.

Marina removed her blades from the sensors' paths and the elevator stopped at the sixth floor. The sentries were reluctant to get off. She peered down through the narrow slit below. The female sentry stood in the path of the bloodstained doors to convince them it was safe.

Marina promptly placed the blades of her daggers in the path of the sensors again. The elevator doors immediately slammed shut on her and crushed her chest. She tried to utter something but blood spewed from her mouth and then she died.

Marina removed her daggers from the door sensor's path and the doors slid open. One by one, the sentries dove off the elevator, wary that it could close on them. Two of them dragged the corpse of the female sentry clear of the elevator. None were willing to enter for the dismembered corpse. Once all were clear, the elevator doors closed normally.

Marina listened as one of the sentries reported the incident to Klingman over his transmitter. Another recommended sending the elevator down to 'five' for their companion. They received orders to disable the alarms on the stairwell briefly so the sentry from the fifth floor could join them.

Marina opened the hatch and dropped down to the elevator floor. The sentries were alerted when her boots struck the floor. Before they could enter, the doors had already closed. She alertly pressed 'five' before they could press 'open' and trap her.

Marina stared down at the legs and hips of the dismembered sentry. Then she noticed all the blood on the doors and felt a certain satisfaction. "Not bad," she uttered to herself. She stepped aside in front of the control panel and out of direct sight as the door slid open on the fifth floor.

The waiting sentry gazed in horror into the elevator at the corpse. Marina reached out and grabbed him by the throat. Before he could react, she sliced his abdomen open and then threw him away from the elevator. An alarm sounded and several lasers fired from within the walls, cutting off the man's knees and head. When the man's body was flat against the floor, the alarm cleared and the lasers ceased firing.

"Impressive," Marina commented to herself. "And then there were seven." She had to find her next vantage point before they came looking for the sentry. By now they surely knew an intruder had penetrated their defenses. *Even Klingman might be smart enough to realize I'm here*, she considered.

Stowing her dagger, she stepped out of the elevator and lay on her stomach. She scanned the corridor and found a door marked ' Stairs'. She shimmied across the floor below the lasers toward the door, wondering how she'd know if it was safe to enter.

After three nerve-wracking minutes, she heard the sentries on the dead man's communicator. "We're in position at the sixth-floor stairwell. Shut down the alarm system now."

Marina n o w stood close to the door to avoid the sensors and waited anxiously. Another voice on the communicator reported, "There's no one in the elevator, sir. We checked the service hatch and it's clear."

"Continue to search!" blared Klingman.

Her heart raced as she placed her hand on the door handle. The voice on the communicator replied, "Alarm system will be disabled in three, two, and one. The alarm is disabled."

Marina opened the door and stepped into the stairwell cautiously. She heard the door on the floor above open and hurried down a flight of stairs to the fourth floor. Waiting for another clue as to their location, she paused in the doorway with the door open slightly and listened.

The sentries rushed down to the fifth floor and began a search of the floor. One sentry remained in the stairwell and peered out toward the elevator.

Marina quietly closed the door and inched back up the stairs toward the man, her daggers in both hands. "Looking for me," she said calmly. Before the sentry could react, she slit his throat and sliced open his abdomen. The man stared at her with a horrified expression as he slid to the floor and bled to death. She removed one of her flash grenades and then the man's dog tags. While holding in the button on the silver ball, she prevented it from triggering. Carefully, she slid the chain through the ball and released the button. Grinning sadistically, she placed the dog tags around the man's neck and stowed the flash grenade under his shirt.

Marina took his communicator and turned it off. She stowed one dagger but held onto the other. She then removed the man's pulse rifle and hurried up the stairs to the 'tenth' floor. Pausing at the door, she turned on the communicator at a low volume.

As she peered out onto the tenth floor, she noticed red smoke emerge from a vent. Curious as to what was happening, she continued to watch. The smoke then took the shape of a person and took clarity. "Holy shit!" Marina blurted in a low voice. Kat emerged from the smoke.

Kat peered both ways and then glided down the corridor. Marina was stunned that she had those kinds of powers and grew wary of her. Then she heard Kat's voice in her head. "This was much easier than the way you chose."

Marina thought, *Just what I need for an ally, a smart-ass witch.*

Kat responded to her thought, *Better than a dumb-ass witch.*

Marina chuckled but her thoughts were interrupted by a flash in the stairwell and screams. A voice on the radio reported frantically, "Blackie's down! Coop and Drake are badly injured!"

Klingman's voice responded, "Leave them and get back here now."

"But, sir, they need help!"

"Get back here now!" shouted Klingman. "That's an order."

"Yes, sir."

Marina was pleased as she knew there were only four sentries left to deal with. Still, the odds weren't in her favor. And then she wondered what Kat was up to. With powers like hers, maybe the odds were in their favor.

Marina stepped through the doorway onto the tenth floor and proceeded cautiously in the opposite direction as Kat. Klingman's voice blared over the page system and startled her.

"Marina, I know you're here. If you want to see your girls alive, come to the Control Center on the tenth floor, if you aren't already there." After a brief pause, he continued, "Oh, and kill or injure one more of my men and I'll start butchering your little friends."

Marina felt her adrenalin run through her body and her rage build. She continued down the corridor, reading the signs on the doors as she passed them. When she finally reached the double doors to the Control Center, she had another vision from the girls. The vision showed the remaining four sentries beating her to the ground as Klingman cut each girl's throat.

Panic set in as Marina feared she was dealt a losing hand. She was stumped as to how they could ambush her like this. She checked the pulse rifle and pressed the 'open' button. As soon as the doors slid open, she burst through, ready to fire at Klingman. Suddenly, she realized she stepped into a trap. The room was empty.

She quickly retreated to the corridor but the four sentries were waiting with their weapons pointed at her. "Fancy meeting you boys here," she remarked cynically.

"Drop the weapon or we'll shoot," ordered the senior sentry.

Another of the sentries lowered his weapon and punched her in the mouth. Marina shrugged it off and spit the blood from her lip at him. "That's no way to treat a lady," she taunted him.

The sentry rammed the butt of his rifle into her stomach and slammed the side of her head. Marina fell to the floor, dazed from the impact. She instinctively reached for one of the flash grenades on her wig. The assaulting sentry swung his rifle at her arm and injured it badly. Marina cried and rolled on her side in intense pain.

"That's for what you did to my wife on the elevator," the sentry shouted at her and kicked her in the ribs.

"That's enough," ordered the senior sentry. "Klingman wants her alive."

The other two sentries ushered her into another room at gun point. She clung to her arm in desperation, realizing they didn't care how much pain they inflicted on her.

The room had a table and two chairs. Marina recognized it as an interrogation room and took a seat. One of the sentries grabbed her by the hair and yanked her to her feet.

"I didn't tell you to sit," he shouted at her and threw her against the wall.

The second sentry backed into the corridor and quipped, "Better leave something for the boss or he'll have your ass."

"We'll see about that," he replied arrogantly.

Marina knelt down as if protecting her arm but subtly drew one of her daggers. Keeping it hidden behind her, she waited for the right moment.

The sentry approached her and grabbed her by the hair again. Marina lashed out with the dagger and shoved it under his ribs. The man's eyes bulged as he realized the wound was lethal. He clutched weakly at her throat with his free hand and attempted to choke her but Marina continued to push and twist the dagger further into his chest.

"Don't worry," she said mockingly. "Your wife wasn't into men anyway."

The sentry's eyes widened with one last burst of rage and then he fell to the floor in a growing pool of blood.

"Hey, Flores," the sentry called from the corridor. "It's awfully quiet in there. You two making out or what?"

Marina leaped through the doorway and plunged her dagger into his throat before he could finish his sentence. The man staggered backwards, frantically clutching at his wound. "I'd say 'or what'," Marina mocked him as he fell to the floor, gasping with his last breath.

Marina leaned against the wall and slid down to the floor. The pain in her arm was unbearable. "Only two left and then Klingman is mine," she reminded herself. The pain overwhelmed her and she passed out.

★ ★ ★

Kat paused in front of a fancy oak door with a gold nameplate with 'Tripp Sexton' etched in fancy font. She turned the door handle slowly and peered inside. Sexton sat at his desk, studying the monitor in front of him. He was pleased by the images of Fleet and alien vessels, floating aimlessly with heavy battle damage. "Soon we'll control everything!" he blurted victoriously.

Kat stood in front of his desk and startled him. "How the hell did you get in here?" he uttered in surprise. "Why are you even alive?" he added and stood up.

"I have something for you," Kat informed him. "I think you'll appreciate it."

Sexton took a pulse pistol from his top desk drawer and pointed it at Kat. "This time I'll make sure I finish you," he swore.

"You have no idea who I am, do you?" she challenged him.

"Sure, I do," he replied. "You are someone who is about to die."

Kat held her hand in front of her mouth and a wisp of smoke formed. She blew on the smoke and it spread. "We shall see who will die," she responded with a sinister laugh.

Sexton fired the pistol at her but she was gone. Suddenly he felt a cold chill overcome his body and then he was paralyzed. Only his eyes could move as he tried to locate Kat.

When the last of the smoke vanished, Kat was standing in front of him. "I told you I have something for you," she repeated to him. She smiled, bearing sharp fangs like those of a cobra. Stroking his cheek briefly, her eyes widened with hunger and she bit into the artery in his neck.

After the bite, she backed away and waved her hand in an invisible circle. Sexton fell to his knees and dropped the pistol. He shuddered violently as his face contorted.

"Please, help me," he pleaded.

"Of course," replied Kat. She knelt next to him and bit the other side of his neck. He fell over on his side and shook with severe spasms. "Consider my debt paid in full," she informed him and left the room.

Sexton's skin turned red and blood seeped from his pores. His clothes turned red with blotches of blood as he gasped for air. Soon, he vomited purple chunks that were once his organs before the poison liquefied them, and then he passed. The flesh from his face fell away and only the skeleton and clothes remained intact. The dark purple fluid spread across the floor, accompanied by a horrible stench.

★ ★ ★

When Marina opened her eyes, she was strapped to a chair in the Control Center. Klingman sat across from her with Kara and Ginna also strapped into chairs.

Monitors behind him showed images of damaged ships, many of them Fleet or alien. Klingman was pleased to see Marina awaken.

"You're a stubborn woman, Marina," he said disappointedly. "Those men you killed were the best that money can buy."

"Then you'd better get your money back," she uttered.

"I told you what I would do to your little friends if you harmed any more of them," he reminded her. "You just don't listen, do you?"

Marina summoned her strength and pleaded, "Let the girls go, please."

Klingman stood and walked around her, eying her meticulously. "The way things are progressing, I may not need your stinking chip," he said confidently. "That's why we abandoned the GSS. No one in the galaxy will know where the weapon is controlled from. None will have the power to stand up to my forces."

"I don't care about your petty plans," she replied dejectedly. "Just let my girls go and I'll do whatever you want."

Klingman laughed at her. "After all the trouble you caused, I'm gonna make you suffer." He slapped the side of her head and left the room.

Marina cried for the first time in a long time. Tears streamed down her cheeks as she felt defeated. Kara and Ginna felt sorry for her and projected a vision of peacefulness to her.

Marina looked up at them and said sadly, "I'm so sorry. I let you girls down."

"No, you didn't," replied Kara. "This was our fate. It has to be."

"Why did you let Kat die?" inquired Ginna. "She cared about you very much."

Marina realized the girls didn't know about Kat. Knowing that there must be a reason that Kat withheld her survival from the girls, Marina said nothing of it. Instead, she replied, "I had to make a choice. When you get older, you'll realize that we can't always have what we want."

"But you need her," responded Ginna. "She is important to your success in uniting the galaxy."

Marina countered their logic with a surprising statement. "Kat and I have lived to be adults. You and Kara deserve that same chance," she remarked. "Maybe I can't save everyone, but perhaps you can."

"That's very noble of you," said Ginna proudly.

"Not really. I made many mistakes in life," Marina confessed. "Consider this my atonement." She closed her eyes and passed out from pain and exhaustion.

In a vision, Marina found herself drifting through an asteroid field in *The Reaper*. She stared at the odd shaped asteroids and felt as though she was one of them. With no sense of purpose, she just drifted.

The girls entered the flight deck and knelt down next to her. Marina glanced at them with a disinterested expression and then resumed her blank stare into space.

"You are our queen, Marina," Kara informed her. "You must lead everyone to build that which is good." Marina disregarded her comment and remained lost somewhere in space.

"We have come so far and yet you feel empty," Kara remarked.

"Look at me," answered Marina angrily. "My arm is useless. Yord is in shambles. The militia and the Fleet sold us out. My own people hate me! Why shouldn't I feel empty?"

Ginna stood and leaned over her with a somber expression. "All these people don't have the strength and conviction that you do. When you are victorious, many will learn. Many will be different because of you. Many will be humbled by your determination."

"And if I fail?"

"You won't fail," Ginna told her sternly. "You don't know how to fail."

"But what if I do?"

"Then we will lose faith in you," she replied pointedly. "Is that what you want?"

"Self-pity is an excuse for quitters," Kara chastised her. "We are here because we believe in you."

Marina became enraged by their persistence and jumped out of her seat to shout at them. As she stood, they vanished. The asteroid field vanished. The ship vanished. She opened her eyes and was in the Control Center.

Kara and Ginna smiled at her. She nodded to them and then fumbled with the straps that bound her hand. Suddenly, her injured arm didn't feel so bad. She felt renewed strength. The straps became loose and she worked her hands free of them.

Klingman entered the room with his remaining two sentries. "Well, look at you," he taunted. "Marina, the escape artist."

The sentries pointed their pulse rifles at Marina and forced her to back away toward the wall. Klingman took a short knife from his belt and walked behind the girls. "You made quite a mess of things on the fifth floor," he said disappointedly. "Now, it's time to pay for your sins." He grabbed Ginna by the hair and bent her head back.

"Please, no!" Marina shouted.

Kat entered the room and startled them. "Leave the girls alone," she ordered.

Klingman chuckled at her and resumed his hold on Ginna. He placed his blade against Ginna's neck until a small bead of blood formed.

Kat's eyes turned white and she mumbled words in a strange language. Klingman and his sentries were mesmerized by her as if under a spell.

Marina rushed at Klingman and knocked him to the floor. She attempted to wrestle the knife from his hand but couldn't. The pain in her injured arm was too much. Frantically, she head-butted him and the spike in the amulet pierced his forehead. She head-butted him a second time, but still he refused to let go of his knife. Marina weakened from fatigue and, feeling desperate, she bit his cheek. Finally, she inflicted enough pain on him to weaken his hold.

Kara and Ginna were in deep concentration and melted away their straps. They stood and approached the sentries. Kat continued to repeat her cryptic words and the girls disarmed the sentries.

Klingman punched Marina in the side of the head to break her bite on his cheek. Marina instinctively head-butted him again and stunned him. Three holes in his forehead seeped blood down his face. He finally weakened enough. Now she had the opportunity to roll him over and pry the knife from his hands.

Klingman appeared stunned from the head-butts and lost his strength. Marina got up and kicked the knife away. She was pleased to see the sentries tied up on the floor and the girls standing over them.

Marina took one of the pulse rifles and aimed at Klingman. "Get in the chair now," she ordered him.

"I don't take orders from an orphan whore," he uttered sarcastically, still lying on the floor.

Marina fired a shot into his knee, evoking a cry of pain. She fired a second shot in to his other knee and left him rolling across the floor. He clutched at both shattered, bloody knees, while sobbing.

Marina took the chip from him. "I doubt you'll be needing this."

Kat ended her rant and noticed one of the monitors displayed the approaching battle at Orpheus-2. "Marina, you might want to see this," she suggested somberly.

Everyone anxiously looked up at the monitor. Klingman crawled up onto the chair and grinned sadistically between sobs. "Now, you'll witness the end of your little regime, Marina," he taunted. "I win!"

Marina placed the barrel of the pistol against his head and patiently waited for the outcome. "You can't change fate, Marina, no matter what," he said defiantly. "Kill me and you're just like me, a murderer."

"He's right," Ginna announced. "But you aren't like him, Marina."

"Wanna bet," she said, fighting the urge to pull the trigger and blow his brains out.

On the monitor, Kronos' forces engaged the remaining militia and Fleet vessels defending Orpheus-2. Then the *Argo*, the *Mantis* and *Hydra* appeared from behind the attacking force and engaged in the battle.

"Sheena did it!" shouted Marina. She grabbed Klingman by the chin and mocked him.

"It won't matter," he uttered feebly, his life slipping away from him.

Marina hugged Kat and the two girls. "There's our saviors, girls. Sheena came through for us."

They watched the monitors anxiously, still aware that Sheena's forces were outnumbered.

★ ★ ★

Sheena stood defiantly on the bridge and ordered the three vessels to stand fast between the attacking force and the space station. Sheena warned the invaders to depart the area immediately but the warships continued to approach.

Sheena knew better than to expect a surrender or a withdrawal. "Fire!" she shouted. The order was quickly relayed to the *Mantis* and the *Hydra*. Intense pulse fire erupted between the two forces. Four Kronos vessels were immediately crippled but then Sheena's forces took on heavy damage.

Lt. Kannel panicked and pleaded, "Can't we retreat, Commander?"

Sheena stared at the monitor with a cold, glaring gaze. "We'll fight to the end, Lieutenant. This is where it ends."

"But what are we trying to accomplish?" he asked again, hoping to change her mind. The other crewmen and officers on the bridge listened intently for her response.

The ship rocked violently and threw them to the floor. "Answer me, Commander!" shouted Lt. Kannel, nearly in tears. "We don't want to die in vain."

Sheena stood up and regained her poise. She took notice of the eyes on her crew and replied sternly, "We're buying time. That's all we're doing - buying time."

★ ★ ★

In the ComSec room, Lilith, Drago and Harville worked feverishly to reprogram the targeting system. A holographic cylinder formed around them. They now moved panels and images through the air as if they were real.

"We're ready!" Lilith cried out excitedly. "Start the targeting process!"

The space around them became the battlefield around Orpheus-2. They placed their fingers on the enemy ships one by one. They waited anxiously as the system performed the necessary calculations and placed a yellow ring around each targeted ship. Unfortunately, the targeting took a few minutes for each vessel.

"We've got to go faster!" Harville yelled frantically. "Those Fleet vessels won't last much longer."

Then, two more Kronos vessels exploded briefly and vanished.

"Stay focused," Lilith instructed them. "Their number dwindles and increases our chances."

"Can't we fire now and decrease the number of attackers?" asked Drago.

"No," replied Lilith, still focused on the targeting process. "It will take too long to program a second blast. We have only one shot at this."

Drago and Harville glanced at each other uneasily. A call from the control room interrupted them. One of the officers urgently requested Harville's presence.

"Damn it!" he shouted and left the room.

Lilith and Drago continued to select targets when the system prompted them.

★ ★ ★

The battle continued for hours. The Fleet vessels continued to fire until every one of their cannons had been silenced. The battered ships drifted aimlessly apart with nothing to indicate that anyone survived. There were no exterior lights or red cannons. The main aft and auxiliary engines no longer glowed orange as their power was extinguished. The battle was over and twelve Kronos ships still remained. Each had sustained heavy damage and with limited firing capabilities.

In the ComSec room, Lilith announced, "It's time! Activate the firing system, Drago!"

★ ★ ★

Marina rushed to the panel and turned on the comm/nav system. She attempted to contact Sheena on the *Argo* but there was no response. Her eyes teared up as she feared her friend's demise.

Twelve Kronos vessels remained and closed on Orpheus-2. The voice of one of the Kronos captains was heard over the speaker calling for Orpheus-2 to accept surrender terms. Ensign Harville's voice responded, "We're offering 'you' one opportunity to surrender or be destroyed."

"Then prepare to die," the Kronos captain responded.

Everyone in the Kronos control center watched nervously. Klingman mumbled arrogantly, "I've waited for so long for this moment."

Marina pressed her face against his and taunted," You'll regret that remark, I promise you. Either way, you will die a thousand deaths."

Kat pulled her away from him, fearing what Marina might do in front of the girls.

Suddenly, dozens of laser bursts from a variety of directions struck the Kronos ships and, within seconds, destroyed all of them.

"No!" cried Klingman. "It can't be!"

Marina was stunned by the effectiveness of the weapon. She turned to Kat and both cringed in fear at how effectively it wiped out the twelve ships.

Marina smiled at Klingman and chided, "You know, it's worth it to keep you alive to savor the fruits of your plan."

Klingman glared at her and requested that she end his life now and be done with it. Marina was more than happy to spare him and bring him back to Orpheus-2 for imprisonment.

"What about Sexton?" Marina asked Kat.

"He's been dealt with. No worries."

Tears streamed down Klingman's cheeks. "I am just one part of Kronos," he blurted. "You have won nothing."

Marina surprised him with a leg kick to the side of the head that knocked him to the floor. Blood seeped from several gashes inflicted by her spiked leg brace. "Anything else you want to say, dipshit?" she inquired callously.

Klingman mumbled incoherently and then passed out. Marina, Kat and the girls hugged each other and then escorted their prisoner back to *The Reaper*.

X
THE AFTERMATH

In the control center on Orpheus-2, Ensign Harville congratulated Lilith and Drago. Fleet officers around them cheered for their success. Their excitement was short-lived as they began the arduous task of retrieving damaged ships and searching for survivors.

Rescue crews were dispatched to Sheena's vessels but the damage they sustained made survivors unlikely. Drago and Lilith arrived in the control room and waited anxiously for news of their friends' fates but none came.

Drago said a brief prayer aloud, knowing the grief Marina would feel when she returned. Everyone in the control room joined in, hoping for a miracle.

Ensign Harville arranged for full military honors to be bestowed upon all those lost in the battle with the ceremony to be held upon Marina's return.

Colonel Lennox returned to Orpheus-2 where she received medical attention but, just like Marina, she was reluctant to stay off her feet.

The Reaper returned to Orpheus-2 and moored at the farthest dock in the transport bay, past the many battle-damaged militia ships. Marina stepped out first, followed by the girls and then Kat. Medics arrived to remove Faust and Marcus' from the ship for medical attention.

The women were appalled at the amount of wreckage to the moored ships. Then it hit Marina that there were so many casualties, including people she cared for. She paused and became pale.

Kat placed an arm around her and encouraged her to continue. Kara and Ginna each held Marina's hand and urged her to be strong. Ginna reminded her that fate already decided the outcome of their destiny and whatever was to be could not be changed.

Marina took exception to her comment and knelt down in front of Ginna. "Look, Ginna, I know you girls have a purpose being Seers and all but I'm gonna tell you something you'd better get used to," she explained sternly. "That's bullshit. Destiny and fate are what we allow them to be."

"That's not true," Ginna countered defensively.

"Everything that happens, both good and bad, is determined by our actions," she continued. "Our mistakes lead to problems and death. Our forethought and wisdom lead to peace and prosperity. Get used to it." Kara and Ginna looked frightened by Marina's stern rebuke.

Marina continued, "I love you girls as if you were my own daughters and I refuse to see you subject yourself to danger because of a false belief."

The girls looked to Kat but she nodded in agreement with Marina. Marina recalled how Kat warned her that it would come to this. She was naive over her future then, but that would never happen again. The galaxy was going to know a new Marina, a Marina they probably won't like.

The four of them took the elevator to the main floor on 'ten'. When the doors slid open, Drago and Lilith were there to greet them.

"Welcome back, my Queen," Drago said humbly as the women stepped off the elevator.

"It's good to be back," Marina replied. "I sense there is something that burdens you to tell me."

"The casualties, my Queen, were extensive."

Harville approached and greeted her sadly. "This is a bittersweet victory, your Highness, but one we must accept with gratitude for the sacrifices our friends made."

"I agree, Ensign. You did well."

"Thank you, my Queen."

Drago and Lilith stood in front of her with sullen expressions. Marina braced herself for the news. Kat placed her arm around Marina's shoulders, knowing what was to come.

Drago continued, "No survivors have been reported from either the *Wasp* or the *Argo*."

Marina's eyes welled with tears. She struggled to keep her composure and asked, "Commander Brice or Sykes?"

"No, your Highness," replied Harville. "I know they were friends of yours."

Marina followed the three of them to the Red Room where they debriefed Ensign Harville on the remaining resources and what needed to be done to secure the targeting system.

A knock on the door halted the conversation. Harville pressed a button on a remote-control pad at the table and the door slid open. Lennox stood there with a cold, almost frozen, stare.

Marina immediately stood and greeted her, "Sandra, come in, please."

"Thank you," she replied stoically and took a seat at the table.

"How did things go with General Witty?" Marina inquired.

"He's retired permanently," Lennox replied feebly. After a brief pause, she continued, "I'm sorry to hear about your friends. It seems we've both lost much."

"And that's why we need to talk," Marina responded. "My mission is to unite everyone under a new alliance."

"You are forever the optimist," Lennox remarked.

"Stubborn is more like it," she quipped to their amusement. "I want you to head the new federation we're going to build," Marina informed her. "I'll bring everyone to the table but I need someone to keep them there. I know you'll do a good job."

Lennox stared down at the table and pondered Marina's offer for several seconds. Marina added, "Ensign Harville did a very good job here at the station throughout the crisis. He'd make a good assistant."

"What about Captain Mallon?" Lennox asked curiously.

Marina turned to Harville and inquired curiously, "Where is Captain Mallon? He's been strangely absent through of all this."

Harville replied uneasily, "We found him in his quarters. It appears he hung himself, but left a note. Apparently, he feared your return, Colonel Lennox, and felt he was better off."

Lennox smiled for once and asked, "Are you married, Ensign Harville?"

Harville was taken aback by her question and responded, "I assume you're concerned about my commitment."

"Yes, I am. We'll be spending a lot of time together and I've been through a lot."

Harville understood that she needed emotional support as well as professional assistance. "I'd be honored to serve under you, Colonel."

"There's one more thing I need to get off my chest," added Lennox uneasily as she turned to Marina.

"You are among friends, Sandra," Marina reminded her. "Feel free to speak."

Lennox twitched and then confessed, "I went to see Klingman an hour ago." She paused and struggled to reveal what she had done. "He needed to pay for what he did to all of us."

"Sandra, you didn't kill him, did you?" Marina responded frantically.

"Of course not, but I had to make sure he never got his hands into Another Kronos project again."

Marina suspected what Lennox was hinting at. "Go on," she urged.

Lennox took a deep breath and then continued, "I took his hands, his feet and his manhood from him with a laser. He'll show much more respect to us in the future."

Lilith and Harville were mortified; Marina, not so much. "Did it change anything?" questioned Marina.

Lennox shook her head and replied disappointedly, "No, it didn't. But it did feel good to see him suffer. Now he's lost everything, just like us."

"I think we'd be hard-pressed to find someone upset about your actions," Marina commented, somewhat relieved. "Just promise me you won't do anything like that again. You have to set an example from here on out."

Lennox stood and shook Marina's hand. "Thank you for believing in me when I didn't."

"Sometimes we all need someone to believe in us," Marina responded.

Lennox smiled and left the room. Marina couldn't help noticing that she was actually a beautiful woman when she wasn't angry.

Lilith chuckled at Marina's expression and remarked, "You have quite a job ahead of you."

"As do you, Lilith. Let me know if you need anything from me."

Lilith smiled and then wheeled her chair out of the room. Harville stood and hesitated as if he wanted to speak. Marina warned, "You'd best keep Colonel Lennox happy, Ensign. She's a good person with a lot of pain inside."

"I'll do my best. I wanted to say thank you for everything you did. I am proud to have you as my queen."

"My days as queen are over. I am turning that responsibility over to someone else."

Harville looked surprised. "But, your Highness..."

"You'll see soon enough," she added. "Things have to be different."

Harville nodded and left the room. He knew better than to question Marina's motives. She proved time and time again to be a very complicated person to him and others at the station.

★ ★ ★

Marina sat in the flight deck of *The Reaper*. Tears streamed down her cheeks as she thought about Britt and Sheena. All this time, she and Britt neglected each other because of bigger things. Now, he was gone. Sheena sacrificed her career to help her and now she was gone as well. "It should have been me!" she cried out and banged her head on the console.

Then she noticed that there was a message waiting for her to acknowledge. She pressed the button and was horrified to hear Britt's voice on it. "I'm sorry, Marina, that I couldn't be there for you. I believe we could have saved many more lives had you considered my suggestions, but I guess that just wouldn't be you. There will always be a place in my heart for you, but we both need to move on in different directions. Take care."

Marina screamed and punched the monitor. "How could you do this to me, Britt?" she cried and fell into her seat. "How could you do this?" she moaned and covered her face with her hands. Then she considered that she was dumped by a dead person, which added to her agony. Maybe he'd be alive if she had listened to him. Maybe they'd be celebrating together in her cabin. Maybe she was doomed to suffer her whole life - a curse to remind her of the hatred she harbored for so many years against her parents.

Kat entered the flight deck with the girls. They surrounded Marina and hugged her affectionately. "You're not alone," Kara informed her. "We're your family now."

Marina hugged them back and cried again.

Faust entered, walking with a cane and looked frail. "So, what do we do now, your Highness?" he inquired playfully, hoping to cheer Marina up.

Marina was relieved to see him. She rushed to him and hugged him gingerly. "I'm so happy to see you, Faust! How did you survive?"

Faust nodded toward Kat and suggested that it just wasn't his time.

Marina looked to Kat and announced, "You are going to rule Yord."

Kat was stunned by her announcement. "But, I can't do that!" she exclaimed.

"You said you enjoyed playing the part, remember?"

Kat responded giddily, "I did say that, didn't I."

Marina placed her hands on Kat's shoulders and continued, "I want you to take the girls under your care and make sure they are well-educated and able to perform their role when the time comes."

"And what role is that?" asked Kara curiously.

"When the time comes, you'll know," responded Marina. "As you can see, survival is the most important one."

The girls glanced at each other curiously. Marina blocked her thoughts from them for the first time ever and left them feeling lost.

"And what will become of you?" Kat asked uneasily.

"I have much work to do to reform the alliance," Marina answered confidently. "It's going to be difficult but I have a knack for coercing people to see my point of view."

"I would like to join you, my Queen, if Kat will permit it," requested Faust.

Marina glanced at Kat, who nodded in approval. "I'd be honored to have you by my side, Faust," Marina winked at Kat. "Although, I think you'll have an expanded role with me. It seems that I require a male counterpart to remind me of my flaws."

Everyone laughed at her joke. Marina informed Kat of Colonel Lennox's new role as military leader of the alliance. Kat also understood that their role was to be guardians of the alliance and all who lived under it.

"We're gonna miss you very much," Kat blurted and hugged Marina tightly.

"I'm sure you will all be there for me when I need you," she replied. "Right now, Faust and I need time to heal, before dealing with Golgar."

"Then heal you must," Kat responded.

Marina and Faust departed Orpheus-2. She knew there would be many more adventures, hardships, and friendships in the future. For several moments, Faust sat in the co-pilot's seat and admired her.

Marina was pleased to have a man by her side. The hurt she felt for Britt would take time to heal but there was no time for remorse. She had too much to do before her next challenge.

"What are you thinking?" asked Faust.

"Kat's black magic does have some advantages," Marina confessed. "I thought we lost you."

"So did I," he responded gratefully.

"It's a shame she couldn't save Marcus."

Faust burst into laughter. "Who says she didn't save Marcus?" he asked playfully. "She's probably with him right now."

Marina realized that Kat conned her. That's why she permitted Faust to join her so easily. "She is such a bitch!" uttered Marina playfully.

"As are you, my Queen."

Marina pulled him toward her and whispered in his ear, "You learn fast." She then kissed him passionately and added, "Let the healing begin."

Faust commented appreciatively, "I'm gonna like this."

Then Marina recalled something that Klingman said to her. "I am just one part of Kronos. You have won nothing." She cringed as she considered what lie ahead. Then she dismissed it and remarked, "So will I, Faust. So will I."

Marina decided that Kronos and Golgar would have to wait for another day. She would reform the alliance and deal with them when the time came. She placed the ship on auto-pilot and turned to Faust, "Time for a nice long rest."

Faust stood up gingerly and asked, "Where are we going, my Queen?"

Marina pulled him close to her and replied, "A little planet where we can be alone, until we're ready to go back to work. But, in the meantime..." Marina kissed him hungrily. "I have needs and you, my friend, will help me with them." She led him from the flight deck to her cabin.

No sooner had they left, the transmitter beeped twice but no one was there to respond. It couldn't be that important, or could it?

Milton Keynes UK
Ingram Content Group UK Ltd.
UKHW020003230724
446010UK00004B/84